9/19

Help us Rate this book...
Put your initials on the
Left side and your rating
on the right side.
1 = Didn't care for
2 = It was O.K.
3 = It was <u>great</u>

_____ LR   1 2 ③
_____   1 2 3
_____   1 2 3
_____   1 2 3
_____   1 2 3
_____   1 2 3
_____   1 2 3
_____   1 2 3
_____   1 2 3
_____   1 2 3
_____   1 2 3
_____   1 2 3
_____   1 2 3
_____   1 2 3
_____   1 2 3

THE EXPRESS BRIDE

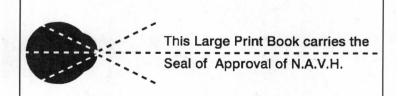

This Large Print Book carries the
Seal of Approval of N.A.V.H.

THE DAUGHTERS OF THE MAYFLOWER

THE EXPRESS BRIDE

KIMBERLEY WOODHOUSE

THORNDIKE PRESS
A part of Gale, a Cengage Company

Farmington Hills, Mich • San Francisco • New York • Waterville, Maine
Meriden, Conn • Mason, Ohio • Chicago

LIBRARY OF CONGRESS CIP DATA ON FILE.
CATALOGUING IN PUBLICATION FOR THIS BOOK
IS AVAILABLE FROM THE LIBRARY OF CONGRESS

ISBN-13: 978-1-4328-6861-1 (hardcover alk. paper)

Published in 2019 by arrangement with Barbour Publishing, Inc.

Printed in the United States of America
1 2 3 4 5 6 7 23 22 21 20 19

DEDICATION

This book is lovingly dedicated to
Becky Germany.
For all you do and all the lives you
touch: Thank you. Never could I have
guessed when we first talked twenty
years ago what God would do through
His gift of story. I'm overwhelmed with
gratitude. You have been an inspiration
and encouragement to me (and your
brilliance in a few simple marketing
sentences sparked my favorite part of
this story). Thank you for giving of
yourself. Thank you for believing in me.
Thank you for *all* you do for so many
authors. You are wonderful and beloved.
Keep on keepin' on, my friend. Your
example is a beautiful thing.

*I consider my life worth nothing to me; my
only aim is to finish the race and
complete the task the Lord Jesus has
given me — the task of testifying to the
good news of God's grace.*
Acts 20:24 NIV

Daughters of the Mayflower

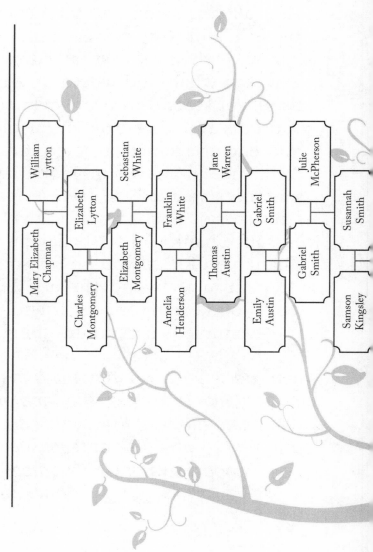

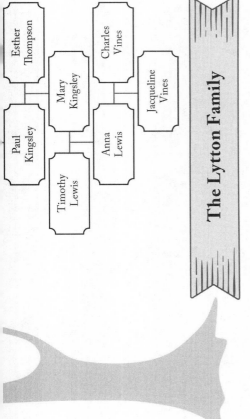

The Lytton Family

William Lytton married Mary Elizabeth Chapman (Plymouth, 1621)

their fourth child is Elizabeth Lytton—married Charles Montgomery (1642)

Their 3rd child born was Elizabeth Montgomery—married Sebastian White (1670)

Their 1st child born was Franklin White—married Amelia Henderson (1688)

Their 2nd child born was Thomas Austin—married Jane Warren (1710)

Their 1st child born was Emily Austin—married Gabriel Smith (1728)

Their 1st child born was Gabriel Smith—married Julia McPherson (1750)

Their 1st live child born was Susannah Smith—married Samson Kingsley (1773)

Their 1st child born was Paul Kingsley—married Esther Thompson (1790)

Their 1st child born was Mary Kingsley—married Timothy Lewis (1810)

Their 2nd child born was Anna Lewis—married Charles Vines (1830)

Their only child was born Jacqueline Vines

Dear Reader,

I'm thrilled to be back in the Daughters of the Mayflower series and to bring you *The Express Bride.*

The Pony Express is a short and fascinating snippet of US history. Full of tall tales, wild characters, and folklore, it's an exciting time to write about.

For my story, I've used the historical location of the Carson Sink station (in modern-day Nevada — the Utah Territory at the time), but most of the people, buildings, and town are fictional as I created them.

Carson Sink (or Sink at Carson) was a relay station back in 1860, but for this story, I'm using it as a home station so you can experience all the ins and outs of the Pony Express.

Not much is known about the original station other than that it was built in March 1860 and a few ruins remain at the site. (For more details, see the Note from the Author at the end of the book.)

What we now refer to as the Pony Express was the Central Overland California and Pikes Peak Express Company. It operated from April 3, 1860 until it was no longer needed when the telegraph was completed on October 24, 1861. Essentially the availability of telegraphs ended the call for the costly but incredible mail service. The Express Service went from St. Joseph, Missouri, to Sacramento, California, in ten days. This is astoundingly fast when you think of the mileage — almost two thousand miles — all on horseback. A rider went about seventy-five miles a day and changed horses at every relay station — every fifteen to twenty miles (sometimes shorter depending on the terrain). Over the nineteen months of its existence, despite a war with the Paiute, dangerous trails, and horrific weather, the Express lost one only mochila (the special leather mail pouch that went over the very small Express saddle and held the mail) and successfully delivered 34,753 letters.

I visited several museums and a couple of actual Pony Express stations that still have original existing structures (Gothenberg, Nebraska, and the Hollenberg Pony Express station at Hanover, Kansas) to research aspects of this story. I hope and pray that life at an Express station comes alive for you through the story.

One interesting thing to note as you are reading is that part of this story is focused on treasury notes. Back in 1860, some banks in large cities issued bank notes from their individual establishments, but there was no national currency. No paper money. People used gold and silver coin to pay for most of their transactions. Then there were treasury notes. The government issued these in times of financial stress (major times were the War of 1812, the Panic of 1837, the Panic of 1857, and the Civil War), and while they weren't supposed to be used as "money," a good amount of the time they were used precisely that way, especially in rural areas.

You'll also notice that my prologue takes place in 1834. For the sake of this story, I took a little creative liberty. Please see the note at the end for more details about the first women to cross the Rockies.

Above all, I hope you enjoy the journey through time as we visit the era of the Pony Express and see once again how God is so gracious to us all.

— Kimberley

PROLOGUE

St. Louis
March 1834

With shaking limbs, she climbed into the plush carriage awaiting her, the precious bundle in her arms worth far more than the money, trinkets, and trunks of clothing she left behind. Time stood still for a moment as the scent of the fresh spring rain filled her senses and transported her thoughts back to another spring day. If only things had turned out differently. How she loved the gardens in spring.

As her memories rushed over her, the gravity of what she was about to do jerked her back to the reality around her with a harsh jolt.

The unmistakable sound of pounding footsteps on the brick walkway above her made her cower into the corner of the carriage.

Oh, why couldn't the driver hurry? She'd

paid him handsomely to take her on the first leg of her journey, and she needed him to get the horses moving. Fast.

Her heart thundered in her chest, knowing all too well what every second meant. Every beat harder and more painful than the last. Footsteps crunched around the carriage and then soft words were spoken to the team. Didn't he realize the urgency?

Oh please, God . . . please. Help us get away in time so —

"Nooo!" The deep, bellowing scream interrupted her prayer and made her shiver.

She didn't dare look. But she couldn't help herself. Opening one eye, she peeked out the window and saw the man she'd loved — and feared — the most, running down the front stairs outside of their massive house, a bottle in his right hand.

"Hurry. Oh, please hurry." Her words were too soft to be heard, but the carriage dipped and gave a little sway, and she could only hope that meant the driver had mounted the box and was preparing to leave. Heart thundering in her chest, she squeezed her eyes against the tears.

Her husband's anger was intense enough to propel even the most timid man into action. She prayed that it would inspire the driver to hurry. And that she would be able to keep herself composed.

"Don't you dare leave me, Anna!" The words were cloaked in a tone that always made her think of the demons of hell itself.

She took a deep breath and looked to his wild eyes long enough to know intoxication had once again taken over his mind. He lifted his arm, and she ducked out of habit — even though he was still a good thirty paces away from the carriage.

Smash!

The shattering of glass against the carriage made her flinch, and she shivered again. Fear that he could yank her from her small sanctuary — her only way of escape — prickled and stung her flesh as if his bottle had smashed upon her very soul.

But the collision of glass against wood was all the urging the horses needed. They took off at a fast pace that threw her against the back carriage wall.

She twisted her neck to peek through the rear window. Not because she regretted leaving but to see if her demon was giving chase. For once, his inebriation was a blessing. He staggered after the carriage rather than running to the stable. His favorite horse — a massive black with a powerful stride — could overtake the carriage in minutes. But either he was too drunk to realize it, or God was answering her prayer for protection.

With a deep breath, she turned forward again. Faced with the very real fact that she would never return, her exhale stuttered and shook. Had she done the right thing? Even with all his flaws, love of liquor, and anger — she'd loved him fiercely. Still did. But her heart couldn't make him change. It didn't stop the bruises and gashes from appearing. She'd gladly lay down her life for him, but now she had to think about more than her own life. . . .

Reaching into the blanket, she stroked the soft skin and tiny fingers. Determined to offer a safe and healthy environment for her little one, she tried to swallow down the fear that she was making a horrible mistake. Grasping the packet she'd stashed inside the blanket in her haste, she felt hot tears burning trails down her cheeks. Inside was the finest piece of jewelry she owned. In the beginning, her husband had showered her with jewelry and trinkets. But none of it could make up for the times he hurt her. Physically and emotionally, she was spent.

Anna glanced at the brooch of solid gold. Inlaid with diamonds, rubies, and sapphires, it was exquisite. Very patriotic with its red, white, and blue, he'd given it to her on their first Fourth of July together. Its worth was a small fortune in and of itself.

She prayed it would provide for her journey and new life. And she prayed he would forgive her for taking it. She'd left everything else.

A twinge of guilt filled her chest. Perhaps she should be feeling some sort of remorse with the thought of selling the treasure. Some sentimental value should be given to the piece — shouldn't it?

It had, after all, been a gift from a loving husband to his bride. Back when their love was new and exhilarating . . . when they could stare at one another for moments on end and dream of the days to come.

As she rubbed the piece with her glove-covered fingers, she turned it over.

Knowing what was there.

Dreading the reminder.

But it drew her, and she couldn't help herself.

Etched on the back of the bejeweled piece was a single word — *"Forever."*

A word meant to signify the commitment and love of their marriage. A word that had made her think her husband would love and cherish her. Just like he'd stated in his vows. But instead, the word was a knife to her heart.

As the carriage raced away from their estate, she clamped her teeth together and tried to rid her mind of the thoughts of guilt. She shouldn't have looked. It didn't matter anymore. Now that engraved word could only symbolize the distance of the chasm between them. She would never return. Never subject herself or her child to his fists. Never live in fear of him again. She was free of him.

Forever.

October 1834

Staring out at the barren, sand-filled landscape ahead of her, Anna pulled the oxen to a halt. Her baby was hungry, and this was as good a place as any to stop. It wasn't like she was in a huge hurry to get anywhere.

As she opened her bodice and snuggled her little one close, emotions flooded her being and fought for center stage in her mind.

Relief at her escape.

Fear of being found.

Elation that she'd made it this far.

Apprehension over whether she could continue on her own.

Guilt for leaving.

They all tumbled around, creating a messy jumble of feelings.

18

Every time she had a moment to herself this happened. Most of the time, she was trying to entertain her little one and focused on the tasks she needed to do. Just keeping the oxen going in the correct direction could be a challenge some days when her precious daughter tugged at her skirts from the box on the floor where she'd basically grown up the past few months.

Some days she was amazed at how far they'd come.

The weeks and months had passed in lack of sleep and constant changes Anna made to her appearance. She'd brought three different wigs with her and sold all her beautiful, custom-made dresses — choosing instead the simple attire of a woman of humble means headed west. As she fed her little one, who grew by the day, her thoughts went back over all that had happened.

She'd been completely unprepared. Even though from the moment she discovered she was pregnant, she'd read every newspaper article she could find on making a new life out West. Attending lectures — without her husband's knowledge — and making lists and plans. But none of it prepared her for the reality.

But she had persevered. She lifted her chin at the thought. Every day she'd changed her looks, hoping she wouldn't be recognized. And while the time had passed in slow moments accompanied by the constant urge to look over her shoulder, at least it had given her body time to heal. The bruising was gone, which meant people didn't stare at her in pity any longer. Not that she'd seen many people lately. The journey was taking her far away from anything she'd ever known and into a vast and unfamiliar frontier.

Now officially in the middle of nowhere, hoping to find an even more remote location, she breathed deeply. Strange that a city girl like herself — one who'd always worn the latest fashion and never had to lift a finger to do anything — had been surviving all this time in a modest covered wagon traveling west. "And we're doing just fine, aren't we, sweetie?"

Her little one smiled and blew a bubble with her pink lips.

Yes, it had been worth it.

After she'd left her home, she had sold the brooch, then paid a man for the wagon, oxen, and supplies. She'd joined two families and traveled with them for a long portion of the trip. The women had taken her under their wings and helped her make poultices for her many wounds. The last bout of her husband's anger had acted like a catapult and thrown her into leaving sooner than planned — she'd feared for their lives more than ever before. If she hadn't left when she did, she was certain she would have been taken out in a pine box.

Once they'd left civilization as she knew it, the work was much harder than she'd ever thought. But she learned. How to care for herself, her child, and the animals. How to cook over an open fire. How to do her laundry on the rocks at the streams. How to shoot a rifle — of which she now owned four with two small crates full of ammunition. Just in case.

"As soon as you are grown enough, I'll teach you too." Never did she want her daughter to know the fear that she had felt for far too long.

Buttoning her bodice, she smiled and cooed at her daughter. This journey had been a wonder even though it had been the most difficult thing she'd ever done. Many mishaps had happened along the way — including encounters with Indians and wild animals — but nothing scared her as much as the thought of her husband finding her. Not even the Indians who looked so fierce — but they'd traded with her little band of travelers and allowed their wagons to move on. Surely that had been a miracle from the good Lord above.

So she'd continued west. Out of the United States and into the Mexican Territories. Never allowing her mind to think about the past or the what-ifs for too long. Praying every moment she could. Over mountains, through valleys, and to what seemed like the very ends of the earth.

A blur. That's what it all had been. Numbing and grueling.

But that was all about to change. It was time to find a place to settle. She'd decided on a new name for herself — one she would recognize if someone called it — and she would finally say her daughter's name aloud. Something she had never done so *he* wouldn't have any clues to find her.

The future sounded like bliss. To actually be able to sleep in the same place. To find a quiet place to call home.

For all this time, she hadn't had the energy to do much of anything but drive the wagon and do daily chores. Keep them safe. Get sleep. Start again the next day.

As she picked up the reins to urge the oxen forward, she looked down at her hands covered in calluses. No longer would she have the smooth skin of a refined lady.

Things like that didn't matter out here. They didn't matter to her either. Not anymore. With a resolved sigh, she tucked the blanket more securely around her precious daughter. The months and miles had rolled past as her child had grown. Cuddly and active, her baby would never know the grand estate they'd left behind. And that was for the best. The more distance between them, the better. It was a good thing her sweet child was too young to remember anything.

With a glance around her, she took another deep breath. The scraggly hills seemed barren and forbidding. Small, scrubby bushes dotted the desertlike landscape. No signs of life except for the small outpost ahead.

It was like . . . a wilderness.

She clucked the oxen forward once again.

The wilderness was a great place to hide.

CHAPTER 1

Kansas City
Twenty-six years later
May 6, 1860
Elijah Johnson watched his employer struggle from the chair to the window. He reached out a hand to assist. He was saddened to see the man who had always been brimming with life appear weak and sickly all of a sudden.

"No. Don't even think about helping me. I can do it." Even though Charles Vines's health was in decline, most of the time he refused Elijah's help. The doctor had already been to visit twice this week. It was no wonder. His boss had been running ragged for far too long. "At least my *mind* is still telling me I can." The older man chuckled.

"Yes, sir." Elijah smiled along and shook his head.

"I see you smirking at me, young man. This stubborn ol' coot knows he's being a cantankerous fool, but under it all, I still want to be my own man. It's hard to give up independence and swallow pride to ask for help." Pulling back the lace curtain, he let out a sigh as he looked out the window. "So forgive my gruff manner. I just need a few minutes to think. I have something to share with you that may come as a shock."

"Understood, sir." *May come as a shock?* That was a phrase he hadn't anticipated. He'd been asked to come for an important conversation, and he had no trouble waiting. But what could be shocking? They'd been doing the same kind of business for as long as he'd known him.

Taking a seat across from his employer, he studied Charles, who'd taken him under his wing more than a decade before when Elijah was a mere eighteen years old. It was hard to see the man he respected most not be his normal robust self.

At fifty years old, Charles Vines was a self-made millionaire. For years Elijah had followed him around the country as they looked into each latest and greatest business venture. They'd expanded Vines's vast empire in every way possible. Charles's love of business deals and seeming obsession with bigger and better made him a force to be reckoned with. Elijah admired the man's work ethic. And Mr. Vines was wise. Often-times he would speak about how he'd gained that wisdom — through great loss — but he never went into details. Then he also spoke of his mistakes. Again, never in great detail, but enough for Elijah to glean that Charles Vines was a respectable and profit-able man *now* because he'd learned from his past.

Wasn't that what the Lord wanted from them all? To learn from their sinful mistakes and repent? While he and Vines had dis-cussed God and faith on many occasions, Elijah was positive that there was something in his boss's life that kept him from truly forgiving himself. So the need to fill the hole inside him was assuaged with the accumula-tion of business successes. Why? Elijah wasn't sure. And even as close as they were, some subjects had never been broached. He began to feel a niggle of concern. This was very unlike his boss.

After a few more excruciating moments of stillness, Mr. Vines turned from the window and took slow steps back to his chair. "Elijah, my boy. We've accomplished a lot these past few years, haven't we?"

Normally, that was his boss's prelude statement to a new and exciting business venture he wanted to try. Which normally meant a good deal of traveling and negotiating. "Yes, sir. That we have. And I'm grateful for all you've taught me." He leaned forward and placed his elbows on his knees. Was the man up for more of the same? Elijah couldn't imagine that he was. How was that shocking? How could he politely convince his boss to pay attention to his health and cut back on work? Let Elijah handle things?

"I know this will sound a bit unlike me, but I've decided to go a different direction than usual."

Elijah couldn't help it — his eyebrows shot up. "Oh?" What could the old man be getting himself into now?

"As difficult as the rest will be for me to say, I think of you as a son, so I'm hoping you'll hear me out."

"Of course." This was not one of their normal let's-head-out-on-another-grand-adventure-and-buy-every-company-we-can talks.

"As you've undoubtedly noticed, my health is deteriorating. The doctor says it's gotten worse the past few months because I've refused to slow down. In my own mind, I thought if I ignored it, it would go away, but I was wrong. Apparently just because I *thought* I could outlive all of my contemporaries doesn't make it so." Mr. Vines wiped a hand down his scruffy face that had always been clean-shaven until the past week. "So I'm ordered to rest and see if I can regain some strength."

"That sounds like a good plan." Certainly that wasn't all of the story. What was so difficult and shocking about all that? But Elijah knew his employer. Something else was motivating the man. Something other than his normal business frame of mind.

The older man took several deep breaths and looked away toward the window again. "In light of all this, I have a very important job for you. Probably the most difficult and challenging I've ever put before you." He tapped the arm of the chair with his bony forefinger. "I need you to find someone for me. And you'll have to do it alone." He sighed again. "I'm afraid to tell you there's a lot more to my past than I've let on."

Finding someone in this vast country could prove to be challenging. But before he jumped to conclusions, he needed to hear the man out. "I believe we all have more to our pasts, sir."

Vines's wry chuckle crackled in the air. "Yes, I'm guessing you're probably correct. Before I get to my request, there's something else I need to say. Something I've been needing to say for a long time."

"All right." Elijah just smiled at his employer. Charles loved to keep people on the edge of their seats, making them wait for whatever it was he wanted to share, building up the anticipation. Because of that, patience was something Elijah had learned early on with his employer. Vines's eccentric and full-steam-ahead ways made for very interesting conversation. But something in his boss's manner made Elijah feel . . . unsettled.

"Forgive me for overstepping my bounds, but peering death in the face will do that to a man."

Elijah raised his brows. While the man was sick, yes, he didn't think he was knocking on death's door. At least not yet.

"You're special to me, my boy. And I'm sorry I haven't always shown you the way I should. I know you stand to inherit a good deal from your father, yet you have worked for *me* in a humble manner for more than a decade. You're a good man, Elijah. And I've watched the last couple of years take their toll on you. How you've searched for the meaning in life — thinking it should be coming from your great success."

Elijah swallowed. Had he really been that transparent?

"When you shared about how horrible your parents' marriage had been when you were a child, I kept my mouth shut, but now I'm beginning to believe that I should have spoken up then." He leaned forward in his chair and pointed a finger in Elijah's face. "Don't you dare waste your life as I have mine. You don't want to end up a lonely old man like me." His voice cracked on the last word, and he paused, looked away, and put a hand over his lips.

Elijah wasn't sure what to think. Charles Vines had always been a godly example to him. Such a hard worker — he poured himself into his businesses and took a hands-on approach. Always making sure that he had the right men in place for the jobs and that they weren't overworked. Every Christmas, he took care that every man had a bonus and presents for his family. Vines was wealthy and smart, but above all he loved the Lord.

In fact, ever since Elijah had met him, he'd wanted to be like him. Generous, wealthy, and self-reliant. So what was Charles talking about? It didn't add up in his mind.

Vines lowered his hand while he took a shaky breath. "I know you've endured great pain when it comes to love. Remember, you told me all about Miss Martha Smith and Miss Laura Winslow — now Mrs. Manchester. And while I applaud you for wanting to marry for love and for standing your ground for what you believe, I can't say that I support the stance you now take. You can't run away and hide forever. Pretending you have no feelings. I should have said something long ago . . . but it was too easy not to. We got along just fine the way things were, and it was to my benefit to keep you running ragged right along with me."

Heat filled Elijah's face. Bringing up the past brought up all the emotions with it. "Mr. Vines, I'd prefer —"

"I'm going to interrupt you right there. I'm sorry for bringing it up. You shared that in confidence and I didn't mean to embarrass you, but again, I'm just trying to be honest. God saw that it wasn't good for man to be alone, Elijah. I think it's high time you thought about that. Frankly, with the knowledge of both of our pasts, I've used it for my — yes, our — gain. But we've been chasing the wrong things. Now, God in His infinite wisdom saw fit to bless us through it, but it's high time I got my priorities straight."

What could he possibly say? Charles knew him better than anyone. And he was right.

They'd both been guilty of using whatever had shaped them in the past to drive them forward. Even if it meant ignoring and shoving down their feelings.

"You need to get yours straight too, son. I'm sorry for how I've failed you in that area of a mentor. You've actually done a great deal to mentor this old coot when it comes to spiritual things. You've made me more of a godly man. Challenged me. Respected me. Honored me. And I need to thank you. While I'm at it, I need to ask your forgiveness because I feel like I've used you. You don't need to stay single to continue working with me, because things are going to change. In fact, I'd like to bring you on as a partner, if you'll have me."

Elijah's heart picked up its pace. He'd dreamed of this day. "Partner? Sir, I'm honored, and truly, there's nothing to forgive —"

"You've been my right hand for too long and I'm sorry I didn't do it sooner. The papers are already drawn up. It's time we stopped working ourselves to the bone and put a little more focus on other areas. Like family . . ." He looked away toward the window and let out a long sigh.

The word *family* made Elijah's chest sting in a way he wasn't expecting.

"That brings me back to my request." The older man leaned back in his chair and just stared toward the window. "There are a few horrible things I've kept to myself for much too long." A haunted look came over his face. "I kept it quiet, but I'm tired of hiding. And I don't know how much time the good Lord will give me. The doctor has told me that if I don't rest and recover, I may only have a few months left — but if I do as he says, there may still be some time for me to rectify some of my failings. That's why I need you to go on this search — I desperately need to see this through. It's *very* important to me."

"If it's that important, I will do whatever I can." Elijah wasn't sure what to make of all of it. Embarrassment, fear, excitement, and shock had all moved through his mind in the past few moments. He shook his head for a moment to clear his muddied emotions. Thinking through everything the man had said before, he tried to steer the conversation back to the reason he was here. "Didn't you say it was a difficult and challenging job? In *addition* to finding this someone? Hopefully you know I would do anything within my power to help you." And he would. He would give his life for the man

34

in front of him. "What do you need me to do?"

"I'll get to that in a minute. But first I need to show you something."

Grief! The man could be infuriating. Always drawing out and dangling the crux of the matter like a carrot until he struck with his point. Elijah had witnessed it in negotiations for years; he just hadn't expected to be on the receiving end of it.

Charles reached into his pocket and pulled out a handkerchief-wrapped bundle. With slow, methodical movements, he unfolded the square.

When the last corner of cloth was lifted, light from the window made the object sparkle. Once again, Elijah's eyebrows shot up. He stood and walked closer to Mr. Vines. Rubies, sapphires, and diamonds covered the gold brooch. Each catching the light and sending brilliant refractions around the room. He tilted his head to see the design. "That's an incredible piece, Mr. Vines. Don't you think it should be locked up in the safe?"

"Oh, it has been, my boy. For many, many years."

Funny, Elijah had never seen it and he'd helped his employer catalog all of his valuables on multiple occasions. Where had it come from? And what did it have to do with whatever new job Elijah was to do? And whoever it was he needed to find. The questions in his mind grew. "It must have some special meaning to you?"

"Yes. And no." The older man took a ragged breath and shook his head. "I gave it as a gift, with the best of intentions . . . but it brings me great grief. Guilt. Shame." A tear slipped down the man's weathered cheek.

A sight Elijah had never seen in his strong, take-charge employer. "When did you purchase it?"

"The first time? Thirty years ago . . ." His voice trailed off.

The first time? What did *that* mean? Elijah couldn't fit the pieces of the puzzle together.

"It is my most prized possession, yet it haunts me. I have nightmares. I love it and hate it at the same time."

Maybe the man's sickness was worse than he thought, because now he wasn't making sense. Elijah shook his head. "I'm sorry, sir. I'm afraid I don't understand."

Mr. Vines looked up at him, the sheen of tears making his eyes shine brighter. There was no confusion or doubt in them. "I had a wife. I gave it to her. But then I did some terrible things."

CHAPTER 2

Utah Territory, forty miles from Virginia City
October 2, 1860

Wadding up the piece of paper in her hand, Jacqueline Rivers scolded herself for once again being too feminine in her language. That wouldn't do. Not for a letter of this magnitude. She had to be convincing.

Her conscience pricked. Honesty had always been her way of life. That's why she was struggling so much with this letter. But her station was at stake. What else could she do? What would Dad want her to do?

A new idea struck as she thought of her father. Perhaps it was the length of her missive. Short and to the point would be better. More manlike. Just like Dad.

With a clean sheet in front of her, she dipped the quill back into the ink and pondered her words. A drop of the black liquid made an unseemly splat on the paper. Gracious, now she would have to start again.

She let out a huff and reached for another clean sheet.

Shaking her head, she stopped herself in mid-grab and determined that men wouldn't worry about a blot of ink on the page. It was wasteful. Station managers didn't waste.

New resolve squaring her shoulders, she set back to the task of writing and tried to ignore the blob.

October 2, 1860

Mr. William Russell
Mr. William Waddell
Mr. Alexander Majors

Gentlemen,

It is with a heavy heart that I tell you of my father's passing. Marshall Rivers was the best of men as I'm sure you are well aware. In his absence, I will continue to run the station for the Central Overland California and Pikes Peak Express Company.

On the loop of her last *y* she chided herself. She should have used the initials COC&PP rather than the long and tedious name. Or better yet just used the familiar-

38

sounding Pony Express. Did she sound too formal by naming the company? Would they guess?

The clock struck the hour. There wasn't time for yet another draft or for her to keep second-guessing herself. The next rider was expected within the quarter hour. Best to keep it short and to the point. It needed to go out on the Express today.

I have worked by my father's side since the beginning of the Express Route and I consider it an honor to serve in his stead. I will keep to the highest standards of the Pony Express and vow my allegiance just like my father before me.

Your humble servant,
Jack Rivers

The twinge of guilt she felt as she signed her name lasted only a second. It would have to do. It was the truth. Marshall Rivers was her father, and he was dead. All the riders liked to call her Jack — like her father had — even though she insisted she preferred Jackie. Tears pricked the corners of her eyes. She hadn't really preferred it. It had just been her way of arguing the point. In her small world surrounded by mostly men, she liked to make sure everyone knew that she liked being a girl.

Jack. Jackie. Jacqueline.

She'd never get to hear him call her name again. Perhaps from now on, she'd take on the beloved nickname with pride. At least it would always bring a smile.

Using the blotter to keep the ink from smearing as it dried, she felt the rumble under her chair. The rider would be here any moment, and it was her job to greet him.

With a flick of her fingers, she had the letter folded and stuffed into an envelope she'd previously addressed and stamped with the Pony Express stamp. She tucked it into her apron pocket. Moving toward the door, she retied the ribbon around her thick braid and threw it over her shoulder.

Everyone scurried about with their jobs as she exited her home, which was also the office for the station. The station served as a home station for the Pony Express as well as a way station for the stagecoach line.

As she surveyed the goings-on, she saw a fresh horse ready and waiting, along with a new rider. Like clockwork, everyone was prepared.

As young Timothy practically flew in on his mount, he pulled the California mustang to a halt and hopped off.

She checked her watch and noted the time in her thoughts.

Timothy had the leather mochila — which was the heart of the Express — wrested off the saddle in seconds and passed it to John with a nod. "I'm glad that run is over." The skinny young man seemed to be covered in an inch-thick layer of dust. "Eighty miles today. I'm starvin'." He headed to the cleaning station they kept for the riders to wash the dirt and grit from their faces.

The small group of people laughed along as everyone did their duties. Checking the new mount, the saddle. Taking the exhausted horse for a good brush-down, food, and water.

Theirs was a full home station. It meant they provided food, housing, and help to the riders. Several of the riders called this home as they made their runs to either the east or west and returned. They kept numerous horses for the riders since they needed to be changed out every ten to twenty miles. The success of the company rested on the speed of the journey. Day and night.

Two scheduled runs came through every day, but being part of the Pony Express meant being ready for emergency runs — the specials — at any given time. And they happened a good deal. Especially if any news of import came through for government officials. With the threat of states seceding, the arguments over slavery, and a presidential election coming up, everyone felt the tremors of the possibility of war on the horizon.

Jackie opened the way pocket on the mochila with a key from around her neck as John positioned the leather pouch over the small Express saddle on the new horse. They were all used to attending their duties together and in tandem — even as everything moved from one mount to another. She pulled out the oiled silk bundle and checked for any correspondence for them. Then she tucked her letter inside. She took the time card and documented the arrival time and checked her watch for the departure time and wrote it down as well. Wrapping everything back up in the oiled cloth to ensure no water could damage the important missives that people paid a pretty penny to send, she then finished the job by placing it back into the pocket and locking it up.

John mounted and waved his hat at everyone as he took off at a breakneck pace. "See ya back here tomorra!" Off he went. A cloud of dust in his wake.

With a hand above her eyes to shield her from the sinking sun, Jackie watched the rider until she couldn't see him any longer. Something her father had always done, and she'd kept up the tradition. It only seemed fitting. The sadness that engulfed her at the thought of her father made it difficult to see. But she blinked away the tears and focused on the horse's elegant stride.

Every time she watched a rider head out, she prayed until he was out of sight. The number of riders and horses it took to cross the two-thousand-mile trail was extravagant. But to get the news in a week rather than a month or more was huge. It never ceased to amaze her, so every day she found herself praying for these young men who sacrificed so much.

"Hey, Jack" — Timothy's call made her turn around — "you got anything good to eat?" The grin that spread across his freshly scrubbed face made her giggle. The boy was always hungry.

"You know better than to ask that, Timothy Peterson." She brushed at the new layer of dust on her skirt from the exchange of riders. "Get on inside. I've got biscuits and gravy ready and waiting for dinner."

"You're the best." He ran over, lifted her hand, and kissed it. Another habit from her father. He'd taught all the young men to treat her like a lady even though they were in the middle of nowhere and, yes, even though they called her Jack.

The memory made tears prick her eyes again. Her only hope was that eventually the pain of his passing wouldn't hurt so much.

"Marshall loved your biscuits and gravy. *Almost* as much as I do." Timothy offered his arm.

Jackie took it and smiled. "Well, I made three pans of biscuits this time. Try to save some for the rest of us, all right?"

As she walked back into the station, the scent of freshly churned-up dirt was familiar and comfortable. She prayed that the owners of the COC&PP would leave the station in her hands. There was no need for them to know she was a woman. At least not right now. They had too many other troubles on their shoulders without worrying about one station keeper. Especially way out here. As long as she kept the Express going, fed and housed the riders, took care of the horses, and kept the Indians at bay, she should be safe continuing as she pleased. No one had ever been sent out to check up on them, so she wasn't too worried about that. But her conscience still niggled at not disclosing her gender.

They couldn't very well shut her down.

Who would run the station? Besides, the stage came through from Virginia City as well, and her outpost was needed. Her rooms were needed. As well as the meals.

But even while she washed up and greeted everyone with a smile as they came in for dinner, she realized that all the reasoning and lists in the world couldn't deny the truth.

She was an unmarried young woman. With no parents. No family. Not a soul to claim her.

As soon as the owners found out that she hadn't told the truth, she could very well be out of a job and kicked out of the only home she'd ever known.

October 10, 1860

The stage rocked back and forth. Another stage. Another town. With every bump and rut in the trail sending a jolt through every bone in his body. If Elijah hadn't felt old before, this journey certainly did the trick. He felt like he'd aged two decades with all the uncomfortable forms of travel he'd had to employ.

He took out his handkerchief and wiped his face. It had been impossible to keep the dirt and grime from seeping into every crack and crevice as soon as he'd left civilization and the train line. Which had been ages and hundreds of miles ago. If they could ever get a train line built that traversed the entire country, that would be a glorious thing. But it would also be a daunting and very costly task. The government had been surveying for a good while, and how or when they would even begin connecting the East and the West was up in the air.

As he looked out the window and watched the barren land pass in scrub brush and rolling hills, he prayed that he would be able to accomplish his job. There weren't any telegraph lines connecting him to Kansas City, and so he'd had to rely on the Express — with their ponies and skinny riders — to get his messages back to Mr. Vines. Grateful that such an extravagant service existed, it still didn't help him feel any better about having nothing positive to report.

At first he'd sent messages every few days. Especially when he found someone who remembered a woman with a baby traveling alone. But the descriptions of the woman varied — it *was* a long time ago — and he always hit a dead end. Back in 1834, all of this would have still been Mexico. The thought had crossed his mind on several occasions that it seemed almost crazy for a woman to journey this far on her own with a baby. But then again, if she was trying to hide, what better way than to leave the country? Even though the United States owned all of this land now, it was still quite desolate.

With a sigh, he sat back on the seat. It would be another couple of hours before he'd make it to the next stop. He left the flap over the window open and allowed the crisp, clean air to fill his lungs. That much could be said for leaving the city — the fresh air had done his health good. If only Mr. Vines had been strong enough, the change in scenery might have done the same for him.

Elijah wanted to please the man who'd given him so much, but this quest had also brought up a flood of his own memories and feelings. Feelings he wasn't quite sure what to do with. For years it had been easy to put it all behind him. Those names, Laura and Martha. He shivered, wondering if they would forever haunt him. He thought he'd had a handle on it. Until Mr. Vines brought it up.

He shook his head and tried to focus. *Why now, Lord? I don't understand. This isn't about me. It's about Charles Vines. Please help me to ease his mind in this difficult time.*

The prayer for his boss brought their last

conversation back to the forefront of his mind. His thoughts tumbled over all that had transpired.

As he closed his eyes to the rocking of the stage, their exchange of words rushed back to his memory.

"But then I did some terrible things."

Elijah's heart thundered in his chest. The look on Mr. Vines's face said it all. Something truly awful had happened. Elijah swallowed and waited.

"You see . . . I had a problem with liquor." The older man stood, an angry frown etched into his features. "No. It was more than a problem. Let's face it. The devil himself had a hold on me through the bottle. I was rich and successful with a beautiful wife, yet I had this hole inside me that seemed unquenchable. I tried filling it with anything and everything. Eventually, drinking was the only way to numb the pain I felt from being hollowed out. And I turned into someone I didn't recognize. A monster. I did . . . unspeakable things to the only woman I've ever loved."

For years Elijah had wondered about his boss's lack of interest in romantic relationships. Even though women practically threw themselves at his feet. For the longest time, he just thought it was because he was focused on his businesses, and then there was the fact that he was a devout Christian man and wanted to honor the Lord. But Elijah had also noticed that Vines often acted like a recluse. It all made a bit more sense now. But how could the man in front of him have done horrible things? The facts didn't equate in his mind.

"I hurt her." His voice cracked.

"You don't have to tell me anything more if you don't wish to, sir." As much as he was curious to know the whole story, he wondered if rehashing the past would make his boss sicker. What if it killed him? Elijah cared for the older man too much to see him in this amount of pain.

"No. It's important that you know the truth. I said horrendous things to her when I was drunk, and it escalated over time. I began to take out my vile temper on her." The man choked on the last word and tears slipped out of his eyes. "I threw things at her. Hit her. One time I even shoved her down the stairs. It was a miracle she lived." Great sobs took over, and Charles Vines shook like a leaf.

Elijah went to his employer's side and laid a hand on the man's shoulder. Consoling wasn't an option, but he could listen. "What happened?"

"One night when I was exceedingly brutal, she must have decided that enough was enough. I don't remember much, but I do recall running outside and throwing a bottle at a carriage as she left. I never saw her — or our daughter — again." Charles swiped at his face with his hands and took a long, shaky breath.

"You had a daughter?" Nothing could have shocked Elijah more. Not only had his employer kept the secret that he'd had a wife, but to find out that there was a child as well? The magnitude of it swirled in his brain.

"Yes. Sadly, I know nothing about her. I was too imbibed for the short span of her life that she was here. I felt empty inside. Useless. So increasingly, I turned to the bottle. You don't know how many times I've wished I could go back. . . ."

Things began to fall into place in Elijah's mind. "What happened to your wife and daughter?"

Mr. Vines held up the beautiful piece of jewelry and stared at it. "After they left, Anna sold this brooch — I'm assuming to pay for whatever she needed to survive. I found it several months later, bought it back, and paid for any information on her I could find. I followed the trail of her purchases and discovered she'd headed west. But after that, no matter how many men I sent to find her, they all came up empty-handed. She'd changed her appearance as far as I could tell by selling her custom clothes and paid people to keep quiet — at least that's what the investigators discovered. Then the trail went completely cold. West of the Rocky Mountains, she vanished without a trace.

"Then one day — years later — I received a cryptic letter in the mail. All it said was that he — the sender — thought I should know that my wife had passed on and she'd been happy the last few years of her life. No return address. No name. No word on our daughter. It broke me. I would never have the chance to show Anna that I'd changed. No way to apologize. No opportunity to make amends. Then I began to question the validity of the letter. Maybe she wasn't dead. I had hope that she was still alive. Perhaps because of my horrific behavior, she'd faked her death so she could be free of me. But it was odd to me that the letter said that my wife died and never mentioned our daughter. The investigators all agreed. They believed the letter. After all this time, I'd love to know that my Anna is alive. But I have more hope that perhaps our daughter is."

Elijah opened his eyes, and his boss's voice faded from his mind. What horrible tragedy had brought the man to his knees. And having to face what he'd done and that he'd never see his wife again. But even through it all, good had come out of it for Charles Vines. Because he'd changed. Even though he'd committed unspeakable horrors, the man had found God. And through Him — repentance, faith, hope.

Then God had brought Elijah to Charles Vines's door. The encounter had changed Elijah's life as well. The least he could do was fulfill this wish for his employer — now partner.

Pulling out his notes and a pencil, Elijah studied the details of all Charles had shared.

Charles had confessed that during the first fifteen years after their disappearance, he'd secretly investigated — hoping there was a slim chance his child had survived and lived happily somewhere. He'd spent large amounts of money on what proved to be futile endeavors. This search drove him to succeed in business. The more he expanded his empire, the more money he had to finance his search.

But it had been to no avail. So Charles halted all the investigations and poured himself into growing his already enormous and wealthy empire with full gusto. All the while hoping for the day that there would be news.

Then his health declined.

Watching his boss and beloved mentor wrestle with the thought of his own mortality had been difficult for Elijah. But he'd supported and encouraged him as much as he could. Meanwhile, Mr. Vines made the decision to put everything he had into finding his child. And the man had quite a fortune. He was one of the richest men in America.

The shock had been great. Elijah hadn't believed the stories at first. It all seemed surreal. But as he'd now spent months on the trail, traveling from one stage stop to the next, he found all the conversations he'd had with Mr. Vines replaying in his mind. It made him think about how *he* would feel if he were in the same situation.

To think that he'd worked for the man for a decade and hadn't understood the motivation behind his actions. The man he thought of as a mentor — even a father figure — had carried his horrible secret for so long that Elijah believed the weight of it had caused the man's health to fail.

Vines's daughter would be all grown up now. Possibly married with children. Elijah made a note in the margin. She would be twenty-six years old. What if too much time had passed?

But her father wanted to apologize and

tell her the truth himself — no matter her age. And he wanted to be able to pass on his wealth to someone who deserved it, because he stated in no uncertain terms that he believed he *didn't.*

Elijah laid the pencil down in the crease of his book. The shocking news from his employer had made him examine his own life. For years he'd thought that working with Charles Vines was such an excellent career choice. He'd made more money than he could use because his boss was so good at investing and encouraged him to invest and buy as well. But while all the other young men were settling down with wives and having children and getting their businesses started, he'd been too busy working. At least that's what he kept telling himself. The hurt and pain from the past had quite a bit of influence as well. Two women had made him decide that marriage was not for him. Ever. He'd rather be alone than be hurt again. That, his employer knew, was hard enough to deal with. But given how much time had elapsed, he felt like life was passing him by. How had he gotten to this point?

The past few months he'd traveled thousands of miles searching and investigating. All the while remembering the misery in

Vines's eyes. Even after all Elijah had been through, his boss's testimony pricked his soul. Realizing he did want a family for himself, Elijah cringed at the thought of ending up like his parents. But the clock was ticking. At twenty-eight, he had nothing to show for himself except wealth. That thought in light of eternity didn't make him feel like he'd accomplished much of anything. He wouldn't be taking any of the wealth with him when he died. So why wasn't he investing in a relationship?

Why? Because it hurt. Because he might be just a tad bit afraid.

That thought irked him. God didn't want him living in fear. Yet that was exactly what he was doing.

With a deep breath, he picked up the pencil and focused back on Vines. He couldn't deal with his own emotions right now. There'd be plenty of time for that later. But Charles might not have that luxury. With new determination, he promised himself that as soon as he fulfilled this search for his employer, he would change his priorities. God willing.

If he'd learned anything from his boss's revelation and their subsequent discussions, it was that first and foremost he needed to keep God as his focus. He'd worry about the rest later.

Right now, he had a woman to find. And he was close — he could feel it. Looking at the list of possible sightings of the woman and child, he tapped the page with the pencil.

She couldn't have simply disappeared.

Outside Virginia City

"Whatcha think?" The fat man squeezed himself into a chair as he puffed on his cigar.

Taking a look at the forged treasury note in front of him, Carl tilted his head. He walked over to the window, took a magnifying glass out of his pocket, and positioned it over the document. With a lift of his brows, he gave a slight nod. "Much better than the last. Still might need some work around the edges." He put the magnifying glass back.

"It's gonna cost ya. That's detail work and I can't just make these out of nothin'." A puff of smoke accentuated his words.

Whipping his Colt out of its holster, Carl leveled it between the man's eyes. "We've already agreed on a price, my friend. The agreement was for acceptable documents, and you know quite well what happened to the last man who crossed me, so why don't you rethink that statement?" He pulled back the hammer and let his words sink in.

Two pudgy hands lifted in the air. "You don't have to get snippy with me. I'm just trying to put food on the table." The man didn't seem at all fazed by the threat of a loaded gun pointed at his head.

"Food on the table? Looks like you've had plenty. Seems to me you're just getting greedy."

"You gotta admit my work is worth it." A slimy grin spread across his face.

"I don't need to admit anything. Not until it's complete and I'm satisfied." Carl clicked the hammer back into place and lowered the gun. "The last guy was good. Real good. But sadly, we had a difference of opinion, and he no longer works for me."

A deep chuckle made the man's thick belly shake. "He ain't workin' for anyone from six feet under."

Carl narrowed his eyes and studied the man. The brash confidence and lack of fear made the man more dangerous than he wanted to admit. He'd have to keep a close eye on this one. But his work was top-notch. Not that he had to admit that. Tossing the forgery back on the table, he took a deep breath. "Fix the scrollwork on the edges. It needs to be perfect. I'll be back in two days for the lot." Not waiting for a response, he walked over to the door and let himself out.

Let the man think whatever he wanted. As long as Carl had the forgeries in his hands and completed on time, his plan would go off without a hitch.

Chapter 3

Carson Sink Station, Utah Territory
October 12, 1860

Jackie smoothed her apron over her skirt as she stood outside the station and the stage rumbled toward her little stop. Everyone in their small town — if they could even call the gathering of a few buildings an actual town — came out to watch the stage and of course to see what kind of mail, passengers, and news would be brought from Virginia City. The arrival of a stage was always an exciting event because it connected them with the rest of the world.

Sometimes out here in the remote area of the Utah Territory, she'd long for something new and different. But in reality she just felt alone. Especially since her father's death. Then she'd feel guilty because her friends — the few people who inhabited their little community — were all like family. And even though she longed sometimes to see the cities that she read about or to wear the fine fashions from *Godey's Lady's Book,* all she really wanted was to stay in her home and run the station. She loved this barren, salt-covered desert area. They were close to a lake and had a nice spring for fresh water, and the craggy hills always made her feel welcome and safe. Because it was home.

Hopefully the men who owned the Pony Express would send word soon and she could continue on with their permission.

Guilt twinged in her stomach at the thought. Was it wrong to have signed her name as Jack when that was her nickname? She hadn't outright lied to them.

Well. Maybe she had. Because omitting the truth was just as much a lie, wasn't it?

Everything she stood for was based on honesty. It had been her way of life. So it shamed her to think that she hadn't been completely honest with the owners. The truth was, she *had* run this station at her father's side. She *did* know what she was doing and she wanted to serve her country by helping with this very important service. Her father was also very much dead.

But she hadn't told the men who hired him the truth. It wasn't just an omission. She'd misled them by signing her name as Jack. And when she wrote the letter, she'd been determined to sound masculine. There weren't any excuses.

Did it matter that she was a woman? Wouldn't they simply be concerned that there was someone to run the station who knew the rules and regulations of the Pony Express?

The argument could go round and round in her mind. With a deep breath, she focused on the team of horses that snorted and huffed as they came to a stop. God forgave her for her sin. She'd just have to confess it to the owners.

Someday.

It wouldn't do for her to be wringing her hands in worry when she had customers to attend to.

"Carson Sink Station!" the driver of the stage yelled. He secured the reins and then started grabbing luggage from the top of the stage and lowering it to the boot to be handed down.

The door of the stage swung open, and a handsome, middle-aged man ducked as he exited through the opening. His tall, wide-banded top hat gleamed in the sunlight. Which was quite the feat considering he'd been riding in the dusty stage.

Jackie admired his neat attire. A pair of blue checked trousers peeked out from underneath his navy blue knee-length over-coat. He must be from the city. The thought made her smile to herself. What was it about her and fashion? She loved to look at it in the magazines and often asked Dad to buy her a stylish dress out of one of the catalogs. Shaking her head, she sucked in a breath as another man exited. His eyes landed on her and she couldn't help but appreciate what she saw there. The light color of his blue eyes in contrast to his dark hair made them very striking.

Younger than the first, the second man wore a top hat that wasn't quite so shiny. Perhaps he'd been traveling for longer so it had accumulated a bit more dust? But his suit was made of fine material and appeared custom tailored. Both of the passengers seemed to be men of wealth. What were they doing in this area of the country? While she'd had plenty of guests travel through here, the arrival of two gentlemen from the city was rare. Especially at the same time.

The owners couldn't have sent them . . . could they?

No. They wouldn't have had time to get here. And why would they send anyone out? It was too costly. She needed to banish her worry and welcome the customers.

Stepping forward, Jackie greeted them.

"Welcome to Carson Sink Station, gentlemen. I'm Miss Rivers. How can I help you today? A hot meal and a place to stay?"

The older man nodded at her and smiled. "That would be lovely. Thank you, Miss Rivers."

"And you are?"

"My name is James Crowell. It's a pleasure to make your acquaintance."

The man with the striking eyes stepped forward after their exchange and gave her a bow and a smile. "Elijah Johnson, Miss Rivers. It's indeed a pleasure."

"Where do you hail from?"

"Washington, DC," Mr. Crowell tipped his hat at her.

"Kansas City."

"I see." A tiny bit of relief filled her mind as their responses confirmed they couldn't be from the COC&PP. She could relax and be herself. "I run the station and stop here. Are you here on business?"

"Yes." Mr. Crowell nodded his head and looked back at the other man. "At least that is my understanding of Mr. Johnson as well. We just met on this last leg of the journey here from Virginia City."

"Yes, business for me as well." Mr. Johnson gave her a slight nod.

She motioned her hand toward her home.

"It's nice to have you here in our little part of the Utah Territory. If you'll follow me, I'll get you situated for the evening."

"Thank you."

"Thank you." The men's voices blended in a bass and baritone harmony that made her feel comfortable and feminine.

Michael, who'd worked for her dad since he'd been orphaned at age seven, carried the men's luggage behind them. "Will you be putting them in the two larger rooms, Jack?"

"That would be perfect." As she entered the home she loved so much, she gave the men a smile. "This is the parlor, dining area, and kitchen. Feel free to make use of the parlor, and all meals will be served at the dining room table." The large open area always made her think of large families gathering together and how wonderful that would be. She loved when all the riders were back at their station and they could have dinner together and share stories and laughter.

Leading them to the counter by the front window that they used for the way station and Express mail business, she gave them the details. "It will be fifty cents a night or three dollars for the week. That includes breakfast and the evening meal. If you would like to join us for lunch as well, that will be an additional five cents. How long will you be staying with us?"

"At least two nights for me." Mr. Crowell gave her a smile.

"I'm not sure." Mr. Johnson studied her for a long moment. "It could be at least a week. And I'd be very grateful to partake of all meals here. Thank you. In case you need to let the cook know."

She gave him a smile. He'd know soon enough that she was the cook as well. She turned the open ledger to them and dipped her pen in the ink. Handing it to Mr. Crowell, she pointed to the line he needed to sign. "Would you please sign in?"

"Of course. Thank you." Mr. Crowell wrote his name in the finest penmanship she'd seen in a long time. "Will you be requiring a deposit?" He passed the pen to Mr. Johnson.

"For the first night, yes. We can settle the rest tomorrow."

Both of the men paid and she checked off the ledger.

"Gentlemen." Off the main area were two hallways. One to the right and one to the left. "If you'll follow me to your rooms." She led them down the left hallway, quite lengthy and lined with well-furnished guest rooms, six in all. It was a large place for an area of the country where most people lived in one-room cabins or adobe-walled structures. The other hallway off the parlor led to her room and personal parlor. They used to be her dad's rooms, but since his death, she'd changed them around and spruced them up, trying to make the spaces as homey as she could without him. The change had been hard, but she wanted to try to move on. It was proving to be much harder than she anticipated. And some days she longed to have left the living spaces as they had been.

Emotion clogged her throat for a moment and she swallowed against it. She went to the first room on the left and stood at the entryway, "This can be yours, Mr. Crowell. Mr. Johnson, yours is the next down the hall."

"Thank you."

"Thank you, Miss Rivers."

"Make yourselves comfortable. Dinner will be served in an hour." As she glanced back and forth between the men, her stomach did a little flip.

For one, she didn't understand what business these fine gentlemen could have here, and having such wealthy customers made her a tad bit nervous — she hoped with all her might that she would live up to their standards. And two, they were both handsome men. Especially the younger one.

"Miss Rivers?"

She turned back to find Mr. Johnson with his hat in his hands and felt heat creep up her neck at her previous thoughts.

"Thank you again."

"You're welcome, Mr. Johnson." As she gazed at the man, her stomach did that weird little flip again.

"Do you run the station alone?"

"Um . . . yes. But as you can see, I have lots of help." The question stabbed her and made her miss her father. She hadn't been asked about him since he passed.

"Is your mother around?"

That was an odd question. "No. My mother has been gone since I was a child."

"Oh. I'm so sorry." The intensity of his gaze softened.

The man's attractive features drew her in. Something about his eyes fascinated her. With a nod, she turned and walked back toward the kitchen area. Dad had told her many times over the years that one day she'd find herself attracted to a man. It had never happened. Sure, she'd found plenty of men handsome over time. But none of them stayed more than a night or two, and not one of them sparked her fancy. None until now.

Placing a hand on her stomach to still the butterflies that had taken up residence, she shook her head. "Jackie Rivers, you need to get your mind back on the business at hand. This is no time for silly shenanigans." Just because she found Mr. Johnson handsome didn't mean she should be acting like a silly schoolgirl.

"Talking to yourself again?" Michael's teasing washed over her.

"Of course. No one else listens to me quite as well." She put her hands on her hips. "Don't you have some chores to do?"

"So bossy." He nudged her with his elbow and waggled his eyebrows.

She watched him snag one of the biscuits she'd just taken from the oven. It had only been a year since Dad had brought the stove in here. For years they'd cooked over the open fire in the giant fireplace. The memory made her a touch despondent. Glancing back at the giant cast-iron piece, she wished she could hear his voice one more time.

"You're thinking about your dad, aren't ya?" Michael touched her shoulder. "That big ol' thing makes me think of him too. I'll never forget when we had to drag this monster in here. I got my fingers pinched in the doorframe, and then Marshall set that stove down on my boot. At the time, I wasn't so sure having a cookstove inside was worth it."

The memory helped her to push the sad thoughts behind her. "And then you made Dad laugh so hard with your antics, it took him a minute to lift it off of you."

"I miss him." Michael's voice turned raspy as he wrapped an arm around her shoulders.

"Me too."

He swiped at his face and took a deep breath. "I'd better get back out and check on the horses."

"Thanks. Me too — not the horses . . . but I'd better get back to dinner." Her blunder made them both chuckle. The memories were wonderful, but they also left her feeling melancholy. So far, she thought she'd done pretty well with her grief. She just needed to focus on the boys. They needed her.

At fourteen, Michael was as close to a brother as she'd ever have. Even though she thought of most of the young Express riders like younger brothers, Michael was differ-ent. He'd been with them for a long time, where the Pony Express had just started this year. Dad had taken him into their home and raised him like a son. Jackie hoped that

Michael would stay and continue to help here, but what if he decided to spread his wings one day and leave? He'd always had big dreams. She couldn't imagine that he would actually want to stay in this isolated place. And watching him mourn for her father made her heart ache for him. Sometimes the memories overwhelmed her. Did they do the same to Michael?

Then there were Timothy, John, Mark, Luke, and Paul. Hired to be Express riders, Dad liked to call them his preacher boys. They were all so young, none of them more than seventeen, but they loved studying the Bible with Dad and he had been a wonderful influence in their lives. His passing left a huge void. How would she ever be able to fill it?

As she finished setting the extra plates for dinner, she wondered if she should sit down soon and have a chat with Michael and the other boys. Dad would want her to do the best she could to make sure they had their feet under them. But did she know what to do?

"Miss Rivers?" Her guest's voice brought her out of her thoughts.

She looked up at him and pasted on a smile. "I'm sorry, Mr. Crowell, did you need something?"

"My apologies for interrupting your work, but I was hoping to find a time when we could talk privately."

She swallowed hard. Had she done something wrong? "Of . . . of course. May I ask what this is about?" The silverware in her hands clanked against the dishes as she laid them out.

"I serve the secretary of the treasury of the United States as his secretary." He stood a little straighter after he said his title. "I'm in the middle of an investigation for my boss, and I think you might be able to help me."

Investigation. Out here? For the Treasury? That was odd. "Of course I will do whatever I can to help. Would tomorrow morning be a good time to chat? After I feed everyone breakfast, I have an hour before the Express is scheduled to come through."

"That would work splendidly. I appreciate your willingness to help, Miss Rivers. Thank you." He gave a slight bow and left the room.

Twenty minutes later, her mind had tried to imagine what Mr. Crowell could want to talk to her about. It baffled her. Did it have anything to do with the Express? She hoped not. The company had already suffered financial setbacks.

Thinking about the Pony Express brought the owners to mind. Why couldn't they just respond to her letter by now? It would help her to move forward with confidence.

With a huff, she blew some stray strands of hair off her forehead.

As she brought the food out, the dining room began to fill with all the workers and their two guests. Ten in all, they almost filled the table. When Mr. Johnson ended up in the chair next to hers, her heart sped up its rhythm.

After everyone was seated, she turned to Michael. "Would you ask the Lord to bless our food, please?"

"Yes, Jack." Michael bowed his head. "God, we thank You for this food and ask that You bless our bodies with this nourishment. Amen."

"Amens" rounded the table. The two hurricane lamps filled the room with a soft glow. The sight of food overflowing the dishes made her want to chuckle. She used an astonishing amount of food to feed this crew every day. Steam spiraled upward from the mountain of fried pork chops. Two large bowls with creamy mashed potatoes sat on either side. Then her dad's favorite — carrots she glazed in brown sugar when available.

As the bowls and platters were passed and they began to eat, Jackie couldn't help watching the man next to her out of the corner of her eye. What was it about him that drew her like a moth to the flame? And why? She'd just met the man.

He cleared his throat. "This is delicious. My compliments to the chef."

She let out a nervous laugh. "That would be me. Thank you, Mr. Johnson."

Mr. Crowell nodded his agreement. "This is some of the tastiest fare I've ever had. I concur with Mr. Johnson. My compliments."

"You all are going to make her blush," Michael piped up from the other side of the table. "This is nothin'. You should try her stew or her biscuits and gravy."

Murmurs of affirmation rounded the table.

She felt the heat rising in her cheeks. "How was everyone's day?" The best way to get the attention off her was to get a lively conversation started between the workers who lived like a giant family.

It worked. Mark and Luke started bantering back and forth about the trouble they'd had with two of the horses, and Michael joined them.

Mr. Johnson tilted his head toward her.

"A very deft redirection of the conversation, Miss Rivers."

She quirked an eyebrow at him. "I don't know what you mean."

His soft chuckle and Mr. Crowell's grin made her smile. "May I ask you something?" His light blue eyes sparkled in the candle-light.

"Of course."

"Are you two siblings?"

Wiping her mouth with her napkin, she looked over at Michael and winked. "Not by blood. My father took him in when he lost his parents. But I think of him as my brother. And we squabble like siblings. How's that for an answer?"

Mr. Johnson's smile made her stomach do funny things. "Perfectly sound to me." He looked across the table at the young man. "Michael, might I ask you a question?"

"Sure." Michael shrugged his shoulders and took a sip from his cup.

"I noticed that twice now you've referred to Miss Rivers as Jack. Is that a family name?"

Water almost spewed from Michael's mouth as he laughed and covered his mouth with his napkin. It took a moment for him to gain his composure. "I'm sorry for my manners. But you took me off guard, Mr.

Johnson." His cheeks tinged pink.

"Maybe it's best if I explain." Jackie turned toward their guest and gave Michael another wink. The young man got flustered easily when important men were around. He always wanted to impress them and imitate their manners and behavior — but instead he tended to have clumsy spells with either his actions or words. "My name is Jacqueline, and although I insisted I liked Jackie as a shorter version of it, my dad always called me Jack. It stuck. Most of the Express riders call me that now."

His eyes softened, and he blinked. "I like it."

The connection between them was overwhelming to Jackie. Especially since this man was a complete stranger. She broke eye contact and looked back to her plate. What had come over her?

But Mr. Johnson leaned toward her. "Miss Rivers, perhaps we could take a walk later? I believe I could use your insight on a matter for my business."

Two different men. Asking for her insight on the same day. It all seemed a bit surreal. "Of course. I'd be happy to do anything I can to assist you in your work."

"Thank you." He leaned back and cut into his pork chop.

Turning back to Mark and Luke, she checked in on the happenings in the stables. Because frankly, Mr. Johnson's nearness was doing strange things to her. And she had no idea why or how to control it. As the station manager, she needed to keep her wits about her.

Dinner continued in lively conversation and plenty more compliments on the food. Their two guests seemed to enjoy talking to each of the workers about their jobs and how they liked living and working here. When they were all done, Jackie rose to clear the table.

"Let us help you with this, Miss Rivers." Mr. Crowell rose and nodded to Mr. Johnson. "Mr. Johnson and I discussed earlier how we would like to show our appreciation for the wonderful accommodations. Believe me, the West holds some questionable lodgings, and I've stayed in many of them. Not to mention the food I've been served, which I'm not sure even deserves the designation of edible." The older man began to roll up his shirtsleeves. "It's the least we can do to show our relief and gratefulness for a meal and housing that is so welcoming."

Never in her life had she seen two men — gentlemen, no less — who had paid for their stay, help with dishes. It was unheard of.

Did gentlemen in the city do this? She couldn't imagine that they did. So why were they helping now?

But in no time, the dishes were washed, dried, and put away. As everyone moved into the parlor, Mr. Johnson stepped next to her. "Perhaps we could take that —"

The front door burst open.

Mrs. June Liverpool — the only other woman in their little community and married to the local blacksmith for the Pony Express — sashayed her way into the parlor. "Jacqueline, have you seen the new *Lady's Book*? You simply must read this article about sewing machines." She pulled out the magazine she'd had tucked under her arm, flipped through the pages, and took a deep breath as she glanced around the room. "Oh, you have guests. How nice. Good evening." She nodded and curtsied to each man and then plowed ahead. "Here, on page 174. Just look at that timetable right there." June pointed to the upper-right-hand portion of the page that contained a table showing the hours and minutes of machine usage versus the hours and minutes needed to sew something by hand. "It's astonishing how much time can be saved using the machine. Imagine a frock coat sewn in two and a half hours! That's fourteen hours saved, right there. And imagine sewing a linen vest in forty-eight minutes. Forty — eight — minutes!" Her voice had risen an octave as she stabbed the page with her finger. "Look, the chart clearly shows that it takes five hours and fourteen minutes if we were to do that by hand. It's miraculous. That's what it is. Aren't you enthralled?"

Jackie smiled past June to Mr. Johnson, hoping the interruption hadn't discouraged him from speaking to her again. Because she really did wish to speak with him. Was that inappropriate? Oh, how she wished Dad were here to talk to. If she'd ever needed his advice on men, it was now.

Mr. Johnson appeared amused by their guest.

She nodded to June. "Oh, well . . . yes, of course. That's quite fascinating, isn't it?"

"Just listen to this: 'Seams of considerable length are ordinarily sewed at the rate of a yard a minute.' A yard a minute!" She clutched the magazine to her chest and let out a laborious sigh. "Imagine how much time that will save. I'll have to convince Mr. Liverpool that I simply must order one."

Movement at the door caught Jackie's attention. Mr. Elijah Johnson smiled, clearly entertained at her neighbor's busy chatter.

Tipping his hat in her direction, he slipped out the door, and Jackie wished she'd had more time to speak to the interesting gentleman.

Maybe she could convince Mrs. Liverpool to take a walk with her outside. As soon as the thought arose, June sat at the table and began flipping through the pages of *Godey's Lady's Book*. With a sigh, Jackie sat with her friend. This was going to take awhile.

CHAPTER 4

Elijah took long strides down the dirt path that was the lone road in Carson Sink. Only a smattering of buildings made up this little stop-off point. The stables and barn for the Pony Express were off to his right, while a couple of smaller buildings and what appeared to be another home were on the left across the so-called street.

Then there was Miss Rivers's home and station house. The large adobe building was quite the sight. Impressive too. On the other side of it was another long adobe building — perhaps the bunkhouse?

Miss Rivers.

He paced back in the other direction. She had blond hair and green eyes. Like the description of Anna Vines. But she looked entirely too young to be Vines's daughter and had a different last name. Besides, he hadn't been able to ask her any questions yet. But still . . . she admitted her mother was dead. Then who was the man she'd called Dad? The one who adopted Michael? It didn't make any sense. At least not yet. He realized a bit more investigating was needed. And Miss Rivers was remarkable. He wouldn't mind investigating one little bit.

Looking around him, he took in his surroundings. The station house was well-maintained, clean, and quite comfortable. Whoever had built it had done a phenomenal job. Was her dad still around? She seemed awfully young to be the owner of such a fine establishment, especially as a woman — in most areas, women weren't allowed to be landowners. It puzzled him. But she definitely stated that she ran the place. Perhaps she could be a widow? That would account for the last name. But no. That couldn't be. She'd introduced herself as *Miss* Rivers. There had to be an explanation, and whatever it was, he aimed to find out.

Perhaps she had access to information about other visitors through this area. If her way station even existed back in 1834.

The more he thought about her though, the more he realized she had captivated his thoughts for a different reason. Looking back toward the main building, he wondered what brought her here and why she stayed. Could she have only come out here since the beginning of the Pony Express? There was a definite attachment between her and the young men. The riders all adored her — that was plain as day.

Then there was young Michael. She'd said that her dad had taken him in but didn't mention anything else about him or where he was at dinner.

If only Charles had known what sharing his story would set in motion. Perhaps the old man *had* known what he was doing all along — and that it would plague Elijah's mind on the journey. Ever the thinker, Elijah often overthought many situations and business dealings.

Even though Vines had encouraged him to open his heart and finally settle down, he couldn't have known that Elijah would meet a woman like Jackie. He'd met a lot of eligible and beautiful women in his years, but never one like her.

And she was nothing like Martha or Laura.

Thoughts of his past invaded his mind again. Why was it he'd been able to keep them buried for years, and now everything seemed to be pummeling him in the face like it happened just yesterday? Martha's sweet-smiling face mocked him as he paced. Her betrayal still festered like an open wound every time he thought about it, so he tried to push her as far from his thoughts as possible. As soon as the ache started in his heart again, Laura's face came to mind. The haughty look she wore as she turned her back on him was the only memory he could conjure of her. He deserved it, but still. He closed his eyes against the memories and forced himself to come back to the present.

A vision of Miss Rivers replaced images of the other two women. They were all quite beautiful. But the way Miss Rivers kept her blond hair pulled back in a long, thick braid made her look young and innocent. Especially compared to the other two. If he'd had the wisdom he possessed now ten years ago, would things have turned out differently? Would he have been able to see the lack of innocence in Martha's eyes?

When they'd first pulled into the station at Carson Sink, he thought Miss Rivers was a young girl — someone's daughter out to see the visitors to their corner of the world. When she stepped up to greet them, he'd quickly discovered such was not the case.

That she managed not only the Pony Express station but her own stage stop as well was amazing. Quite simply, she intrigued him.

But what was he thinking? The last time a woman had fascinated him, things had ended in disaster and he'd fled the East. It was probably for the best that he'd been interrupted by the dramatic and loquacious Mrs. Liverpool. It wasn't like he would ever have the opportunity to see Miss Rivers past his visit here. She lived in the middle of nowhere in the Utah Territory. He lived in Kansas City. Thousands of miles away. Even though she fascinated him, he should get his heart in check and focus on the task at hand. She might have answers to help him find Vines's daughter. That had to come first.

But he was weary. The weeks and months of traveling had taken their toll. This quest that he'd been sent on was proving fruitless. And as much as he hated to admit it, he'd have to tell Mr. Vines — in yet another letter — that there was no trace of Anna Vines and their daughter. No matter how many witnesses he'd found, it was all for naught if he couldn't find them. But in his heart, he still knew he was close.

More than anything, he wished he could fulfill this last wish for Charles. He hated seeing the man suffer.

The humility he'd seen in Vines wasn't something one normally saw in a man who had wealth beyond most people's comprehension. The fact that he would trade it all for the chance to see his daughter and wife again showed how he longed to make things right.

The man had truly been broken by his mistakes.

As soon as he'd found out that Mr. Vines had lost his family though, something in Elijah changed. Abruptly. His own heart felt broken by the older man's loss. As much as he respected and admired Charles Vines, Elijah didn't want to end up like him — drenched in regret and seeking forgiveness and restitution.

Pacing the length of the only street at Carson Sink, he let his long legs eat up the short distance and then turned back toward the station. A lake sat close by — or so the stagecoach driver had said — and perhaps he could take some time to hike to it and do some praying. A flicker of something new started in his mind. Maybe he could invite Miss Rivers and Michael. To ask questions, of course. The thought made him smile.

It wouldn't be too terrible to stay awhile. It was definitely quiet here. If he went back to his room tonight and wrote a letter to

Mr. Vines, he could send it out on the Express in the morning and perhaps just tell his partner that he would wait for a response here. There might be news that Mr. Vines had been trying to get to him anyway.

As he thought of the beloved man back in Kansas City, emotion swelled in his throat. It would be hard to lose him. The man was more like family to him than his own. His parents were back east and didn't have much time for things outside their social groups. Especially not after the shame he'd brought on the family. In all these years, they'd never journeyed farther west than Chicago.

Watching Miss Rivers, Michael, and the rest of the crew at the table tonight made Elijah long for something he'd never experienced. Their sibling-like banter and closeness — well, all of the workers at the Express station were close — made him want more of that for himself. Especially when he thought of Miss Rivers. What was it that had gotten under his skin and riveted him so much? How had he been missing out on all this for so many years?

Maybe city life and all his busyness had kept him from seeing it.

Forcing his thoughts back to his employer,

Elijah prayed as he walked and brought the older man to the Great Physician. A steady peace filled him. If Mr. Vines was following the doctor's orders, there was still a chance he could heal and have years left. But if he wasn't? Elijah could only pray that his boss had listened.

"Mr. Johnson?"

Elijah stopped in the middle of the street, his deep thoughts broken by the voice. As he looked toward the sound, he saw a slight figure walking toward him in the twilight. "Yes, Miss Rivers?"

"My apologies, Mr. Johnson. I don't wish to intrude."

Everything else fell away as he watched her approach. "No need to apologize."

"I'm sorry we were interrupted earlier. Mrs. Liverpool normally comes over to share what she loves in the magazine, and we talk about baubles and trinkets, patterns and gowns for hours. She's unaccustomed to many guests staying. And we are the only two women around." She looked down at the ground for a moment. "I just wanted to make sure your accommodations suit your needs. Do you have everything you require?"

"Yes, of course. The accommodations are most gracious." His earlier thoughts warred with the feeling that grew in his stomach.

"Would you care to take that walk now?"

She stepped closer and smiled. "That would be lovely, but I'm afraid it's getting too dark and that would be . . . Well, perhaps we could sit in the parlor, and I could take you up on the offer of a walk tomorrow evening while it is still light. Or sooner in the day if your business is urgent."

His gentlemanly skills were obviously wanting from lack of use. But her generous manner helped cover his faux pas. Of course it was completely inappropriate to ask a lady to walk after dark. What had he been thinking? "My apologies. I have been lost in thought and wasn't paying attention as the hour grew later. It would be an honor to take our walk tomorrow evening."

"Thank you. That would be lovely. I will look forward to whatever it is you need my assistance with."

"I appreciate it."

"If you are planning to stay awhile, I could tell you about some of the unique aspects of our country out here." She turned and walked back toward the station.

He matched her steps. "I have actually decided to stay for a while, yes, so I would greatly appreciate any insight you could give me on the area." Especially since he had Vines's daughter to find. They entered the door into the parlor, where Mr. Crowell sat talking with Michael. "I hear there's a lake around here?"

"Yep. It's pretty neat," Michael chimed in.

"Maybe that's something you all could show me while I'm here."

"Sure. We go out there all the time." The young man stared at him. "Maybe later this week, Jack?"

"Sounds wonderful." She sat in a chair and picked up a piece of mending, but her cheeks were pink and she wouldn't look up at Elijah.

Hopefully he hadn't embarrassed her. The clock on the mantel chimed. If he was going to stay, he'd better write his letter to Mr. Vines. He turned back to Miss Rivers. "How long does it normally take to receive a response from an Express?"

"Two to three weeks. Depending on which direction you've sent the Express from here and where it's going and will return from." She used her hands as she talked. "For instance, if you are wanting to get a letter back east but you put it on the Express that's heading west, it will take a few more days for it to get on the line to return east. I've had several people who've been quite insistent about getting messages on the next Express run, rather than waiting for the one that is headed in the correct direction."

"Still, that's incredibly fast." Elijah nodded.

"It's what we live by. Ten days or faster from San Francisco all the way to St. Joseph, Missouri."

"I'm amazed. Especially to get to see it in action." He cleared his throat. "You should probably count on my needing a room for that amount of time. While I'm here, I might as well learn all about the fascinating Express. My employer has long wanted to know more about it since he is well acquainted with the owners and has invested in them."

Her blond hair in its long braid still made him think of a young girl, but the crinkles at the corners of her eyes attested to wisdom, experience, and a good bit of time spent smiling and laughing. But it was her eyes that fascinated him the most. Green — they practically lit up when she smiled. "I would love to share more about the Pony Express with you. Dad and I were privileged to be a part of it."

"Were? Is this not a stop anymore? Where is your father now? I would greatly like to meet him." Elijah couldn't keep the questions from spilling out.

Her smile slipped from her face. "We're

still a stop. I apologize for the misunderstanding. It's just . . . Dad died a few weeks ago." She turned to the fireplace and brushed a tear from under her eye.

Michael came out of his chair immediately and wrapped an arm around Jackie's shoulders.

"Oh. I'm so sorry for your loss, Miss Rivers." Now he truly felt like a heel. He'd been so determined to get answers that he hadn't used his manners. That was that. She couldn't be Charles's daughter. And now he'd hurt her to boot.

A forced smile back in place, she took a deep breath. "It's been difficult. He was a wonderful man." She looked at Michael. "I'm fine. Thank you."

The lad returned to his seat but gave Elijah a look that clearly said, *Don't you dare make her cry.*

"You run the station on your own now? That must be quite a task for a woman. I'd been wondering how you did it all."

Standing abruptly, she took a deep breath and brushed threads from her skirt. "If you will excuse me, gentlemen." She looked at Mr. Crowell and then back to Elijah. "I'm sure Michael can see to any of your needs, but I am quite spent. I will see you in the morning for breakfast. We dine at seven o'clock." Turning on her heel to go, she grasped her hands at her waist. But not before Elijah noticed them shaking.

Michael walked over to him and sat down. "You shouldn't discount Jack's capability because she's a woman."

"I'm sorry. I didn't realize I had."

"Yeah, well. You said it must be quite a task for a woman." The young boy lifted his chin and sat straighter. "It's been hard enough on her to lose her dad. They were really close. She doesn't need to feel like we doubt her. Because we don't. She's amazing."

The young man stood and his brows were tipped down in a very serious expression.

Elijah was impressed with the young man's closeness to Miss Rivers once again — and this time because he showed his loyalty and love for the woman who was his only family. Elijah wanted to kick himself or simply go back in time and keep from sticking his foot in his mouth. He hadn't meant anything insulting by his comment.

"I agree. My apologies, Michael." Next time, he wouldn't jump to conclusions so quickly.

Tomorrow he would have to apologize and try to make it up to Miss Rivers.

Of course, it was quite possible that she'd

taken his words in the absolute worst way and wouldn't wish to speak to him again. Perhaps ever.

That was a horrible thought.

Mrs. Liverpool entered through the back door and marched into the parlor. She smoothed her skirt as she sat in a chair. "Now, where were we in our discussion this evening? These are my favorite times, you know, when we talk about what we've —" She looked up and twisted her head to glance around the room, a puzzled look on her face. "Where did Jacqueline get off to?"

Michael frowned in Elijah's direction. "She went to bed early."

"Oh." She blinked at him and waved her hand. "Well then, why don't you two gentlemen catch me up on all the news from the East. We haven't had such fine guests in a long time."

Elijah turned and looked to Crowell for help. But the older man was nodding off. No wonder the man hadn't said anything.

"Come now. Don't be shy. I'll be quite entertained, I assure you."

Looked like the duty fell to his shoulders. He would have to write his letter later and figure out how on earth to apologize to Miss Jackie Rivers.

CHAPTER 5

October 13, 1860

The morning had not gone well so far.

Jackie wiped sweat from her brow as she stirred the potato hash. So far, she'd dropped a basket filled with a dozen eggs on the floor, hit her head on a beam as she'd run down to the cellar, and burned her tongue on some coffee. She'd been able to pull breakfast together, but it still felt like a disaster.

These incidents — compounded by her lack of sleep last night — seriously lowered her expectations for the day.

She went back to the thoughts that had her mind swirling last night. First, there was the handsome Mr. Johnson whom she'd left abruptly in the parlor because grief had overwhelmed her. Feeling inadequate to do anything of import while suffering the loss of her father, she couldn't bear his sympathy. Or was it that he thought she was incapable?

Embarrassed by her quick departure — no matter the reason — she figured it best to give the man a wide berth this morning until she fully regained her composure as hostess and station manager.

She also faced the conundrum that both Mr. Crowell and Mr. Johnson wanted to meet with her to ask for her assistance. But assistance with what? And why her? Her little station in Carson Sink didn't amount to much.

It was all a bit overwhelming. And she needed a nap.

She checked the clock on the mantel that she'd asked Dad for last year with its bell-like chimes and fancy gold face. Every time it chimed the quarter hour, it made her smile and think of him, remembering how he would look at his pocket watch and declare, "Well, I'll be, it's right on time."

After looking around to ensure everything was ready, she wiped her hands on a towel and headed toward the door. If she hurried, she could take a moment to gather her thoughts.

Michael sat at the table, reading one of the papers that had come through from the East.

"I'll be back in a few minutes to dish

everything up."

"All right." He never even looked up.

Jackie scurried out the door and headed for the small hill where her parents were buried. A graying wooden cross that had weathered many years out in the harsh Utah Territory read HANNAH, 1811–1837. Next to it was a freshly constructed cross that made her swallow against the wave of grief. It read MARSHALL RIVERS, 1809–1860.

Standing between the two, she let out a long sigh. "I miss you. Both of you. And now that I'm faced with . . . life completely on my own, I have to admit it's a bit overwhelming. Dad, I miss getting to work by your side each and every day. I need your wisdom right now. Hopefully I haven't messed everything up, but I promise to do better." She turned a bit to see her mother's cross. "Mom, I wish you were still here. There's so much I wish I could ask you. So many times I just needed your womanly direction. I always wanted to remember more about you. . . ." Closing her mouth, she realized she couldn't say anything else. Her throat was clogged with emotion. And it wasn't like going out there was going to fix anything. Her parents were dead. *Lord, I don't know what to do. It hurts so much. Please give me strength.*

Turning on her heel, she headed back to her home. She'd have to continue on with what she knew — taking care of the people around her and running the station. At least she could do that. Hopefully without further mishap.

When she walked back in, Michael, Mark, Peter, Timothy, and John were all sitting at the table. Michael quirked an eyebrow at her. "Everything all right?"

"Yep." Dishing up the potatoes into a serving bowl, Jackie heard more footsteps and chatter as the others gathered. She turned back toward the table and put on what she hoped was a decent smile that said, *Everything is perfectly all right.* "Good morning, everyone."

They all spoke at once, which was fine with her. Maybe she could get away with just eating her breakfast in peace and pray that the coffee would wake her up sooner rather than later.

"Would you like me to offer the blessing?" Mr. Crowell's voice boomed over the talkative group.

"Yes, thank you." Jackie placed her napkin in her lap and closed her eyes as the man prayed. Which she realized was a mistake. As soon as her lids closed, she wanted to go to sleep. So she popped her eyes open.

Which was another mistake. Because now she was looking across the table at Mr. Johnson's firm jawline. His eyes were closed — thank the good Lord — but his reverent expression just about took her breath away. What was going on with her? Perhaps she needed a good smack upside her head with a cast-iron skillet to jolt her back to the real world.

As soon as the "Amen" was heard, she picked up her coffee cup and took a long sip. This was not how her thoughts should be going. Scolding herself to wake up and get her thoughts in order, she kept her eyes lowered as they passed around the food.

"What time does the Express come through?" Even looking from the corner of her eye, she saw that Mr. Johnson's question was clearly directed at her.

Blinking several times, Jackie took another sip of coffee and passed the bowl of bacon as nonchalantly as she could. "Which one, the one heading east or the one heading west?"

"Preferably the east one. My letter needs to get back to Kansas City."

"Then you'll want the morning Express. The afternoon Express heads west. Is your letter ready to go?"

He nodded as he chewed a bite of hash.

"Yes. I just need to pay the fee."

"I'll take care of that after breakfast and stamp it."

"Thank you. I'm sure the owners must be thrilled that you have Michael here to help you keep the station running." Mr. Johnson's words pierced her heart and made her blood run cold. His tone made it sound like she shouldn't be allowed to carry such a burden alone.

Michael made a face. "Why would they be thrilled that *I'm* here? I don't even think they know about me. Jack here does all the work. She understands the ins and outs of the Express. I wouldn't want to have to deal with all the boring details anyway. I just do what I'm told. One day, I want to climb mountains or sail the ocean."

As much as Michael's words encouraged her, his defense was because he loved her, not out of admiration for her abilities. He didn't notice such things. Because they were *boring,* as he so graciously stated. But the longer she thought about Mr. Johnson's statement, the more it got her dander up. Was he suggesting a woman shouldn't be in charge? Was that what his comment last night was all about?

He didn't seem to have a problem with her running the place when she introduced herself yesterday. "What is it exactly that you do, Mr. Johnson?"

His eyebrows shot up at her hard tone of voice. "I'm an investor and business owner, Miss Rivers. Is there a problem?"

"No. There's not any problem. I'm simply not entirely certain that I understand what you were implying." She raised her eyebrows and tilted her head. "Do you have a problem with how any of the business here has been handled?"

Mr. Johnson at least had the good manners to look embarrassed. "My apologies, Miss Rivers. I simply meant that since you are a woman here all by yourself . . ." He pulled his collar away from his neck as his words came to a halt.

"Yes? What does that have to do with anything?" Her anger flared — probably from lack of sleep — but she wasn't tired right now.

"Nothing. I'm sorry." The man visibly paled and swallowed. He attacked his plate of food with gusto and didn't look up again.

"I'm sure Mr. Johnson meant no insult, Miss Rivers." Mr. Crowell wiped his mouth with his napkin. "I think I can speak for all of us when I say that I'm quite amazed at your adept and efficient ways of running the station. And I haven't even had the privilege of seeing the Express come through yet."

Jackie felt her nerves ease a bit as she looked at the older gentleman.

Obviously trying to keep the peace, the man smiled at her.

Remorse filled her for her heated words. What was she doing? Throwing a tantrum like a petulant child? She was the station manager. It was time to act like it. She would do her job and do it well. Forcing herself to calm her ire, she gave him a slight smile in return. She decided to go with a more diplomatic response. "My apologies, gentlemen. I realize that I dislike being questioned about my abilities because I'm a woman. I've never had to deal with this before, and I'm afraid it is uncharted territory. Especially since the loss of my father is so fresh." Not to mention the guilt she carried knowing she'd lied to the owners. This wasn't her position. Not truly. Not until they knew the truth and gave their permission.

"You do the best job out here, Jack. Don't worry about what anyone else thinks." This time it was Mark — one of the riders — who spoke up between bites. "No one understands us riders and our jobs like you do. And that's what makes a great station manager. Believe us, because we're the ones who see it. Day in and day out. So who cares what anyone else thinks?" The young man shrugged his shoulders and dug right back into his food.

Pride filled her chest. All the riders were like family to her, and she held a special place in her heart for the gangly bunch who risked life and limb every time they ventured out at crazy speeds. "Thank you, Mark."

She rose from the table and began to clear some of the dishes. She was too embarrassed to even look at either Mr. Crowell or Mr. Johnson. The rest of the table was filled with people who loved her and respected her. But she needed to gather her wits and restore her composure because she had agreed to help Mr. Crowell. Horrified at losing her temper, she took several deep breaths and turned back around.

"I'm incredibly sorry for my outburst, everyone." She made herself look the men in the eyes. "Especially to our guests."

"We should be the ones apologizing, Miss Rivers." Elijah stood. "Well, no, *I* should be the one. I had no idea about the loss of your father, and frankly, I've done a splendid job of sticking my foot in my mouth." He held up a hand and put the other over his chest. "I promise you that my intention was never to insult you. I think too highly of you to do that."

"Thank you. But it's not necessary. I was the one in the wrong." She gave him a half smile and felt her cheeks heat. "I'd best get back to the dishes." With a quick turn, she went back to what was safe. A mess to clean up. She shaved soap into the large dishpan and started pumping water into the bowl. She'd add hot water from the stove as soon as she gathered her wits about her.

Chairs scooted on the floor while plates and silverware clattered together. One by one the boys brought their dishes to the sink and kissed her on the cheek. She half expected Mr. Johnson and Mr. Crowell to follow suit, but the thought made her eyes go wide so she spun around to retrieve their dishes.

Mr. Johnson stood a foot away with a sheepish look on his face and the rest of the dishes stacked precariously in his arms.

"Thank you." The whispered words slipped past her lips.

The left side of his mouth twitched. "Truce?"

After sharing a laugh with Mr. Johnson and having washed, dried, and put away a considerable number of dishes, she took off her apron and headed to the business counter near the front window.

Mr. Johnson met her there with an envelope in his hand. She calculated the cost to mail it, then accepted his money and stamped the letter.

When she was finished, Mr. Crowell entered the room, his top hat in his hand. "Is there a place where we could speak in private?" he asked.

Glancing around the room at the riders and workers fixing two of the small Express saddles, Jackie understood the request for privacy. The man had asked for her assistance, and he worked for the United States Treasury. She just wasn't sure why he needed her help. "Of course. Maybe if we go outside?"

"That would be wonderful." He donned his hat and extended his arm toward the door. "After you."

Clasping her hands at her waist, she took a deep breath and prayed for wisdom. They walked to the other side of the street, which was vacant.

Mr. Crowell appeared very serious. "Miss Rivers, what I need to discuss with you is of the utmost importance, and confidentiality is required at all costs. Are you willing to swear an oath to that extent?"

The question took her off guard. "Of

course, Mr. Crowell." She swallowed. "I swear to you that I will keep the confidentiality of whatever matter you wish to discuss."

The man gave a slow nod and looked off into the distance. "I came here because your father was a trusted friend of the secretary, Mr. Howell Cobb. They hadn't seen each other in decades, but I had the privilege of meeting Marshall a few years ago. We've corresponded frequently on behalf of my boss. I'm sorry for your loss."

She nodded. "You knew my dad?"

"Yes. He was a good man."

Biting her lip, she took a long, deep breath. Oh, how she missed him.

"I apologize for adding to your grief, but time is of the essence. Because the situation is delicate, I had been enlisting your father's help. Because of his unfortunate death, we have nowhere else to turn but to ask you to take up the mantle. In his last letter, he told me that you could be trusted if anything happened to him."

What on earth was the man talking about? It sounded grave indeed. But hearing of Dad's confidence in her bolstered her spirits. "I will do whatever I can to assist you."

"I'm glad to hear that. I know your father

would be proud." He sighed and placed his hands behind his back. "We face two different situations. Both are illegal matters, and we're unsure if they are linked. Regardless, the culprits must be caught, but the only way to do that is to have someone on the inside keeping an eye on things."

Keeping an eye on things? That sounded an awful lot like spying. Maybe not being a full-fledged spy but still doing the work of a spy. Wasn't it? She'd only read of such things in periodical serials. As scary as it sounded, it also seemed a little exciting and quite intriguing. "What kinds of things?"

"I'll get to the specifics in a moment, but it has to do with the Express and the mail it carries."

"Will this put any of my riders in danger?"

"No. I don't believe so. But it is admirable of you to be concerned for them over your own safety."

"Does that mean that you believe I may be in danger if I take on this position?"

"It's highly unlikely because you're a woman. No one will expect it. But I can't say that we weren't ready to insist your father take precautionary measures."

"Such as?"

He held up a hand. "How about I fill you in on the details, and then you and I can discuss such measures if you think they will be necessary."

"All right." Crossing her arms over her middle, she listened.

"We have reason to believe that bonds from the Indian Trust have been used illegally to help finance the COC&PP and cover its debts. That's the first situation."

She sucked in her breath. Could that really be happening?

"The second is that we now believe we have treasury note forgers on our hands. This could be devastating for our country and its economy. All our information to this point leads to a small area. Within about eight stations. That's where you come in. This investigation has been going on for many months. The culprits are probably feeling confident that they've gotten away with it. We need to know if there's any evidence of these crimes, if we can find the source, and if they are connected in any way."

"Am I to assume that one of the stations in the small area is my own?"

Mr. Crowell nodded. "Yes, but your father had been investigated before I asked him to come on. He checked out, and so do you. That's why I've come to you to ask for your assistance."

It pleased her to no end to know that her father had been a trusted friend to this man and that the government had come to ask for his assistance in a matter of such importance. Even as tears of pride for her dad stung her eyes, she straightened her shoulders and said without hesitation, "I am honored to help." But her heart was heavy to think that anyone with the COC&PP could be corrupt.

"Thank you, Miss Rivers." He pulled an envelope out of his coat pocket. "This is what we've gathered so far. Included are both a genuine treasury note and a forged one. It's tough to see the difference, but study them. If you come across any, feel free to examine them further. They may come through the Express, and as the station manager, you have access to the mail."

"You're not asking me to open all the mail, are you?" The thought horrified her and went against everything she stood for.

"No." He tilted his head and gave a little shrug. "I'm not asking you to open it necessarily. But there may be an opportunity to take a peek through the corner of an envelope. Some of the missives are sent without envelopes as it is to make them lighter and thus cheaper to send. I'm simply asking you to look at what you can. Carefully. Be aware of every piece that comes through here. Especially if anyone attempts to use a treasury note as payment."

"Has that been happening?"

"Quite a bit. And right under our noses. But your father never saw any of them here. Only in Virginia City." He pointed to the envelope he'd given her. "There are no names or locations listed so that you are protected should anyone find these treasury notes and information. After dinner this evening I will give you a code to use in case you need to send any missives to me."

"Code? What exactly is the code used for?" She took the packet and slipped it into her dress pocket. "And where will you be?"

"The code is just for backup. We have other people in place. But in case you need us or we need you, you'll have the necessary means. As for me, I'll need to travel to continue my investigation. But this is going to be my home base, so to speak."

It all sounded mysterious and a little dangerous. "I need to make sure we are clear on one important area."

"What is that?"

"I must take care of my station and my riders."

"That won't be a problem."

"They come first."

"Of course."

She stuck out her hand, and he took it with a firm shake. "I'll do whatever I can."

"I know you will. Thank you."

She nodded and felt a slight rumble beneath her feet. "If you'll excuse me, the Express is coming, and he's early." Leaving Mr. Crowell on the other side of the street, she ran back over to the station house. The others were already out the door and attending to their duties.

Mr. Johnson walked out and nodded at her. "Is it all right if I watch?"

"Of course. Just make sure you stay out of the way." She emphasized her words by gently pushing him back a step. "He's going to come in at a fast speed. Believe me, you don't want to be near the horse's hooves."

Mark brought the fresh mount — a spotted gray named Horace — to her and she gave the horse a quick check. The pounding of the incoming horse made Horace prance and shake his head. He knew it was his turn to run.

Elijah leaned up against the station house to stay out of the way as instructed. In all his days, he'd never seen anything quite so exciting. As soon as he caught sight of the Pony Express rider, he marveled at the speed and agility of both rider and animal. To know that these young men — most of whom he'd heard were under twenty years of age — rode at such incredible speeds for upwards of seventy-five to one hundred miles a day. Through all types of terrain, weather, and dangers.

Miss Rivers had been correct to keep him back because the horse and rider didn't slow until they stopped in front of the station.

In smooth and quick motions, the rider dismounted and lifted the mail pouch — what did she call it? Motilla? Mochila? Yes, that was it — off one horse and took it to the fresh mount. Miss Rivers checked her watch, walked with the pouch, unlocked a pocket, and removed a bundle. Opening it up, she flipped through the missives with deft fingers, pulled out a couple, and put them in her apron pocket. Then she put new items into the bundle, pulled out something else, checked her watch again, wrote on whatever it was, and put everything back into the bundle and back in the pocket in a matter of seconds.

Two other Express riders took the horse the young man had come in on to the barn. Miss Rivers handed a small, napkin-wrapped bundle to him as he mounted the fresh horse. He took a sip from a dipper that Michael held up to him.

And in a whirlwind of dust and shouts, the Pony Express rider was back on the trail.

Elijah walked to Miss Rivers's side as she watched the rider speed eastward. "That was exhilarating."

She beamed a brief smile at him and looked back to the horse and rider. "Wasn't it? I never get tired of seeing it all in action. And to think that we do this every day, covering thousands of miles."

"Makes the five-dollar fee worth it just to see it in action."

She laughed — a sound that was full and musical, not like the tittering giggles of the simpering ladies back east. "I bet it does. It takes a lot of people and horses to carry a letter across the country at such a speed."

"Why didn't the rider change out this time?"

"One of the riders from Virginia City was sick, so Luke took the extra leg."

"How do you keep it all straight?"

"Lots of organization and lists."

"I can imagine. Thank you for giving me the privilege of watching."

"Of course."

He ventured into uncertain territory. "I'm looking forward to our walk this evening,

Miss Rivers." Would she still agree to it after he'd offended her not once but *twice*?

She held up a hand. "Please. We need to stop with the 'Miss Rivers' title. It's exhausting just to hear it. Why don't you call me Jackie?"

"All right, I'm looking forward to our walk this evening, Jackie."

"I am too. That is, I'm hoping I will be able to assist you." Her smile didn't make her eyes shine, but it was a start. "I must apologize for —"

"Please." It was his turn to hold up his hand. "Forgive me for interrupting. There's no need to apologize again. It was my fault for not thinking before I spoke."

Jackie ducked her head for a moment, and when she raised it, the smile reached her eyes and made her face glow. "My dad taught me to believe in second chances. It's only fair since God does that for us each and every day." She held out her hand.

He took her offered hand and shook it, trying to keep his face from showing his amusement. But it didn't work — he felt the smile creep out. "That is definitely something I can shake on." He bowed, and before he could say anything else, she removed her hand and walked away toward the barn.

"I wish I understood women better. . . ." The mumbled words tumbled out.

"Good luck figuring her out." Michael stepped from behind Elijah and patted him on the arm. "I've known her all my life and I still don't understand her half the time."

CHAPTER 6

Kansas City
October 13, 1860

Charles Vines stared out his study window. Since Elijah had left, the months had passed in an achingly slow repetition. He missed the man he thought of as a son. He missed the strength and health that he'd taken for granted for far too long. He missed . . . life.

Why God had chosen to spare him when he'd been such an atrocious human being was beyond his comprehension. But he was grateful.

His wife had left him more than a quarter of a century ago, and he'd thought for a long time that she would return sooner rather than later. But the months passed, and when she didn't return, he fell into a deep depression. After a year and a half of drinking himself into oblivion, Vines was found in a gutter by the pastor of a nearby church. He could only imagine the state he'd been in at the time.

But the pastor took him home, dried him out, and cleaned him up. If only all men of the cloth were so loving and steadfast. Pastor Wright had challenged Vines to be the man God made him to be. And as the pastor dared him to quit the bottle and get right with God, Charles began to understand that repentance was his only hope.

So he'd gotten on his knees and done just that. Repented. His deeds had been ugly. But thankfully, God dealt with ugly all the time and loved humanity anyway.

Vines and Pastor Wright became close friends. Charles turned his life around.

But the damage had already been done, and he knew it. His wife was nowhere to be found, and Charles didn't even know his daughter's name because he'd been too drunk to try to find out. He was a successful businessman surrounded by wealth, but he felt empty and hollow until God entered his life.

Determined now to do something for others with his wealth, Charles understood that whatever legacy he left needed to testify to God's grace and nothing of his own merit. Money and things vanished. But people . . . they had the opportunity to spend eternity with Almighty God.

He wanted to wait until Elijah returned to implement his plans, but he'd had a lot of time to think about the future. His hope was that his long-lost daughter would be part of that.

"Mr. Vines, sir." Colson's voice at the door interrupted his thoughts. "I've found something I thought you would want to see immediately."

"Of course. Come in." Charles waved him in and sat back down in the chair by his bed. He reached for his spectacles on the nightstand and put them on.

Colson held out what looked to be a small painting.

Charles reached for it and gasped. His heart clenched at the sight. After all these years, he thought he'd never see it again. But here it was. In his shaking hands.

The portrait of his Anna. The small one he'd had commissioned to put on his desk because he wanted to have her with him everywhere. Back when he was young and first in love.

Memories and guilt flooded him as he gazed at her beautiful face. *Oh Anna. I'm so sorry.* Not long after they were married, he'd turned into a monster. He couldn't blame her for leaving. It was his own doing. But when he found that she'd burned all the pictures of herself in their home, he'd been angry. Then grief had set in when he realized she wasn't coming back.

He thought he'd never see her again.

With a trembling hand, he swiped at his eyes and held the small portrait closer.

He'd loved her so much. If only he'd given his life to God sooner. Maybe he could have avoided all the pain and sorrow. And the loss of Anna.

But there was still hope. He took a deep breath. This portrait could help him find his daughter. And maybe Anna too — there was still a chance she lived, wasn't there?

Where could Elijah be? The West was a vast frontier, and it had been weeks since his last letter from Elijah. But everything had changed with Colson's discovery today. This could be exactly what Elijah needed.

The necessity of getting the portrait to his new partner sent his mind to whirling. He *must* get the painting to him. Before his time ran out.

In the barn, Jackie went into Romeo's stall to have a moment to herself. Picking up the brush, she gave her prized horse a quick rub-down. His black coat turned shiny again as she brushed away the dust and dirt. He was a beautiful animal. Dad had bought him for her birthday last year, and they'd had an instant connection. "How are you doing, boy?" she murmured.

The horse nickered and rubbed his head up against her hair.

"Yeah, me too." She held his face between her hands. "Maybe we can go for a ride later. It would do us both some good."

Romeo huffed in response.

Jackie laughed. "I know I've neglected you, but I promise to do better." She laid one hand on his nose while reaching with her other hand into her pocket. "Right now, I need a quiet place to read this letter. And *you,* my friend, are great at keeping secrets, so that's why I came out here."

His head bobbed.

Tearing into the envelope, Jackie took a deep breath. Hopefully it would be good news.

October 9, 1860

Mr. Rivers,

We are very sorry to hear of your father's passing, but also grateful that you are there in his place. Please continue to run the Carson Sink Station with our full approval. Payments for your services will continue at the same rate we paid your father.

Thank you for your service to the COC&PP as well as to your country.

Sincerely,
Mr. William Russell

She let out her breath in a whoosh as she reread the short letter. *Thank You, Lord.* She looked heavenward. At least she had their permission to carry on as she had been. Jackie folded the letter up against her chest and closed her eyes. Releasing a long sigh, she felt relief and another surge of guilt. Yes, they'd granted her permission to keep running the station — which was a wonderful thing — but they also still thought she was *Mr.* Rivers.

As good as the news felt, she knew that soon she'd need to tell them the truth. The thought of doing that wasn't pleasant. What if they didn't allow her to stay?

Being a woman all on her own wasn't easy out here. But Dad had left detailed papers signed by him and a lawyer that legally gave her their home. Because of the Preemption Act of 1841, he'd been able to obtain the legal title for the 160 acres surrounding their stage stop and station. He'd paid $1.25 per acre and named Jacqueline his heir. The lawyer had been clever indeed in the will and showed that Marshall Rivers had taken in young Michael and had sworn Jacqueline to raise him and take care of him should Marshall be incapacitated or die while Michael was still under age. That made Jackie a head of household when Marshall died, and that allowed her to now own the land.

The COC&PP hadn't paid for a station here because Marshall Rivers had already been here with the stage stop and boardinghouse. Maybe that would keep them from trying to kick her out. She could only hope. The Pony Express station was what really kept things moving daily. Could the owners and officials do something to her because she was a woman? When they found out that she hadn't been honest, would they use that against her to try to take her land away?

Maybe she could ask Mr. Crowell to write her a letter of recommendation when she sent her apology. If she was working honorably for the secretary of the treasury, surely she could be trusted with the station as well.

The thought of her job for Mr. Crowell brought his instructions to the forefront of her mind. She'd read the packet, but without the code it didn't make complete sense. This much she knew: she would travel to nearby stations and ask some questions. The people at those stations knew her and had respected her father. If she kept things as normal as possible, they would never suspect she was doing any investigating. So what excuse could she use for the visit?

"Miss Rivers . . . Jackie?" The voice of Mr. Johnson made her heart flutter.

She exited the stall and found him waiting at the entrance to the barn. "How can I help you, Mr. Johnson?"

"I insist you call me Elijah." His smile was warm.

Even though she knew the rules of etiquette, everyone out here was on a first-name basis. Besides, she'd insisted that he call her Jackie. "Elijah. Of course. Now what can I do for you?"

"The stage driver told me about a nearby lake. Could I possibly convince you and one of the other young men to ride with me out there? Since I'm going to be here awhile, I'd like to explore the area a bit."

"That would be lovely. I have business to attend to after lunch, but I'll be free tomorrow morning after the Express."

"Thank you. I'll look forward to it." He clasped his hands behind his back as they exited the barn. "I hope this isn't too forward of me, but I hope you have forgiven me for allowing my mouth to run away with me."

"Of course." Why did he have to bring it up again? The awkwardness between them stretched. "All is forgiven."

"That's a relief. Especially since I will be your guest for the coming weeks. I would hate to be a thorn in your side." His comment was accentuated with a smirk.

"I like your sense of humor. It's quite refreshing" — she leaned an inch closer to him and lowered her voice — "especially since Mrs. Liverpool doesn't seem to understand sarcasm. But she has ears like a hawk."

"She's an interesting character. What brought her here?"

"Her husband is a blacksmith and services all the horses that come through. Since we are a home station, there's a lot of traffic every day. And you'd be surprised how many horses throw a shoe when they're traveling at such high speeds. He's also my stable manager. We wear many different hats out here. As for his wife, she's been my friend for many years. I'm not sure how she has managed being out of the city because she loved it so much. But it is nice to have another woman around."

"To discuss *Godey's Lady's Book,* I'm sure."

"Well, of course, Elijah Johnson. Don't you know it is the foremost publication for women?" She couldn't help but laugh at the look on his face.

"Yes, I've heard that."

"The August issue included a thrilling section about women's headdresses. I found one called *La Belle,* with chenille net and beads, quite charming. I might try it myself." She couldn't keep a straight face any longer and laughed.

He chuckled along with her. "I'm sure it would look lovely on you. As long as it didn't cover up your hair too much." His voice softened. "It is quite beautiful."

Without thinking about it, she put a hand up to her thick braid. When she was younger, she had plaited it and wound it into a knot at her neck because she wanted to look older, but then she started getting headaches from the tightness and weight of it. Dad had said he didn't mind if she wore it down. It wasn't like they needed to follow society's rules out here anyway. "Thank you."

The moment sparked between them, but she was at a loss for words. This had never happened to her before. She didn't have trouble carrying on conversations with other men. What was wrong with her?

She cleared her throat.

Elijah shifted his weight, apparently finding the moment as awkward as she did, and looked away to the station. Then he cleared his throat too. "I haven't seen a church anywhere. Did I miss it?"

"No. We have services in the parlor every Sunday."

"Wonderful to hear. I'll look forward to taking part." He stayed in step with her.

"Just be forewarned that the arrival of the Express often interrupts us, so we take a break and come back to it."

"Duly noted, miss."

The moment turned awkward again. Was this what happened when two grown people found they were interested in each other? She desperately wished her father were still alive so she could talk to him about it. "Well, I'd better get back to lunch preparations. The morning has flown by."

"What if I were to offer to help you? Would that be all right?" The eagerness on his face almost made her giggle.

"That's quite unheard of, Mr. Johnson —"

"Elijah," he corrected.

"Elijah. Yes. But I've never had a male guest offer to help cook. It was enough of a shock to see you and Mr. Crowell doing dishes the other night."

"Is that a no?" He quirked one eyebrow.

"I didn't say that. . . ." Looking into his

eyes, she realized she could get lost in them quite easily. Would it be selfish to want to spend more time with him? Oh, what could it hurt? "I'd be delighted to have your assistance."

His eyebrows rose toward his hairline. "I must admit, I'm a bit shocked that you agreed."

"You're in the wild and untamed West now, Mr. Johnson. I'm sure there will be a great many things that shock you. Just hopefully not my cooking."

"Your cooking is quite the delight."

Since the ease of conversation was back, Jackie plunged into another topic. "Didn't you say you needed my assistance with some sort of business?"

He stopped outside the door to the station. "Thank you for remembering. This might be a bit far-fetched, and I'm sure you are probably too young to know anything, but I'm looking for someone. Maybe they came out here? About twenty-five or twenty-six years ago?"

She puzzled over that. "I was just a baby at that time. I wish Dad were here; he never forgot a face. Was it a man? A family? Do you have any description?"

"A woman and child. An infant or toddler, depending on when they came through."

"Hmm . . . It would have been very dangerous and difficult for a woman to come on her own. Do you know what she looked like?"

"Blond hair, green eyes. I've tracked a young woman and child, but the testimonies vary. Sometimes she has red hair. Sometimes black. It's had me running in circles."

An idea struck. "You know, my father kept ledgers for everything. I wonder if he would have anything documented from back then. I don't even know if we had a stage stop at that point — like I said, I was too young to remember anything. Let's see, the Butterfield line obviously wasn't running. But there had to be one from Virginia City. I remember it coming through as a child."

"And your mother? Would she have written anything down?"

"She died when I was little. I don't have any way to know."

"Oh, I'm sorry. What was her name?"

"Hannah. Hannah Rivers."

Elijah stroked his chin with his hand. "Perhaps your father's ledgers will show something. You never know."

"We can always try." She shot him a smile, but the way he studied her made her feel a bit uncomfortable. "What?"

"It's just that you have blond hair and green eyes."

"It couldn't have been me." She laughed. "I was a child." Something didn't seem right, but at the moment she couldn't put her finger on it.

"No. It couldn't. I'm sorry. I think I've been searching for this woman for so long that my mind is running in circles. But thank you for helping. Do you happen to know anyone else who's been out in the area for a long time?"

"There might be some folks in Virginia City, but I wouldn't know who."

He nodded. "I will ask around when I go back there. Well . . . why don't we get to that lunch? I appreciate your help, Jackie."

"I hope you find who you're looking for. Let me know if I can do anything else. We'll get out the ledgers later." She shrugged and walked inside.

Outside Virginia City

Carl took the stack of forgeries and compared them to the real one. He couldn't see any difference whatsoever. The guy was good. Now if the fat man could just keep his mouth shut, Carl might let him live long enough to create a few hundred more. "How long will it take you to make another twenty?"

The man's double chin grew as he lowered his head and wrote on a piece of paper. "Two weeks?"

"Good. You get to work on those, and I'll have the gold coins ready."

The man stood and stuck his cigar back into his mouth. "Pleasure doing business." Then he picked up the bag full of his latest payment and headed out the door.

As he tucked the treasury notes into his satchel, Carl thought about his next steps. He just needed a few more things to fall into place. Even the rumors of war were playing right into his hands. It wouldn't be long before he'd cash in his fortune.

"Carl, I got the information you wanted." His nephew stood in the doorway. The kid had gotten pretty adept at helping with his business.

"And you've got the letters ready?"

"Yep."

"When did Rivers die?"

"A few weeks ago. So our schedule still works."

"Perfect." Carl walked over to his sister's kid and gripped the young man's shoulder. "You know what to do."

CHAPTER 7

October 14, 1860

Elijah shifted in the saddle. It had been a long time since he'd ridden just to amble along a trail. Usually he was in a hurry to get somewhere.

Michael rode in the lead with Jackie behind him, while Elijah brought up the rear. He really wanted to chat with Jackie, so he pulled his horse alongside hers.

"Oh, that's not a good idea, Mr. Johnson. We need to ride single file for a bit."

"I'm sorry. May I ask why? It's not like we are climbing a dangerous mountain trail."

"Let's just say that there are many areas around here where if you're not careful, your horse can sink up to his flank in the sand."

He immediately returned to his position at the back of their party. "My apologies."

"It's not your fault," Jackie called over her

shoulder. "I should have warned you about the Sink at Carson."

"Ah, so that's why the station is called Carson Sink."

Her laughter filled the air around him. "You got it."

"Wonderful. One of the great mysteries is solved." He spoke loudly so she could hear him.

"No offense, Mr. Johnson" — Michael's voice echoed back to him — "but that isn't much of a mystery. I thought you had traveled all over."

"I have. But I must admit, I've never been anywhere like here."

They rode for several more minutes until Jackie waved him forward. "It's safe for us to ride abreast now."

As their horses moved along through the sandy dirt and nubby grass, Elijah took in the beauty around him. It was unlike anything he'd seen before, and he finally understood that all things could be beautiful in their own way. He turned to Jackie. "You must really love it out here."

"I do. It's been my home my whole life."

"You don't ever wish to go anywhere else?"

She tilted her head a bit and shrugged. "Oh, I think I'd like to travel sometime, but this is home."

"Not me," Michael chimed in. "I want to get out of here and explore one day. I get tired of all the dirt and sand. And it's always so dry. I'd really like to see more green. That's why I like going to the lake so much."

Elijah watched Jackie's face. While she didn't look enthusiastic about Michael's proclamation, she at least had put on a smile for the young lad.

"Where would you like to go?" He aimed his question at the boy, hoping to earn his trust.

"To the ocean. Then the Rocky Mountains. And then all the way across the country. I want to see it all."

"Where do you think you'd like to end up?"

"Oh, I don't know. But it would have to be within a few days of here."

"Why?"

"Because I wouldn't want to be away from Jack forever."

The tender look Jackie gave Michael made Elijah wish she'd pointed it at him.

"Aw, don't go getting all mushy on me, Jack. You know I can't stand it." The young man made a face.

"At least I know that after you've had your adventures, you'll still come around. You're my family, and I'll miss you when you're gone." Jackie's voice did indeed sound a bit mushy.

But instead of the reaction Elijah expected out of the boy, Michael surprised him. "I know. And I wouldn't want any other family in the world. Thanks for being there for me."

Elijah looked ahead, letting them have the moment. For a brief second he found himself jealous of the fourteen-year-old orphan who had experienced a real family, while Elijah, although twice his age, still searched for one.

Different thoughts and emotions swirled through him. Amazing how hearing Charles's story had stirred up so much in him. This trip had changed him, and he wasn't quite sure what to do with that.

"I miss him." Michael's voice was soft.

"Me too."

Elijah snuck a look at Jackie. Her eyes were sad, but she smiled. If their dad had died only a few weeks ago, their grief must be extraordinarily hard for them to bear. "Would you tell me about your father?"

Her eyes brightened. "I'd love to. It seems I haven't been able to talk about him since he died — except for a time or two with Michael — and it's hard."

Michael grinned and interjected, "He was

a big man. Tall and stronger than anyone else I've ever seen." His voice was enthusiastic as he spoke.

Jackie gave a light laugh. "He was definitely that. He had to duck through the doorway when he entered a room, and he could lift just about anything."

The adoration on her face as she talked about him gave Elijah a glimpse into her heart.

"He was smart, thoughtful, caring, and stubborn."

Michael gave Elijah a look and pointed his thumb at her. "We know she gets it honestly."

"Oh hush." But she laughed along with them. "He was a very practical man, but gave in to the whims and desires of his daughter — me — quite often." Her face saddened. "But I would trade away all the things I asked for just to have him back one more day."

"He sounds like a man I would have liked to know."

"He was." Jackie reached up to brush a tear away.

"Your father raised you?"

She smiled again. "Yes. Although I know I exasperated him on more than one occasion. I heard him mutter under his breath how much he wished my mother was still alive."

"You? Exasperating? It's hard to believe." While Elijah wasn't being sarcastic, he wanted to tease her because he loved the smile on her face.

"You have no idea," Michael threw out. "Then there were all those catalogs and newspapers with their drawings of the latest and greatest dresses, dishes, stoves, you name it. Dad — Marshall — often would hide them so we wouldn't have to hear her ooh and aah over everything."

"I like fine things." She shrugged with a laugh. "But my favorite thing was riding with my dad. He taught me everything. From taking care of horses, cows, pigs, and chickens to cooking and even sewing. That's not something you can purchase from a catalog."

"No. It's not." And it wasn't something that could easily be replaced. Elijah noted the respect that both of them had for the man. "What was his name?"

"Marshall. Marshall Rivers." Her voice caught on the last syllable.

"He was the best." Michael urged his horse forward. "Look, we're here." The boy galloped ahead.

At the crest of a small hill, Jackie pulled

her horse to a stop, and Elijah joined her.

"It's quite a sight." The green grass and lush surroundings were a stark contrast to the dry and barren landscape they'd been traveling through.

"Isn't it?" Her gaze was captured by the lake. "I love coming here." She turned her head toward him and looked into his eyes. "Would you like to ride around the lake with me? It's a lovely ride."

"I'd love to. Lead the way." As he watched her direct her horse onto a path that would take them around the body of water sparkling in the sunlight, Elijah studied the fascinating woman who ran a Pony Express station. What was it about her that was so . . . refreshing? He'd never met anyone like her, and he longed to get to know her better. But was that wise? He wouldn't be here for more than a few weeks.

Pushing aside the doubts, Elijah decided that he wanted to get to know Jackie Rivers. And he wanted that more than anything else he'd sought in a very long time.

October 16, 1860

While Michael and the other riders enjoyed some coffee in the kitchen, Elijah sat in the parlor with Mr. Crowell while Jackie and Mrs. Liverpool spread open the *Lady's Book* on the dining room table and discussed some *Zouave* jacket that it pictured. As much as he was trying to carry on an intelligent conversation with the older man, he found himself listening to bits and pieces of the ladies' conversation. Especially whenever Jackie spoke up. Over the past couple of days, he'd gotten to watch her in her regular routine and enjoyed listening to her talk to the riders, dispensing duties and managing things with an experienced and comfortable air. After their time at the lake, he found himself trying to catch a glance from her here and there.

But tonight, he was intrigued. A certain animation came over her whenever she and the blacksmith's wife discussed fashion. Seeing it made him smile. From what he could gather, she had an eye for elegant and beautiful things. Mrs. Liverpool seemed to hang on every suggestion Jackie made and was always seeking the younger woman's advice on hats and dresses.

Jackie Rivers was anything but plain, but she had lived here her entire life and lived simply. That's what made it so fascinating. There was something . . . refined about her.

Her laughter floated over to him. "Oh, you know Dad. He'd always give in and buy the things that I fancied from the catalog."

Mrs. Liverpool twittered in response. "It's a good thing he was a man of such good taste."

The men's conversation stalled and Elijah took that opportunity to watch the ladies without reservation. At ease in her surroundings, Jackie was like a breath of fresh air in contrast to the stuffy women he'd been acquainted with in the city. Mrs. Liverpool seemed to be like an older sister to the vibrant Miss Rivers. Their relationship appeared genuine and warm. It charmed him.

Other than his relationship with Mr. Vines, Elijah hadn't seen too many friendships that were real like this one. In the city, people were always involved in business dealings and meetings, but they seemed to put on their best face and wanted to be seen with the right people for show. Maybe that was why his view of love and romance had been so tainted. Not to mention what he'd experienced growing up with his parents and their hideous social circles where no one really liked the others. They simply got together so the papers would report them in a list of society's best attending an important gala.

But over the past few months, Elijah had witnessed several couples either on the stage or at the way houses who seemed to be truly happy in their marriages. In love. Wanting to be in each other's presence. He'd wondered if that was actually possible. But the way Mrs. Liverpool spoke of her husband suggested that they were very much in love and happy too. So maybe he was the one with the wrong viewpoint.

Mr. Vines came back to mind. If only he could complete this job for Charles and still get to know these people — especially Jackie — better. But sadly, he was most likely going to have to leave soon. As soon as he heard from his boss.

That thought made him frown.

"Johnson?"

Elijah blinked and looked back up at Crowell. "I'm sorry, I was lost in thought there for a moment. What were you saying?"

"I was asking if I heard correctly that you would be staying for a week or two."

"Ah, yes. I'd like to wait to hear back from my partner — Mr. Charles Vines. I've sent him a lot of messages from the road, but as I traveled, there was no way for him to respond."

Crowell nodded. "Good. I'm glad you will be around for a bit. It's been a privilege to get to know you, and I'm hoping I can enlist your help."

"But of course. How can I be of aid?"

Crowell moved his chair closer and lowered his voice. "It's funny that you mentioned Charles Vines. I assume you mean the Charles Vines of Kansas City? Millionaire?"

"Yes, sir, that is correct."

Crowell chuckled. "Good ol' Charles. We were school chums back in the '20s."

"How about that! It's a small world, sir."

"Yes, it is. We've corresponded since then, but mainly because he has had to do a great deal of business with my boss — the secretary of the treasury, Mr. Howell Cobb. Since we reconnected, it's been a privilege to catch up with my old friend."

"Ah, yes. I've written letters to Mr. Cobb in the past on behalf of Mr. Vines. My boss speaks highly of him. I'd forgotten that he was the secretary of the treasury now."

Crowell nodded. "He's a good man. And he's trying to investigate some illegal practices that could do serious damage to the country's economy. This is why I'm coming to you. When I heard you worked for Charles, I knew you could be trusted."

"I'm not sure what I can offer, but I'll do my best. What is it that you need?"

"We've traced the illegal activity to this part of the country, and that's where I need your help. I've already been to Virginia City several times. People there know me and that I work for the Treasury. Frankly, I think they're all getting tired of me asking questions. But when we were on the stage, you said you hadn't spent any time there. Is that correct?"

"Yes. That's correct."

"Could you possibly go there and ask some questions for me?"

"I'm sure I could. I need to ask some questions pertaining to my own business as well."

"I appreciate your willingness to help. I have the names of two men I will need you to meet, and I'll prepare the questions I need answered. It won't be difficult or tedious. I just need someone other than myself to be there. Of course, I'll need your word that you will keep all of this to yourself. You must tell no one."

"Of course." Elijah looked back to the table and saw a smile fill Jackie's face. He turned back to Crowell. "When do you need me to go?"

"In a few days? I need to make a trip to Carson City, and I'm hoping that when you and I return, we'll have some good answers."

"Answers to what?" Mrs. Liverpool tilted her head and looked at the men.

How she'd snuck up on them, Elijah had no idea, but both ladies had joined them in the parlor. The smirk on Jackie's face was unmistakable.

"Oh, just some questions that I have about the area." Crowell looked back to Elijah. "I hear you've been to the lake?"

"Yes. Michael, Jackie, and I went out there yesterday. It's such unique terrain around here, I was shocked to see how lush and green it was around the water."

"Unique?" Mrs. Liverpool clucked her tongue. "Barren wasteland, if you ask me. Personally, I miss my mountains."

"Where are you from, Mrs. Liverpool?" Elijah was thankful they'd been able to turn the conversation away from Crowell's private request.

"Over by Lake Tahoe. It's truly beautiful there." She sat on the settee and brushed at her skirt. "I don't know why Mr. Liverpool wanted to come out here, but he did, and I love that man and would follow him anywhere. So here we are."

Jackie reached out and patted the other woman's arm. "Well, I'm glad you came."

"Thank you, dear."

"And our discussions during Bible study wouldn't be the same without you." Jackie giggled. "Especially the ones about Daniel."

Mrs. Liverpool's sour face turned into a smile that made the woman much more pleasant to look at. "Now, let's not start in about that. . . ." But the woman laughed along.

"Oh, come now, Mrs. Liverpool, you can't leave us hanging on such an interesting topic. Please tell us." Mr. Crowell leaned forward and smiled.

Jackie turned to the other woman. "Would you like to tell it, or should I?"

Mrs. Liverpool straightened her shoulders and sighed. "Oh fine. Go ahead." The amusement on the woman's face contradicted the resigned tone of her voice.

"Well, we were discussing chapter 4 of the book of Daniel. It had gotten quite lively, especially since we noticed that it appears that chapter is written by the king of Babylon himself and it tells such an amazing story of how he learned his lesson. June — Mrs. Liverpool here — had a lot of . . . questions about Nebuchadnezzar's circumstances." Jackie chuckled. "With all sincerity, she asked, 'What do you suppose he wore as he was out there eating grass?' "

The blacksmith's wife's laughter grew as her eyes crinkled, and she put a hand to her chest. "I asked if someone had to change the king's clothes while he was living like an animal or if he was naked. These things plague me, you know, as I study the scriptures. Don't they plague you? I want to know all the details and everything that isn't described to us." The woman's eyes twinkled as she spoke.

"That sent everyone into a fit of giggles and the discussion went all over the place after that. The boys started asking if they penned the king up at night, if he was on his hands and knees or his hands and feet. And whether or not he harmed anyone with his long claws. And what on earth did the people do without a king for seven years? Did they know he was out with the animals? Did they visit him? Pet him?" Jackie leaned over and patted her friend's knee. "The discussion and questions went on for hours. It was one of the most memorable nights of my life. I think the good Lord above has given us curiosity for a reason. And a sense of humor."

After their laughter died down, Mrs. Liverpool stood, which caused Elijah and Mr. Crowell to stand as well. With a sly grin, she admitted, "Well, I'm looking forward to Sunday Bible study even more now, but I'm afraid I must be going. Mr. Liverpool will be looking for me." She curtsied and headed for the door. "Good evening."

"Good evening."

"Good evening." All their voices joined together.

Elijah watched Jackie. "I'm glad to hear that you have such lively Bible studies. It is one of my favorite things to do."

"Mine too." Her eyes softened as she looked at him and smiled. "Dad and I used to sit by the fire every night and read and discuss scripture. I miss that." She looked away for a moment and then turned back to him. "Sunday mornings were our time to study with everyone. It's always been interesting. Mrs. Liverpool asks some of the most intriguing questions."

Mr. Crowell sat back down. "She's an interesting woman. We haven't met her husband yet. You must keep him terribly busy."

Elijah chuckled. "Oh, I can imagine he enjoys the reprieve."

"Elijah Johnson." Jackie covered her mouth to hide her laughter. "She is a wonderful woman." She paused. "Who likes to chat." The laughter returned. "But she and Mr. Liverpool are so very happy together. It's been a wonderful thing for me to see their example over the years. I love how God brings the right two people together at the right time. I admit, they're total opposites. Liverpool is a quiet man, and yes, Mrs. Liverpool does enough talking for both of them. But they love each other and want to serve God together no matter where they are. What is better than that?"

CHAPTER 8

After Mrs. Liverpool left, Michael and the rest of the riders and hands excused themselves to go to bed.

Jackie smiled at each one as they headed out, and her heart swelled with pride. They might be in the middle of nowhere, and their little stage stop and Express station might not even get a mark on the map, but this was home. She was so blessed to be surrounded by a wonderful group of people. Her *family.* Even with the ache still fresh from the loss of Dad, she could smile at the future, just like the woman portrayed in Proverbs chapter 31. How she longed to be like that woman. But she was so flawed and had such a long way to go.

A hazy image abruptly ran through her mind — the image of a blond woman smiling down on her — and for a moment it took her breath away. Rarely did she remember anything about her mother, and when she did, she longed for more. But she'd been only three years old when her mother died. Dad said he didn't like to talk about it because he still loved and mourned her. But oh, when she was younger, how incessantly she asked about her mother.

Mr. Crowell stood, jolting her out of the memory. "I believe all this fresh air has worn me out. If you will excuse me, I shall retire for the night." He bowed toward her, gave a nod to Elijah, and then headed down the guest hallway.

The fire roared in the fireplace as Jackie collected her thoughts. She needed to do the job that Mr. Crowell had asked her to do to honor her father. If Marshall Rivers had been helping the secretary of the treasury before his death, then she wanted to help them finish the job. But how exactly would she go about it? Playing false was never something she was good at. But then, she did pretend she was a man in that letter, didn't she? Besides, she wouldn't necessarily play false. She just needed to do a little investigating — a little spying. She could do that, couldn't she?

As she looked down at her cup of tea, the image of her mother, so dreamlike and beautiful, still hovered at the edges of her mind. If only she could keep it there and remember more.

"Miss Rivers . . . Jackie . . ." Elijah gazed at her from across the parlor. "I hope this doesn't sound too impatient, but have you had a chance to look at any of your father's ledgers?"

His question made the picture in her mind vanish and brought her fully back to the present. "I'm so sorry, Elijah. I quite forgot." As she stood, he came to his feet as well, a look of hope on his face. She smiled and pointed to her room. "Let me go fetch them. I'll return momentarily." She hurried off and wondered about the woman this man was so fascinated with. Or, she guessed, the woman must be a fascination of his employer's. The woman and child must be of some great importance. Who were they? Could she ask?

Grabbing the leather-bound books, she stopped for a moment as memories washed over her. Dad sitting at their table going over the ledgers at night. As he worked, his strong arms lifted her onto his lap, and she would fall asleep on his shoulder as his masculine script filled the pages. "Oh Dad." A sob welled up in her throat. "I really miss you."

Sucking in a breath, she closed her eyes against the tears. Elijah was waiting for her, and she didn't want him to think that she was weak and incapable of handling business. Why did men believe that tears meant weakness? Didn't they grieve too? She'd seen several younger riders shed a tear or two when Marshall Rivers died.

But she was in charge now. It didn't matter that she was mourning her father. Mr. Johnson needed to see her as a strong and capable woman.

With new determination, she left her room and brought the stack of books into the parlor.

"Here they are." She forced a smile she hoped showed she was happier than she felt at the moment. The melancholy feeling just didn't want to go away.

"Thank you for helping me." His smile was so genuine and sweet.

"When did you say they would have come through?"

"Late 1834 or possibly into 1835. Maybe even later?" He winced a bit as he said it. "My apologies. That might take a lot of sorting through. It wasn't my intention to add to your workload."

"Nonsense. I told you I would help, and I am glad to do it." And perhaps it would help get her mind off the overwhelming grief that threatened to overtake her. Maybe she needed this little project to focus on something other than her loss. Because the way she was feeling right now, if she started crying, she might not be able to stop. She picked up the oldest book and read the dates aloud. "This one starts in April 1832." Flipping to the back of the book, she said, "And ends in November 1834. We should begin with this one, I think." Seeing Dad's handwriting cover the pages brought another wave of grief. She swallowed against it. "It's a woman and child we're looking for?"

"Yes."

"If the child was under ten years old, Dad would simply write 'child.' If it was a baby, he would often write 'infant.' Older than ten, he would put the name of the child." She handed the book over to Elijah.

He raised his eyebrows at the proffered book. "You don't mind me looking through this by myself?"

Her emotions were in tumult. She *did* mind. Well, maybe she didn't. But she couldn't straighten out her emotions at the moment. "Go ahead. But please be respectful of my father and his clients' privacy. I trust you'll only be interested in the people you're searching for." Keeping her head down, she didn't look at her guest for fear he would be able to read the sorrow on her face.

"Of course, I'll be discreet." He took the book over to the table and sat down with a hurricane lamp.

Hoping that he was occupied with the ledger, she flipped through the others one at a time. Not reading anything. Not doing anything other than covering up her struggle to hold herself together.

When they'd buried her father, the minister's wife from Virginia City had wrapped her in a hug and whispered in her ear that grief could be a difficult road to navigate and that it took time to heal. Why hadn't the woman warned her that it would come back weeks after and haunt her worse than when he'd first died? How would she overcome the anguish?

She picked up the last book, and as she leafed through the pages, a paper fell into her lap. Her name was there. In Dad's bold script.

Her heart picked up its pace, and she looked over at Elijah. He appeared deep in thought as he looked through the ledger, so she turned toward the fire, putting her back to him, and unfolded the paper.

Dearest Daughter,

As I'm sitting here balancing the ledgers, I couldn't help but think of you and be overwhelmed with joy and gratitude that you are my daughter. I hope I have many years left on this earth before there comes a need for you to read this, but I figured it was time I put things in order. There's so much that I wish to tell you, but I will take the time to write it all out because I'm much too scared to do it in person.

The thought of the strong Marshall Rivers being scared of something made her let out a breath of disbelief. He was never scared of anything. At least, not that she knew of. Was he teasing her? She dove into the rest of the letter.

First, you need to know that I have loved you since I first laid eyes on you as a baby. You captured my heart fully the moment you wrapped your tiny fist around my finger, and it has been yours all these years since. Always remember that. No matter what you think or feel when you find out the truth.

The truth? What could he be talking about? Dad was never cryptic. First afraid

153

and now this? Did he hold some horrible secret she didn't know about? She forced herself to swallow and read on.

Second, your mother was a wonderful person. I wish you could have known her, but I see so much of her in you. Perhaps I will get up the courage to talk to you about her in detail one day. I feel negligent in not raising you to know more about her, but it was such a difficult situation and I loved her very much. I still do. You'll understand more when I tell you the whole story.

The last sentence made her pause. Her mother had died of the fever when she was little. Marshall had never been a man who beat around the bush. Never one for secrets. He believed in honesty and speaking the truth. So what was his hesitation? For many years she'd simply thought he'd loved her mother so much that it was incredibly difficult for him to talk about her. But now? She couldn't really say. This was a different side of him she'd never seen.

She looked over to Elijah, who was still absorbed in the ledger she'd given him. She returned to the letter.

As you've gotten older, I've been thrilled to see her again — in you. And I realize that you are now the same age that she was when she died. How has the time gone by so fast?

A pang filled her chest. Now she understood a bit better why Dad had reacted the way he had on her birthday. She'd turned twenty-six this year. Her mother had died at twenty-six.

Third, if anything happens to me, you know where most of the important documents are. But I've held back one box for you. With help for your future and keys to your past. To find it, you'll have to remember, "A thousand times the worse to want thy light." He who speaks shelters the treasure that I hope to share with you one day — prayerfully in my old, old age. But until then, I'll keep it hidden. Just in case. It's my back-up plan in case I do not garner the courage to tell you in person.

What? The quote made absolutely no sense to her. What was Dad up to? And why was he suddenly interested in keeping some sort of box hidden? His words were so different from anything else she'd ever seen from her father. Maybe he'd become a bit sentimental as he'd grown older.

Perhaps I'll be brave and tell you in person one day, but I kind of enjoy the thought of sending you on a treasure hunt. You always loved adventures and beautiful things. I wish I could have given you more.

Oh Dad. He'd given her more than she ever could have wanted. Her heart clenched.

I always wanted to be a better father. If you're reading this, hopefully I've achieved that before I leave this world.

Follow God's Word. Live with joy and happiness. Don't grieve for me, for if I'm dead, it simply means I'm with my heavenly Father. And your mother. Which is glorious to even think about.

Don't forget that I love you and that you'll always be my little girl.

All my love,
M.R.

Jackie read the note again, then refolded it and tucked it into her pocket. A smile spread across her face as she recalled his strong script. How she missed him. Opening the ledger back up, she went to the pages where Dad had tucked the letter. Sure enough, his check marks showed where he'd caught up balancing the books. She'd put off the job since his death, dreading the effort it took. But between the pages and in the middle of his work, he'd taken time to write her a note. She ran her hand down the page and wished she'd found the message earlier.

The thought of big, strong Marshall Rivers sitting down with pen and ink to tell her he was afraid of telling her the truth puzzled her. Whatever the truth was didn't matter. He'd been a wonderful father, and she'd adored him. That he wanted to send her on a hunt for something he'd left for her was wonderful and gave her heart a lift.

But the more she pondered his clue, the more confused she became. Dad had been a simple man. For him to go to such lengths was out of character. Then again, he'd done a lot of things out of character for his little girl. The thought made her love him all the more.

Turning back toward Elijah, she realized she hadn't been looking in the ledgers to help him. So she laid down the most recent book and picked up the ledger that continued from November 1834. As she glanced through the first two pages of entries, she noticed that "HM and infant" were listed in the same guest room for several days.

"Elijah, I think I've found something."

He lifted his head and looked at her. "Is it a woman and child?"

"I believe so, but it's just the initials 'HM' and 'infant.' Apparently they started off this ledger staying in room 3. Could you check the end of yours?" She brought the book over to the table where he'd been studying the ledger.

It appeared that he'd made it through the first third of the book. Marking his place, he then went to the back of the ledger. "You're correct. Room 3 has 'HM and infant' listed."

"Let's trace it back to the first stay — perhaps he wrote the full name on the first night." Excited that they'd found a clue so quickly, she couldn't wait for him to turn the page back.

But as he placed his finger at the top of the previous page and slid it down, she saw the same thing listed at the top with ditto marks written beneath.

Elijah turned back another page, then another. After he turned back the fourth page, his finger stopped. "Look!" His voice was animated.

Jackie leaned in. "On the eighteenth of October 1834, a woman named Hanna Morris signed in with her infant." The words in front of her made her pause. Hannah was her mother's name. But it was spelled differently. How strange. Hannah was a common enough name.

"That's got to be her." Elijah's words ended on a sigh.

"How can you be so sure?" She hated to squash his excitement, but it couldn't be that easy, could it?

He leaned back into his chair. "Her name was Anna. I know that much. Could your father have misunderstood her name and written Hanna instead?"

"No. Dad was pretty accurate. Why do you think it's the same person?" She pointed to the page. "It's clearly written as Hanna here."

"Because the time period fits." His brow lowered and he came forward again. "Let's check your book. How long does she stay?"

Caught up in the fun of the mystery, Jackie placed her ledger on the table. Flipping through the pages, she discovered that the same guest room was occupied with only ditto marks through the entire ledger! "So our mystery woman stayed here for" —

she checked the back of the ledger — "two years?"

They exchanged glances and both went to grab the other ledgers.

Elijah opened the next one and flipped through it quickly. "There's not even a listing for room 3 in this one."

Jackie was discovering the same thing in the first few pages of the ledger that followed. "It's not in this one either."

Elijah held up his book for her to examine. "But he obviously had a busier stage stop, because this one fills up after nine months. See?"

She looked at the dates as he pointed to the beginning and end of the ledger. It was true, their stage stop must have been a busier route starting that year. Jackie went back to the one she held. She continued to flip through the pages. Room 3 wasn't listed on the first ten pages. But then, on page eleven, it appeared again. She gasped. "Look!"

He leaned over her shoulder. "September 1837. All of a sudden room 3 is available again." Elijah backed away and Jackie studied his face. What was he thinking?

As he sat down in his chair, he looked from book to book. "Almost three years . . ." His words were mumbled.

"What? What are you thinking?" Now she was completely intrigued. Who was this woman, and why were Elijah and his boss so interested in her? Better yet, why had she stayed here, of all places, for close to three years? Hanna or Anna? It didn't make sense.

"It couldn't be. . . ." His gaze shot to hers. He didn't say anything else. Just studied her. A look of marvel on his face.

As she stared back at Mr. Elijah Johnson, she started to feel uncomfortable. What was he up to?

CHAPTER 9

His scrutiny had made her uncomfortable. He could see unease etched clearly on her face. "My apologies, Jackie. I was thinking it all through." Shaking his head, he tore his eyes from her, smiled, closed the ledger, and patted it. "Thank you so much for taking the time to help me, but I believe we found what I was looking for."

She gave him an odd look. Like she didn't quite believe him. "Of course. It's been my pleasure to help." She gathered the books toward her. "Will there be anything else you might need?"

He breathed deeply. "No. I don't think so. But I might like to look at those again, if you don't mind." He backed away from the table. He couldn't allow her to know what he was thinking.

A frown furrowed her brow at his retreat. "I won't mind. Just let me know when." Her voice sounded hurt as she hefted the stack of books into her arms. She looked young, innocent, and like a girl carrying her books to the schoolhouse with her thick blond braid curling over her right shoulder.

"I appreciate it. Now, if you don't mind, I believe I will head to my room." He gave her an awkward bow. "Thank you. Good night." He couldn't bear to look at the puzzled look on her face anymore, and while he hated to distance himself, he had to think. He took quick steps toward the guest hallway and followed it down to his room.

Once he closed the door, he leaned against it with a sigh. But he couldn't stand still. So he paced the length of his bed and back.

One question haunted every step and thought.

Could Jackie be Charles's daughter?

The thought was almost too much to absorb. He'd dismissed it easily enough when he first arrived, but now?

The woman who came here with an infant could very well be Anna Vines. Even though her name was written in the ledger as Hanna Morris. A few other thoughts raced through his mind, so he went to his case and looked through his notes. Anna Vines's maiden name was Morrison. Could she have shortened it so it would be easy for her to remember yet still familiar? But could it be that simple? She'd gone to great lengths to cover up her identity as she fled. Why would she give a name so similar to her own? So she would recognize it if someone called out her name?

If only he could talk to Anna or Hanna herself. If only she were still alive, the mystery could be solved.

He shook his head and continued pacing. How long had it taken her to reach this place? The stage lines back then were nothing like they were today. And she hadn't stayed on a coach. She'd purchased supplies and a wagon. If his assumptions were correct, she would have arrived at Carson Sink seven months after she'd left Kansas City. It was not an easy location to get to — especially back in 1834 with a wagon full of supplies and a baby — and it was truly out in the wilderness, away from society. Probably exactly why she chose to stay here. Hanna Morris *had* to be Anna Vines.

It was the only logical explanation. Jackie was blond with green eyes. Just like Anna. And the woman — Hanna or Anna — had stayed here. At Marshall Rivers's stage stop. For three years. That would line up with about when Charles suspected she'd come down with the fever. All they had to go on was the letter he received that said his wife had died and the postal markings that traced it back to the Utah Territory. Elijah wished he could look at that letter. Maybe there was some other clue. They didn't have exact dates to go on, but this couldn't all be coincidental, could it?

Even though his instincts were telling him there was a very real possibility that Jacqueline Rivers was Charles Vines's long-lost daughter, two obstacles stood in the way.

One — he didn't have any proof.

Two — Marshall Rivers.

A man who sounded like the epitome of a wonderful husband and father. Jackie respected him — and mourned him — a great deal. How could Elijah possibly tell her that the man she loved — the man who had raised her — wasn't her real father?

He couldn't.

At least not yet. Not until he had proof. It would take time. But what if Mr. Vines didn't have much time left? Could he break the old man's heart by not following his instincts and finding out the truth as quickly as possible?

Jackie's face floated to his mind. He'd only known her a few days, but he already held her in high esteem. He didn't want to hurt her either. And pushing on such a delicate matter might drive her away completely. She'd said her mother's name was Hannah. Did Anna change her name to Hannah? They sounded very similar. Was that why it was in the ledger that way? A last-minute decision as she was signing in? Just another piece of the puzzle.

As he sat on his bed, he shook his head and looked at the ceiling. *Lord, what am I to do?*

Allowing himself to admit the truth only added to his consternation: for the first time in a long time, he found a woman intriguing and quite appealing. He'd wanted to spend time with her and get to know her.

But if his gut was correct, he would have to shove his personal feelings aside. He couldn't exactly tell Jackie the truth about his feelings when he was trying to find his boss's heiress. If Jackie did indeed turn out to be Vines's daughter, she might think the only reason he came was because he was after her money.

And who was to say that Jacqueline Rivers wouldn't end up being exactly like Martha or even Laura? They'd both trampled all over him when the truth came out. It was the reason he had decided to pour himself into his work all those years ago — just like Mr. Vines.

But then, that was the reason he'd missed out on so much of life, wasn't it? It was the reason he hadn't settled down. Hadn't searched for love. He had been hurt in ways he hadn't even thought possible. Couldn't Jackie be different though?

His mind volleyed back and forth with each argument until his head hurt.

Elijah sat on the bed and put his head in his hands.

Maybe getting to know her better wasn't such a bad idea. He had to wait here for any word from his boss. He wouldn't cause any harm by using the time to find out about her character. Not just for himself — but for Charles's sake. And she might be able to help him discover other clues about the mysterious Hanna Morris who stayed here for so long.

Pushing his thoughts aside, Elijah knew he needed to let Charles know about his progress. If the man didn't have a lot of time left, perhaps the hope that Elijah was getting close to discovering the truth would encourage him to keep gaining strength. Sitting at the desk in his room, he put pen to paper and wrote a quick note to his partner.

A knock sounded at his door. That was odd. It was getting late. He went to the door and opened it a crack.

Mr. Crowell stood there in his nightclothes and robe. "My apologies, Elijah. But I forgot to give you this." He held out a piece of paper. "It's the names of the contacts I need you to meet with."

Elijah had completely forgotten about the job he had promised to do. "Oh, yes. Of course. When do you need me to go?"

"I received a note today on the Express. In five days' time, you'll need to meet with them. Will that work with your schedule?"

Nodding, he opened the paper and glanced at the names and locations. "That will be fine. So on the twenty-first I need to be there?"

"Actually, it is the twenty-second. My apologies. I leave for Carson City tomorrow and will hopefully return in a fortnight or less. I understand that is a long time, but things have come up that I must handle personally. If you need to leave before I return, would you please leave a sealed missive for me?" Crowell held out a hand.

Elijah shook the man's proffered hand. "I'll do as you ask. Perhaps I'll still be here as well."

Crowell smiled at him. "Good. Well, I should return to bed. Thank you, Mr. Johnson, for your assistance."

As he closed the door again, Elijah narrowed his eyes and pondered all that was going on. Too many mysteries intersected at this Express station in Carson Sink, Utah Territory. He'd already thought there were too many coincidences between Jackie and Mr. Vines's wife and missing daughter. This couldn't be another coincidence, could it? Or were they all connected somehow?

Virginia City
October 17, 1860

Carl fired off a clean shot into the man's chest. As he holstered his Colt, he walked over to the man, whose shocked gaze was beginning to glaze over, and spoke to his still form. "Sorry about that, Mr. Williamson, but we don't need you telling anyone the truth, now, do we?"

The man's breath left him in a hiss and gurgle of blood. Then his eyes stared at nothing.

As he crouched over the lifeless body, Carl reached into the man's waistcoat pocket and removed the papers. Perusing them, he found that the Treasury Department had learned more than he thought. They knew the treasury notes were being forged in this area. But at least the documents didn't say anything about who was supplying the forgeries. "So they think they have it all figured out. Well, we'll just have to make sure we send them in a different direction." He stood up, brushed off his pants, and straightened his jacket.

A chuckle sounded from behind him. "Yeah. Your plan is really smart. Blame all the forgin' and killin' on a dead man while we head to Mexico."

Carl looked over his shoulder at his nephew. The goofy grin on his face needed to be wiped off with a good, hard slap. "I don't want to hear you say anything about my plan out loud *ever again.* Especially not another word about Rivers. This won't work if you can't keep your trap shut. Do you hear me?"

The grin gone, the young man straightened his shoulders. "I hear ya."

With a flick of his wrist, Carl threw the papers into the fireplace where a roaring fire licked at the pages until they were completely engulfed. He stared at the flames. "Good."

"Want me to burn it down?"

The kid's eagerness for destruction needed to be tamed. "No. That would bring unwanted attention. Besides, we need it. He's a contact, remember? Which means that someone will be coming to meet him at some point."

"Yeah." His nephew nodded. "Do you wanna have me pretend I'm Mr. Williamson?"

Carl shook his head and laughed. "You? You couldn't clean yourself up enough to play the part. Besides, you talk like you never made it past the first grade. No, this calls for someone who is a bit more . . . cultured."

"You and your stupid clothes and fancy speech. Ya know I made it to second." He crossed his arms over his chest, the gleam in his eyes a look of pure evil. "Who needs schoolin' anyway? It don't help me make money like stealin' and killin' does." The younger man dared to step closer and puff out his chest. He was a big guy. Strong and scary. Exactly why Carl needed him.

Carl ignored his comments and stared at the fire. No. Schooling never helped him with his chosen line of work. But it *did* help him pass himself off as a gentleman. Something that the authorities seemed to miss every time. Seemed they always expected the serious criminals, thieves, and murderers to look the part. Filthy, disgusting, and uneducated. Just like his nephew here. Who stank to high heaven and hadn't washed his clothes probably . . . ever.

The thought made him chuckle.

After this job was over, he'd be set for life. As long as he could keep this kid from doing anything stupid. Then he'd just get rid of him too.

Chapter 10

Kansas City
October 18, 1860

Charles sat in his chair and looked out the window. The doctor had been checking on him this morning and so far hadn't said a word. "Well?"

Dr. Nathaniel Newberry had been his friend for a long time now. He swiped a hand down his face and sat down across from Charles. "Your symptoms haven't worsened. In fact, it seems you are improving —"

"Wonderful." Charles clapped his hands together.

Newberry held up his hand and halted any further words from Charles. "Wait just a minute. I'm not finished, Charles. Yes, you're improving, but if you don't continue to follow my recommendations and fully heal, you can easily go back to where you were."

"I've followed your instructions for months now, and I've been feeling so much better."

"I understand that. And I couldn't be happier for you, but if you want to continue to improve and have a life to actually live, then you need to listen to me. Otherwise, I'm afraid you will decline rapidly and you'll be facing the end." Nathaniel raised his eyebrows. "I know that's not what you want to hear, but I've got to be honest with you. It's imperative that you rest. Just because you're feeling better doesn't mean you can go back to your busy schedule from before." He stood up. "My orders remain. And I will make sure that Colson knows. What about your other man . . . Elijah? Do I need to inform him as well to keep you from doing anything foolish?"

Colson chose that moment to enter the room. "I'll be happy to enforce your orders, Dr. Newberry." The smirk on his face made Charles squirm.

"I'm not an invalid."

"Yes, you are. At least for now you are." The doctor shook his head and had the gall to laugh. "You are one of the most stubborn men I've ever met. But you've met your match now. Sickness and death are much more stubborn than you, and it's high time you realized it." He picked up his bag. "I'll be back in a week to check on you. That is, unless I get a bad report from Colson. Then I might just have to come see you every day again. And we don't want that, now, do we?"

Charles glared at his friend. "No, we most certainly do not. Especially if you make me drink any more of that nasty castor oil."

"Then it's agreed. You do as you're told, and I won't come and give you castor oil every day."

"Fine. But how long will I have to endure this?"

"Weeks. Months. I'm not sure. But if you refuse to listen, it will take longer. Understood?"

Charles rolled his eyes at his friend. "You speak like I'm a child."

"Well, don't act like one."

"It's a good thing I've known you as long as I have, or I might have Colson throw you out."

"I don't think Colson is on your side on this one, Charles." The doctor chuckled and headed to the door. "Behave yourself. We all would like to see you back to full strength. I'll see myself out."

As he turned back to the window, Charles heard his friend's footsteps echo down the hallway. "Colson?"

"Yes, sir?"

"How many more of the attic trunks do we have to go through?"

"There are at least twenty more, sir."

Resigned to his life of resting and recuperating, Charles nodded. "Good. At least that's something to keep us occupied for a while longer." Especially now that he felt so much better. He needed to be doing something.

"Very good, sir. Would you like luncheon now?"

Weariness washed over him in a sudden wave. Even though he'd been feeling much better, as much as he hated to admit it, the doctor was right. It would be a good while before he was full strength again. If ever. "Yes, that would be nice. Then perhaps after a nap, you can bring down another trunk for us to rummage through."

Colson smiled at him. "I would be happy to, sir."

Charles gazed out the window again and watched the branches with their colorful fall leaves dance in the wind. So much time had passed already. But if he could just hear from Elijah — perhaps with even a hint of good news — then he could endure whatever the doctor ordered.

Pounding on the front door made him turn.

"I'll see who that is, sir." Colson bowed and left.

He listened to the retreating footsteps and heard the door creak. Muffled words followed. Straining to hear whatever he could, Charles realized he was leaning toward the sound. Whatever had come over him? Never in his life had he been so interested in a simple knock on the door. He shook his head at the thought. He had entirely too much time on his hands. The doctor's words slid through his mind again. Perhaps he'd better pay a bit more heed to his wise friend. Charles longed to live his life — which meant he'd better rest so that he could get well and actually live.

Colson's quick footsteps approached. "Sir, this just arrived via Express."

"Thank you." He recognized the script as Elijah's.

"Do you need anything else, sir?"

"Not at the moment. Thank you." He studied the postal markings on the envelope.

As he opened the letter, he realized how much he had missed Elijah Johnson's presence in his life. Charles had relied greatly on the younger man, the son he never had. When he sent him away on a far-off journey

177

with an almost impossible task, had he been fair? He quickly scanned the words:

October 12, 1860

Mr. Vines,

I regret to inform you that I still haven't found any clues as to the whereabouts of your daughter. But I feel the good Lord prompting me to stay here for a while and continue to investigate. Please respond as soon as you are able with any other clues you might have thought of to help me in my search. I look forward to hearing from you.

I'm staying at the Express station in Carson Sink — in the Utah Territory — until I hear from you.

I pray you are doing well and listening to the doctor's orders. I fully expect you to be back to your normal self upon my return.

Sincerely,
Elijah Johnson

"Colson!"

The man appeared at the door in mere seconds. "Yes, sir?"

"I need that miniature painting and some paper. I used the last of it in my correspondence this morning." Since he'd been ordered to rest, he'd taken the time to write more letters than he ever had before. A task he'd normally pawned off to Elijah or Colson. He moved slowly to the desk in his room, even though his heart raced with excitement. He no longer felt like a weak little pup every time he tried to move around. Maybe he'd just needed something to look forward to. Could the good doctor be wrong? "Do we have time for you to get this to the Express heading west this afternoon?"

Colson checked the clock. "Yes, sir. I believe we do. I will hurry."

Writing as fast as he could, Charles explained the portrait and told Elijah of the project they had undertaken. Removing the painting from the small frame, he tucked it in with the letter and closed the four flaps of the envelope. He poured melted wax over the intersection of the flaps and pressed his seal into it. Now more than ever, he hoped that perhaps another clue presided in the attic above. Maybe, just maybe, he'd be able to meet his daughter before he died.

Carson Sink Express Station
Jackie sat next to Michael on the wagon seat as they left the Express yard and headed to

the Sand Hill station. Mr. Crowell had given her specific instructions about the questions she should ask, and she spent time studying the two treasury notes in the confines of her rooms at night.

What plagued her the most was the thought that this note forging and stealing from the government was happening in such a remote area where the small stations and towns were like family. The notion made her mind spin with questions. But then again, she guessed it made sense. Yes, gold and silver coin was often hard to come by out here. The treasury notes were used more for payment in remote areas like hers, but still the idea of foul play plagued her.

Who was behind all this? Could one of the owners of her beloved COC&PP be involved, or was it just a coincidence? If there were as many forgeries being made as Mr. Crowell suggested, someone was stealing thousands upon thousands of dollars from the government. That amount of theft could bankrupt any number of businesses or even small banks that cashed the notes for the thieves.

Another thought made her pulse race. What if the culprits were dangerous? And why wouldn't they be? If a lot of money was at stake, she assumed they would do just about anything to protect themselves. The thought was not pleasant. Maybe she shouldn't have agreed to help. What if she put any of her boys at risk? They were all so young. And not one of them weighed more than 125 pounds per the regulations of the Pony Express. Could they put up much of a fight if they got caught in the middle of something? Yes, they were always armed, but they were also usually flying at breakneck speed on the back of a horse.

A million different scenarios rushed through her mind. She hadn't heard of any suspicious deaths lately, and none of the stages had been attacked since the last Paiute uprising in June.

Granted, the Paiute wars had shut down the entire Express and all the stagecoach runs for almost two months, and tensions still ran high in their area of the Utah Territory, but the stage and Express had resumed and hadn't had any other issues for months.

Even so, the stage drivers traveled with rifles and pistols tucked under the seat for good measure. Could the men behind these unlawful practices be using the scare of attack by Indians to keep people afraid? That new thought intrigued her even more. Had Mr. Crowell and his men thought of such a scheme?

With a sigh, she clutched her reticule tighter. She hadn't wanted to risk bringing anything with her, so she'd memorized the code and the documents. It had taken her a couple of days to find the subtle differences between the real and forged treasury notes — enough so that she hoped to be able to recognize a forged note again if she saw one. She'd brought a small paper in her reticule with her own thoughts about what to look for. But it wasn't like she had become an expert at forgeries overnight.

Michael nudged her from his seat beside her. "Why exactly are we going to Sand Hill Station?"

"I need to speak with the station master." She stiffened her shoulders and used a take-charge voice, hoping he would take her word for it. Sworn to secrecy, she didn't want to betray her promise to Mr. Crowell, but she also needed to protect Michael. He hadn't signed up for any of this.

"Why are you so secretive about this? It's not like you." While she had no desire to deceive him, it really was for his own good.

"I'm not being secretive." She shrugged. "I'm just tired. That's all."

He raised his eyebrows. "Sure. If you say so. But we're family, Jack. If you're in some kind of trouble, you need to let me know.

Maybe I can help."

She relaxed her posture after hearing the concern in his voice. Smiling at him, she softened her tone. "I'm sorry. I'm not in any trouble, and I appreciate you being concerned." She looked out at the scrub brush and barren terrain. With a sigh she turned back to him. "I've volunteered to help Mr. Crowell with something. That's all. No need to worry."

Michael glanced at her like he was trying to figure out if she was telling the truth. "But you'll let me know if you need my help, right?"

"Of course I will." She wrapped an arm around his shoulders. "Like you said, we're family. And we always will be." Tucking her hands back in her lap, she took a deep breath and smiled. "Now why don't you tell me about all these dreams you keep talking about with the other men in the evenings?"

For the next thirty minutes, Michael went on about how he'd love to explore their country. He wanted to travel as far west as he could go and then head all the way east. Since he'd never been any farther than Virginia City, she understood his desire to see the rest of the world. Especially when travelers often came through who talked about the Rocky Mountains or the great cities of the East.

"I thought you wanted to be an Express rider." She tilted her head.

He shrugged. "Yeah, well, who knows how long it will last? I mean, once they get the telegraph all the way across, there won't be much need for the Express anymore. Don't ya think?"

Glancing back at the road in front of them, she realized he was correct. Something she hadn't put much thought into. It was a good thing she had a business with the stage stop as well. Otherwise, what would happen when the Express shut down? "It's not that close to being done, is it?"

"You don't read all the news that comes through here, do ya? They've already granted more money for it to be completed."

"How long do you think it will be?"

"A year or two at the most. Times are changin', Jack. Before you know it, we'll have the railroad crossing the whole country too. Then there won't be anything standing in my way of heading out on an adventure."

"You'd really want to leave? What if I need you? Won't you miss us?" She knew her voice sounded whiny and uncertain, but the thought of Michael leaving tore her heart in two. First Dad . . . now him. What would she do?

"Aw, fiddlesticks, Jack. I'm not leaving anytime soon. So don't get your dander up. Besides, you could always come with me."

"You know very well that I'm supposed to keep an eye out for you, young man. So don't start ordering me around. My home is here." Her big-sister-station-master voice was back in place. "There's plenty of time for us to discuss this later. You know I'll support you in whatever you want to do. As long as it is God honoring and upstanding, that is."

He laughed. "You should know me better than that, Jack. You and Marshall raised me better than that." He shook his head as he slowed the wagon and they approached the station. "It wouldn't surprise me if Marshall reached up from the grave to give me what-for if I were to choose anything *other* than God honoring and upstanding."

"You're right. Then you'd have to deal with both of us." Once they stopped, she climbed down from the wagon. "I'll only be a few minutes. Why don't you get the horses some water before we head back?"

"Always so bossy." He jumped down like the young kid he was.

"Don't you forget it either." Turning to the station, she left him at the wagon and hoped he'd stay there. It wasn't like there was much of anything to do out here. Sand Hill was smaller than Carson Sink. It was a Pony Express station and nothing more. The thrown-together, lopsided building looked like it could blow away with a stiff wind. The barn was in better shape, and that was saying a lot because the barn only had three walls.

Tom — the station manager — greeted her over the top of his paper when she walked in the door. "Whatcha up to today, Jack?" He looked back at the newsprint. Out here it was months before they received any papers from back east, but it was always good to catch up with the news when they got it.

She approached and spoke in the calmest voice she could muster. "I'm actually wondering if you've had anyone come in with treasury notes."

Looking up at her, he spit tobacco juice out the side of his mouth to the spittoon on the floor. "Treasury notes? What fer?"

"Have you seen any? Anyone trying to pay with them or needing to cash them in?"

The gruff man scratched his stubbly chin. "Nah, not for a while. I don't see much of that. They'll go to a bigger station most times."

186

"But you have seen some?"

"Not some. But one, yeah."

"When was it?"

"About a month or so back. I took it into Virginia City and cashed it in."

"Oh." She felt a bit deflated. How was she supposed to get a look at it if it wasn't even here?

"Marty out at Sand Springs Station brought in several at the same time I did. Thought it was rather odd that he'd have so many, but you know how it is out here. People pay with whatever they can get their hands on." He snapped the paper closed. "Why you askin' about it anyway?" Tom raised his eyebrows at her.

"It's not any big deal. I've had several come through my station lately. I'm just curious." She felt the heat rise up her neck. Why hadn't she prepared a better answer? Of course he was going to ask why she wanted to know. So much for her being a good spy for Mr. Crowell. Grief, she should stop thinking of herself as such.

"You women. Always nosing around." Tom turned back to his paper. "Best to keep to yerself if you ask me."

"Thank you for your advice." She attempted to keep the sarcasm from her voice, but she didn't care what Tom thought.

They'd known each other for too many years, and Tom was stuck in his ways and didn't care much for other people. Turning on her heel, she left him to his paper. "Good afternoon."

"Uh-huh."

Well, that proved completely unfruitful. At least it felt that way. She stopped in her tracks and looked down the trail. She wasn't a spy. She was being nosy. Just like Tom said. Mr. Crowell needed information, but he hadn't asked her to take this any further than that. Maybe she should stick to that.

But why would someone pay with a treasury note out here at Sand Hill Station? Yes, the Express was expensive, but no one lived out here. Most people paid for their Pony Express mail at a station that had a town around it.

Even farther east was Sand Springs. Several had been cashed in from there? This was definitely news she needed to share with Mr. Crowell. While Sand Springs was bigger than this station, she couldn't imagine people having access to treasury notes. Or was this a new trend? People always paid her in gold or silver. She knew that in large cities the banks had issued their own bank notes, but that wasn't national. The treasury notes were from the government.

Mr. Crowell's suspicions had to be correct. There was a forgery ring out here. And while she had seen a few of the notes come through in the mail, she hadn't looked at any of them. That kind of thing came through all the time. But after Mr. Crowell asked her to keep her eyes open, she'd become suspicious.

Exiting the station, she thought about the other stops she needed to visit. She'd committed to this job and should see it through. Sand Springs sounded like a good place to stop next, but what reason could she give for going all the way out there? She figured the most likely place to get information would be Virginia City. Especially if more of the treasury notes had been cashed in there. Even though that wasn't what Mr. Crowell had asked her to do, it seemed the logical choice.

Maybe she should go there next instead of any of the other stations.

Climbing back up into the wagon, she looked over at Michael.

He raised his eyebrows. "Well?"

She shrugged. "Nothing to tell. We'd better head home. I want to be there for the afternoon Express."

"And perhaps to talk to Mr. Johnson some more after dinner?"

Blinking rapidly, she took a deep breath. "What is that supposed to mean?"

"Aw, come on, Jack. I've seen how the two of you like to talk each evening. How long has he been here? Five, six days? No one ever stays out here that long."

"I don't know what you are insinuating, Michael, but there is nothing untoward going on."

He blew out his breath. *Pftt.* "I never said there was. But it seems to me that when a gentleman pays attention to a woman, it means he likes her."

Sitting up straight on the wagon seat, Jackie looked down at her adopted brother and then back ahead to the trail. "He's just being nice. Besides, he won't be out here forever and then we'll probably never see each other again." As soon as she said the words, her heart plummeted.

"But don't you like him? I've seen the way you like to sit at the fireplace. You two talk about scripture and all kinds of things. All evening. And the others notice it too."

She wasn't sure how to respond. "Well, of course I like him. He's a nice man. But he's only staying until he hears something from his employer. Then I'm sure he'll be on his way and we won't have the pleasure of his company anymore." The thought made her chest tighten.

It was true. She'd come to enjoy their chats each evening. Elijah was just as interested in studying God's Word as she was, and his insights were always helpful. He'd said the same to her. And even though logically she knew that he would leave one day and never return, she had to admit that he interested her much more than as just a guest at her station house.

Tilting her head, she tried to think of something else. Because the thought of the handsome Elijah Johnson leaving was enough to make her want to cry.

CHAPTER 11

October 21, 1860

As everyone from the small station of Carson Sink gathered around the fireplace for Sunday Bible study, Elijah couldn't help but watch their hostess.

The more time he spent with her, the more he admired her. But then the battle within his mind would rage again. What if she was Charles's long-lost daughter? Would she think he was only interested because of that?

He still had no idea how to prove it or how to broach the subject with her. But his gut told him he was correct.

Each day it was growing increasingly difficult to persuade his heart not to spend more time with her. Even though he'd convinced himself to keep his distance, he'd find himself searching her out. Whether it was watching her navigate and coordinate the Express when it came through or sitting by the fire in the evenings and discussing scripture, he wanted to spend as many moments with her as he could.

Blinking his eyes and breathing deep to rid himself of the thoughts, he looked back down at the Bible in his hands. *Lord, I need Your divine help here. I don't know why I'm so drawn to this woman, but please keep my mind and heart in check. If this isn't of Your will, I don't want any part of it.*

If only he would hear from Mr. Vines. So many things hung in the balance, and he needed to hear from his mentor. Especially now that he'd seen the ledgers. He'd sent off three different Express letters to his boss. He hoped they would all reach him in a speedy manner and he would have something to send Elijah in return.

Thoughts of Vines brought him back around to Jackie. Getting to know her better wasn't hurting anything or anyone. It might even come to his aid later on. Especially if there was proof that she was indeed Jacqueline *Vines.* Not Rivers. She would need someone to trust. And that could be him.

As much as the thought made him smile, it was another reason he shouldn't think about having feelings for her. How could he be trustworthy as her friend if his theory proved correct and she found out he'd kept such a huge secret from her? That it was the whole reason he had come here in the first place?

This conundrum was unlike anything he'd ever experienced. If only there were an easy answer.

But life wasn't full of easy answers. He'd learned that early on through his relationship with Martha. With the thought of her name, a whole slew of memories rushed forward.

As the group around him settled in to read from Daniel, Elijah found that he couldn't keep his focus on the passage at hand. Instead his thoughts took him back a decade. To a time he'd stashed in his memories, hoping to forget.

A time when he'd been in love with a young working girl. She wasn't even remotely close to his "class of people," as his mother and father termed it. They'd arranged for him to marry the beautiful and rich Laura Winslow. While he thought Laura was pretty and nice enough, his heart already belonged to Martha Smith. He'd been young, yes, but society demanded advantageous marriages, with no exception for Elijah Johnson.

Over the months, he'd begged his parents

to allow him to marry for love. When he told Laura how he felt, she'd put on a good performance of being gracious but told him in no uncertain terms that he was not to humiliate her in any way. She would find some way to end the engagement, and it would be on her terms.

His parents, however, didn't appreciate his feelings. His father even threatened to disown him. Elijah had stood his ground and faced his father — telling him that he'd already asked Martha to marry him and it would be dishonorable to turn back. They finally acquiesced and figured they could weather the storm as long as Elijah held up his end of the bargain and took over the family business dealings. Money could buy a lot of things. Including loyalty and the press.

But life had crashed around him when he'd gone to tell Martha the news. Finding her in another man's arms, he'd overheard the words that crushed him and pointed him to the path he'd been on for all these years.

"Nothing will change between us, my love. I promise. We can go on as lovers. . . . I'll simply be rich and married."

When he'd confronted her — his heart broken into a thousand pieces — her hard and callous nature came out. She tried to convince him to follow through with their marriage and threatened to tell everyone about how he'd promised to marry her but had taken advantage of her. Her threats could do no more damage than what his heart had already been through. Realizing she had never cared about him at all, Elijah left her and went home.

The greeting from his parents was nothing like he'd hoped. He'd prayed they would forgive him his foolish ways and help him rebuild his life. But no. They'd scolded him and been more worried about the scandal and their reputations than about their son's future or his feelings.

So he'd gone to Laura and apologized. She'd laughed in his face and told him he got what he deserved.

The next day, every paper in town reported that Miss Laura Winslow regretted to announce the termination of her engagement to Mr. Elijah Johnson in light of his affair with a working-class woman.

There'd been nothing scandalous between him and Martha, which Laura well knew. But the truth — that he simply didn't love her — was humiliating. So she publicly pronounced him a scoundrel, ensuring he felt as mortified as she did. According to her, he was pretty much evil itself.

The next day, he'd emptied his savings account and left his trust fund sitting in the family bank. He'd left everything behind — even his parents — and headed west to make a new life.

And he'd promised himself never to fall in love again.

Over the years, he'd wondered what would have happened if he had gone along with his parents' plan to marry Laura and how long it would have taken him to recognize that her pretty smile disguised a miserable character.

As soon as he'd told her the truth, her devious, conniving nature surfaced. She'd bragged about ruining more than one of her servants' lives. Gossip was her best friend. And as Elijah matured, he realized he would have been miserable under such circumstances.

He discovered through that awful situation that character was what mattered.

It didn't matter that his family had money. That society loved them because of it.

What mattered was that one day he would need to stand before God. And his actions were his testimony.

An elbow to his right arm brought his thoughts promptly back to the present. He blinked. It took a moment to realize he wasn't that young man starting out fresh on his own, with his heart broken in two.

Michael leaned over to him. "It's your turn to read."

Clearing his throat, Elijah looked up at the group. "My apologies. Where were we?"

"Daniel chapter 5, verse 24." Michael showed him in his Bible.

Elijah cleared his throat again and gave a weak smile to the group as he focused on the reading. Daniel was speaking to King Belshazzar about the writing on the wall. " 'Then was the part of the hand sent from him; and this writing was written. And this is the writing that was written, Mene, Mene, Tekel, Upharsin. This is the interpretation of the thing: Mene; God hath numbered thy kingdom, and finished it. Tekel; Thou art weighted in the balances, and art found wanting. Peres; Thy kingdom is divided, and given to the Medes and Persians.' "

As he finished the chapter, everyone looked up at each other.

Jackie raised her eyebrows. "Can you imagine seeing that hand writing on the wall?"

Elijah nodded and pushed the remnants of his past from his mind. "It's hard to imagine. Then the king's life is taken that very night."

"Because he didn't listen," Mr. Liverpool interjected. "We're so good at doing whatever we want because we think we can. It makes us no better than King Belshazzar here."

Affirmations were heard around the room.

The blacksmith continued, "It's been a fascinating study of Daniel so far. But let's review a bit of what we've learned for our guests here." He nodded at Elijah and Mr. Crowell.

Michael chimed in beside him, "Well, for one, we know that the first half of Daniel is historical. The second half is prophetic."

"That's right," Mr. Liverpool agreed. "And in the first six chapters of Daniel we see kings dreaming and Daniel interpreting. Then in the second six chapters we see Daniel dreaming and an angel interpreting."

Elijah watched as Jackie made notes across the room. Her pencil flew across the sheet of paper she had laid over her Bible.

Liverpool's wife gave a heavy sigh. "It's great to understand that about how the book is divided, but why is this second part so difficult? The stories in the beginning are much easier to understand than all the prophecy later on. Doesn't God want us to make sense out of this?"

Several of the riders nodded, but they all sat with their arms crossed — almost a challenge not to ask them any questions.

Their posture amused Elijah, but he looked back down at the chapter.

Jackie spoke up again. "What if we talk about the favorite thing we've learned so far?"

Mark — one of the riders — leaned forward. "I'll start with my favorite. I think it's interesting how King Nebuchadnezzar changes throughout the first four chapters. Especially his view of God."

Elijah was impressed with the young man's response, and recollections of the beginning of Daniel came to mind. Since he hadn't been here when the group first started the book, he flipped back to Daniel chapter 1. "I'd like to hear more of your thoughts on that." He turned to Jackie. "Would you mind writing this down for me so I can use it as I study later?"

"Of course." She went back to writing on the paper.

Mark shrugged and looked down at a Bible he shared with John. "Well, I don't think I have anything really profound to say, but as we've been studying this together, it's stood out to me in a progression. In the first chapter, after Daniel and his friends don't eat the king's food and determine not to defile themselves while they're in captivity, they prove that God is better and His ways are the right ways. When King Nebuchadnezzar communes with them, he finds them ten times better than all the others. So at least he's understanding that their God — the God of the Hebrews — is worth something. It's almost like they've now got the king's attention.

"Then in chapter 2, Nebuchadnezzar acknowledges God. Here in verse 47, he says, 'Of a truth it is, that your God is a God of gods, and a Lord of kings, and a revealer of secrets.' So he's taken a step closer. He at least realized who God is. Then in chapter 3, the good ol' king of Babylon goes a step even further and says that Shadrach, Meshach, and Abednego are 'servants of the most high God.' He blesses God and says that 'there is no other God that can deliver after this sort.' He's beginnin' to really understand that Daniel's God is the one true God. Even if he hasn't grasped it completely for himself yet."

The whole group sat mesmerized, hanging on Mark's every word.

The young man didn't look up — he just kept pointing to the Bible in front of him. "And finally in chapter 4, after Nebuchadnezzar has learned a mighty lesson — after being a beast for seven years, which was a consequence of him not listenin' — it's pretty clear that Daniel and his friends' God isn't just their God. He's Nebuchadnezzar's God as well. The king has finally come to understand the full truth."

Mrs. Liverpool's mouth dropped open a bit. "Young man, that's amazing."

He shrugged. "Ain't much, ma'am. Just tellin' ya what I think is my favorite part of Daniel."

"But that puts it all in a whole new perspective for me. I never saw that before." Once again, her mouth hung open.

Mr. Liverpool glanced at his wife and chuckled to the rest of the group. "Mark, you've done an extraordinary thing."

"What's that, sir?"

"You've rendered my wife speechless."

The group laughed together as Mrs. Liverpool swatted at her husband. He wrapped his arm around her in a sweet side hug and kissed her on the cheek.

Mrs. Liverpool's cheeks turned pink, and she looked at her husband with an expression of love that stunned Elijah.

He looked over to Jackie, who took in the expression of affection like it was a normal, everyday occurrence.

Elijah compared the simplicity of this group to the stodgy church services he'd attended at home. Oh, there were definitely some positives about having the hymns played on the beautiful pipe organ or hearing the smooth voice of the pastor as he read from the Bible, but for the most part, the services were cold and unwelcoming. Whereas here he felt like part of a family. Like an actual part of the Church. "Do you think this meeting is like the gatherings of the first church that we read about in Acts?" He hadn't meant to ask the question aloud, but it was out.

Everyone started talking at once, and he had a hard time keeping up. He held up his hands. "My apologies, but perhaps we could speak one at a time?"

Mrs. Liverpool was speechless no longer. "That's exactly what I've been telling Mr. Liverpool every time we come together like this." She gave her husband another adoring look. "We always wanted to be part of something like that. And wouldn't you know? We found it out here in the middle of nowhere."

Jackie smiled. "Dad used to say he preferred church in a home because that was how many in the first church did it, not in many fancy buildings."

As the conversation continued, Elijah watched the animated faces and genuine smiles around the room. There was something so different about the people here. It made him crave a family even more.

But was that what God had for him?

Could he trust himself to fall in love again?

After all he'd been through with Laura and Martha, he had never thought it was possible. But then his mind shifted back to Daniel. He'd overcome insurmountable obstacles, survived seventy years of captivity, and continued to serve God no matter what came his way. Daniel chose God over everything.

Maybe that was where Elijah needed to focus. Instead of focusing on his work or on pleasing Vines, perhaps the answer was in keeping his eyes on Almighty God. Acknowledging Him at every turn.

With new resolve, Elijah sent a prayer heavenward. No matter what happened from this day forward, he wanted to serve God with the same passion Daniel had.

As he looked around the room, a fresh new thought crossed his mind. Maybe God hadn't brought him here to finish his quest for Mr. Vines. Maybe God had brought him here to change him from the inside out.

CHAPTER 12

"Amen," Jackie echoed after Mr. Liverpool finished his closing prayer for their little group. She stood to her feet. "Michael and I have planned a picnic for everyone at the lake today, so we'd like to invite everyone to join us. If I can get all the men to help carry the food and blankets to the wagons, we can make our way there."

"How lovely." June clapped her hands.

"What a nice thing to do, Jackie." Elijah gave her a broad smile. There was something different in his expression. She couldn't tell what it was at the moment, but hopefully she'd get the chance to talk with him at the lake. Their conversations had been brief lately, and she found herself longing for more.

In a flurry of activity, everyone scrambled about. Some went to their rooms or the bunkhouse to put away their Bibles. Some went to the kitchen where she had baskets of food ready to be taken out to the lake. Some went to the stable to get the wagons.

In a matter of minutes, everyone from their little station at Carson Sink was loaded into wagons and headed to the lake to enjoy the beautiful day. As she looked from person to person, her heart overflowed. And another pang of grief hit her chest. *Oh Dad, I wish you were here.*

It wasn't just missing him on such a lovely, fun day. It was the fact that she wouldn't have the chance to discuss with him her questions about scripture anymore. It had been his idea to study the book of Daniel.

He wasn't there to advise her about the work she was doing for the Express. And she wished she could talk to him about what she'd discovered as she worked for Mr. Crowell. Would he approve of her spying for the government? If he'd already been helping, then surely he would.

Her mind spun with all the what-ifs. Especially when it came to the fact that she'd lied to the COC&PP owners. A matter she needed to fix, and soon. Why did she keep putting it off? Her excuse had been the busyness around the station. Maybe it was time to swallow her excuses and just do it. Dad would want her to be honorable and honest.

Thoughts of him as they drove out to Carson Lake only brought her grief to the forefront again. Jackie shook her head of the sad thoughts. Grief had reared its ugly head a few too many times lately. And she was tired.

Heavenly Father, I don't know why this has been such a difficult time for me. You know how much I miss Dad. I know I've made a lot of mistakes. Please forgive me, Lord. Forgive me for all the ways I've failed You. And God, if You would, please help me to get past the grief that is wearing me down. I know Dad wouldn't want it. But I miss him.

Her wagon hit a large bump and she almost let go of the reins. With a deep breath, she pulled herself together. It would be a good day. A fun day. A short time of Sabbath. And they all needed the brief respite despite the fact that the Express had to function seven days a week.

Marshall Rivers had instilled in all of them a strong work ethic. And while their business indeed required seven days of work a week, he insisted that they all take a brief time of respite — or Sabbath — each day. Especially on Sundays. Jackie realized how important it was and how she had neglected it. No wonder she felt weary.

The ride out to the lake took the better

part of an hour, but the wagons were filled with laughter, silly songs, and wild stories from the riders. They told so many crazy stories they'd heard as they rode the Express that Jackie wondered how many of them were actually true.

As they emptied the wagons and laid the blankets out on the ground, she caught sight of Elijah out of the corner of her eye. He hammered a stake into the ground and yelled, "Who's up for a game of quoits?"

"As soon as we eat, I'll take that challenge." Michael ran a basket over to her and threw a thumb over his shoulder. "I think I need to teach this city boy that out here we use horseshoes."

She laughed at the face he made. "I'll cheer you on."

Their luncheon of ham sandwiches with pickles and thick slices of Mrs. Liverpool's prized dairy cows' cheese was laid out in short order. Michael joined her on her blanket, and even though she'd secretly hoped that Elijah would sit with them, she deflated a bit when he sat with Mr. Crowell. Why did she care so much anyway? She'd get to see him the whole time they were here, and then perhaps he would join her at the fireplace tonight — since that had been his habit since he arrived. Pasting a smile on her face, she determined to enjoy the picnic.

Lunch was consumed in what seemed to be record time. Then everyone headed to the area where Elijah had placed the stakes.

As she lifted the edge of her skirt to make her way over the rough terrain, Jackie's mind wandered to what it must be like to live in the city. With all the beautiful gowns the women wore, the headdresses, beaded jackets, and embroidered hats that matched each outfit. They probably never had to worry about purchasing boots that were sturdy enough to withstand the prickly ground of the West. Or keeping their skirts and petticoats free of the sagebrush and tumbleweed.

While she'd never had a chance to wear anything fine like that, she did enjoy talking about the latest fashions with June and looking through *Godey's* every time a new issue arrived. She'd often peruse each one for months and dream up her own elaborate dress complete with jewels and a handsome man at her side.

The romantic side of her wasn't something she let anyone see. But oh, she could dream. Perhaps Mother was a woman who loved fine things as well. She definitely didn't get it from Dad. Marshall Rivers was as down to earth as a man could be. And while he cleaned up good, he was always about the practical. Whenever she asked for new ribbons for her hair or a new dress, he'd often give her a look she couldn't quite decipher. But being the doting father he was, he usually gave in and ordered her something pretty. She'd never forget the first time she asked him to buy a china tea set. His face had been almost comical.

Cheering and the clanking of iron against iron brought her attention back to the small group in front of her. They might not be wealthy by any means or dressed in finery, but they were happy and together.

Joining the spectators for the exciting tournament of horseshoes, she glanced at Elijah as he held a horseshoe in his right hand. He cut a fine figure in his blue suit and leather shoes with the contrasting toe caps and heels. Her mind automatically imagined what it would be like to dress in something fancy and accompany Mr. Johnson to an elegant affair in Kansas City.

"What's put the smile on your face, Jackie?" June Liverpool walked up to her side, one eyebrow raised and a hand on her hip.

Jackie felt a blush rising to her cheeks at the realization that it had been far too easy for her thoughts to jump to that daydream with Elijah. "Oh, just thinking about a new dress that we saw in *Godey's.*"

"Oh, which one? The 'Extremely tasteful dress of white glacé silk; the skirt in nine flounces, pinked in large scallops; the berthé finished by a bouillon of violet silk, and a bow of the same shade, with flowing ends, placed in the center of the corsage below it. Simple wreath of violet primroses, without foliage, in the hair'?" She took a deep breath. "Or did you mean the 'Dinner-dress also suited to a concert or opera. Dress, itself, of lustrous blue glacé silk; the bottom of the skirt trimmed by six narrow puffs, or bouillons of the same material; corsage rather low, with a tucker of white muslin, drawn by a narrow black velvet ribbon'?"

Jackie laughed. "Did you *memorize* the magazine, June?"

Mrs. Liverpool laughed along. "Almost. I tell you, I get so bored most days, I find myself rereading the *Lady's Book* every chance I have." A dramatic sigh followed. "I cannot tell you how much I miss being closer to a city and society. But poor Mr. Liverpool's constitution would never be able to withstand it. And I wouldn't be able to withstand life without him." The woman fanned herself with a delicate pink fan even though there was no need for it in the beautiful fall weather.

"I'd imagine that your cheese-making would take up a good deal of your time. It is quite scrumptious, I must say."

The fan moved at a faster pace. "Why, thank you, my dear. It does take a decent amount of time, but you know me. I like to be busy, busy, busy and keep my mind and hands occupied."

Indeed. Jackie suppressed a giggle.

"Are you certain that the reason for the smile on your face wasn't due to a certain fashionable gentleman?"

"June . . . I . . ." Had she been so transparent?

Her friend put a hand on her arm. "I'm sorry. I didn't mean to pry — well, maybe I did a little. Just know that whenever you need someone to talk to, I'm here. I *am* the only other woman around." The older lady laughed at her own joke. "I haven't been able to have any children of my own, and I'm much too young to be your mother, but I'd love to fill a role as maybe . . . older sister. Now that your father is gone. If you'll have me."

"Thank you, June. You are very dear. You've always been like an older sister to me, and I can't imagine what I would do without you."

"I hope you know I feel the same about you. It's just different once both your parents are dead. You always were such a daddy's girl — following him around like a little puppy. And he adored you. For the longest time, I didn't feel like you needed anyone else in your life."

"Oh June. I'm so sorry. I never meant to make you feel that way. I need you more than you can imagine." They hugged, and the clank of a horseshoe against a metal stake made the group cheer. Jackie looked over to see a huge grin spread across Michael's face. He must be winning. Clapping along with the others, she glanced over at Elijah, whose face was in a serious-looking scrunch as he got ready to fling his horseshoe. He released it, and it flew through the air.

Another resounding *clank* made their little group cheer all the more.

"Well, it seems we have ourselves quite the competition." June walked closer to the game, never to be left out of anything important. She waved Jackie forward.

Jackie followed along, not just dutifully as the only other woman, but as a friend. And because secretly she wanted to see Elijah win.

As soon as the thought filled her mind, she wondered where it had come from. But it was true. She couldn't cheer for one and not the other though. Michael was, after all, family. Oh, what was she thinking? Mr. Johnson would be leaving at some point in the near future, and he would probably never return. She needed to get her head out of the clouds and back on solid ground.

After several rounds of horseshoes were played and the men had all touted their successes, Jackie realized it was about time to head back if she wanted to ensure she was ready for the Express — just in case it was early. Which happened more often than not.

Just as she was about to call out to everyone to gather their things, a ball of mud-colored fur raced past her. What in the world?

Trying to make out whatever the blur was, she got bumped from behind.

"Sorry!" Michael's voice rushed past her as he went in pursuit of whatever it was.

Letting out a huff, she put her hands on her hips. What was he up to now?

Mark ran up to her side. "It's a puppy. . . . We found it over there" — he spoke between gasping breaths and jerked his head to the left — "and must've scared it, because now it just runs and runs . . . while we chase it."

He bent over and put his hands on his knees. "But the only one with any energy left is Michael."

"I thought your whole job was delivering the mail faster than anyone else, yet you can't keep up with a puppy?" she teased.

"Give me a horse, and I'll chase him down any day of the week." Laughing, he lay down on the ground. "But on foot? I'm plum tuckered out."

By this point, everyone was watching the chase and laughing every time the small canine outmaneuvered Michael. Jackie watched along with them, laughing and cheering with their group as they loaded the wagons. But her breath caught in her throat when, in a split second, the pup jumped off a ledge into the water below. A scream formed in her throat. "No! Michael, don't —"

Splash!

Michael followed whether he wanted to or not, the momentum of the chase preventing him from stopping.

She covered her mouth with her hands and started running toward the water. The lake was deep on that side.

Jackie had no idea if anyone else knew what was going on, but she had to help him. As she reached the ledge where they'd

215

jumped off, she reached down to tear off her shoes.

A strong hand stopped her. "He can't swim, can he?" Elijah's voice cut through the fog in her brain.

Shaking her head and biting her lip against the tears that threatened, Jackie implored, "Please . . . help him."

Elijah nodded while he took off his shoes, and in the next moment, he dove into the water below.

The seconds that passed felt like hours — even though it couldn't have been that long because she held her breath the entire time. Hoping and praying that Michael would be okay.

Nothing could have prepared her for the way she felt. The pain of losing Dad came flooding back. Tears raced down her cheeks as she thought of losing Michael too. *No, God, please, no.*

Just when she thought her lungs would explode, she saw Elijah's head come to the surface, followed by Michael's. He sputtered and coughed. Then she saw that Michael held the wiggling pup in his arms. Gasps were heard throughout the group.

Elijah glanced up at her.

She mouthed, *Thank you,* her hands clutched at her chest. How would she ever repay the man?

Elijah swam them over to shallower water where they could climb out.

Grabbing Elijah's shoes, she then ran over to the soaked men.

Michael caught her gaze and shot her a smile. "Can I keep him?"

CHAPTER 13

Virginia City
October 21, 1860

The puff of smoke from the fat man's cigar wafted up into the air.

Carl watched the man thumb through the forged notes. "Are you finished with them?"

"Quite." The man handed over the documents, his pudgy hands covered in ink.

"Good." Carl walked back behind his desk and examined each one. The guy was good, he'd give him that. "The last order needs to be ready in four weeks."

"It's gonna take longer for an order that size. You should know that. Six at the very least." Another puff of smoke filled the air with a gray haze.

Carl eyed the man. "Six weeks. Not a day more." That would be cutting it close, but if he played his cards right, he could make do.

"Fine. I'll be seein' ya next week for the deposit." The man waddled out the door.

They'd agreed at the beginning of their business arrangement that they wouldn't know each other's name. That way, if either one of them was confronted, they had nothing to give up.

But this guy was greedy. Carl wished he did know who he was so he could find him and take care of him quietly when all was said and done. He narrowed his eyes and turned to his nephew. "Did you make sure all the letters were delivered?"

"Yep. They should make for lively discussion whenever someone comes lookin' for the forged treasury notes."

"Good." Carl tucked his hands into his tweed coat pockets and went over to the window. "Pretty soon we'll be on our way to Mexico, and no one will be the wiser."

His nephew chuckled. "Can we get a place to live by the water? It's so stinkin' dry here. If I see one more tumbleweed, I'll be tempted to shoot it."

"It's called the beach." The imbecile. If even a bit of brain lodged in the kid's head, Carl would be surprised. "And yes, I think it would be nice to walk out every morning and gaze at the ocean, a cool breeze on my face. But we will get separate houses. I'm not living in filth."

"I'll get me a senorita or two. They can

clean up after me."

Carl shook his head. There was no chance he wanted to live anywhere near members of his family. He hadn't spent ten years of his life getting educated and learning how to be part of high society just so he could live out his days in a pigsty. No. He enjoyed the finer things in life, and he planned to have them.

Just because the rest of his family looked the part of criminals didn't mean he had to like it. His nephew had served a purpose. He and the rest of the family could rot in jail for all he cared. They were a means to an end.

As soon as he had all the forgeries, he'd finish cashing them in. Plenty of idiots were jumping at the chance to obtain the notes in hopes that they could get more of the interest from the government. Since he was willing to get rid of them for a fraction of their worth, distribution had been easier than he'd thought. He'd take the last bunch to San Francisco before he left for good. Enough ne'er-do-wells waited there to do business that he could easily get lost in the crowd.

When those stupid men who worked for the Treasury finally figured out they'd been duped, he'd be long gone. They'd find the letters incriminating Marshall Rivers as the mastermind and the box at the bank in Virginia City full of a stack of forgeries. All in Rivers's name. There'd be no reason for them to look anywhere else.

He could live the life that he deserved in the lap of luxury.

No one could ever talk down to him again.

Carson Sink Station

Sitting in front of the roaring fire, Jackie worked on darning one of Michael's socks. Michael had a blanket wrapped around his shoulders as he lounged on the floor with the puppy. It really was a cute little thing, but Jackie wasn't sure they needed a pet underfoot in such a busy station. What if he got caught under the hooves of an Express horse? Or what if he ran out in front of the stage? But for now, she couldn't deny Michael the little fellow.

At least the pup had finally calmed down after their little dunk in the lake. And it had stuck by Michael's side ever since.

The young man she thought of as a little brother had done nothing but shiver ever since they returned home — even now, after he was in clean, dry clothes, wrapped in a blanket, and sitting only a foot or so from the warmth of the fire. She prayed he wouldn't catch his death from his little swim.

Poking her needle back through the heel of the sock, she watched him play with the little ball of fur. "He sure is adorable."

"Yep. And fast too. Did you see how fast he could run?" Pride rang in Michael's voice.

Footsteps sounded down the hall. Elijah came around the corner and headed for the fire. "He definitely could outrun you. We all had the privilege to witness that."

Michael laughed and held out his hand. "Thank you, again, for saving me today."

"Think nothing of it. You're welcome." Elijah shook his hand.

Jackie raised her eyebrows at the comment. "It most certainly will be thought of, Mr. Johnson. You saved Michael's life, and I will be forever grateful." She went to the kitchen and poured a cup of coffee.

She walked back to the parlor area and handed it to the man who'd jumped in the lake to save Michael. The man she couldn't seem to stop thinking about.

He took it from her, and as she went back to her seat, the fresh scent of his hair pomade, soap, and . . . something else very masculine and appealing lingered in her senses. He'd taken a hot bath when they'd returned since he too had been soaked to the bone. Jackie found that she liked the way he smelled. The soap that they made out here for themselves wasn't all that pleasant, and most of the Express riders and workers smelled like sweat and leather. But whatever cologne Elijah Johnson used was just another reminder that he was a gentleman and not from around here.

"What happened to calling me Elijah?" He tilted his head at her as he smiled. "And you've thanked me enough. Now, I believe I may just need to teach this young man how to swim." Elijah took a long sip.

"Would you?" Michael sat up straighter and yawned, holding the now sleeping puppy close.

The cup still close to his lips, Elijah nodded. "Of course. Everyone needs to know how to swim. But if the water is this cold all the time, we might have a problem. Especially as we draw closer to winter."

"The creek is warmer. Not a lot, but at least for now I could stand it. And it's deep enough to swim in." The eagerness in Michael's tone couldn't be denied.

"All right then. It's settled. When I return from Virginia City, I'll teach you how to swim."

His words brought her head up from her

sewing. "You're going to Virginia City?"

"Tomorrow, yes." With a nod, he set his cup down on the small table beside him. "I have a few simple errands, and then I'll return."

"Oh. That's nice." She pushed the needle back and forth through the sock. The thought of him gone from the station did weird things to her stomach. She'd gotten used to his presence. Even though he'd only been there slightly more than a week.

"Will you hold my mail for me?"

"Of course. Are you expecting to be gone long?"

"No. Probably just tomorrow. But I'm hoping for a letter from my employer. Although I doubt it could get here this quick." He took another long sip of coffee. "Let's see, I sent it out on the twelfth. It's only been eight days."

A snore from the direction of the fire captured her attention. Sure enough, Michael was fast asleep on the floor with the puppy lying on his chest. She laughed. "Sorry about that. He always could fall asleep at the drop of a hat. I guess today wore him out."

"It's no wonder. The fresh air was glorious, but then Michael chased that little dog for a good while, and then of course he took a dunk in the lake. It makes me tired just thinking about it." He leaned forward and put his elbows on his knees, the china cup between his hands.

"Dad used to take us to the lake. . . ." She couldn't finish.

"Might I offer my condolences again for the loss of your father? I hope it's not too personal for me to comment, but I've noticed that it has affected you a great deal of late."

"Yes, thank you." The thought of Dad pinched her heart, but it was special to her that Elijah noticed. No one else had. At least, no one had mentioned it.

"I'm sorry for bringing it up again. But it's made me wonder if you plan to stay here."

"Of course." She glanced up at him. "This has been my home my whole life."

"Would you like to travel anywhere? Perhaps experience the big city?" His words were soft and gentle, so why did they feel like a knife?

Why was he asking these questions? Was she not doing an adequate job here? Did he think she was inferior because she hadn't experienced society? She studied his gaze. The warmth she saw made her think something altogether different. Perhaps he was asking because . . . he was interested in her? Wondering if she would ever consider leaving? Her heart warmed with the thought. And while she'd spent entirely too much time daydreaming about the handsome Mr. Johnson, logic had prevailed, and she'd come to the conclusion that a man of his caliber would never be interested in someone like her. Especially since he would be leaving soon.

"Jackie?" He leaned a bit closer, his gaze intense.

She blinked. "I'm sorry. I'm afraid I was lost in thought." Laying the darning in her lap, she took a deep breath. "I admit I've always wanted to travel. But this is my home, and I have responsibilities here."

"But what if you didn't have responsibilities?" he pressed. "Would you want to go?"

Not knowing what to think of his train of thought, she decided to just be honest. "I'm sure I would. I've always loved the idea of traveling and going to the opera in the city. Dressing up and dining at a fancy restaurant." She took a long breath. "But I don't know if I'd enjoy staying there. While I might appreciate fine things and love the beautiful dresses and attire of the wealthy, I'm still just a simple country girl. I enjoy the quiet pace of our lives out here."

"I can see that."

"What about you?" It was high time she turned the tables and asked him a few probing questions. "Will you continue in your job? It sounds like you've done nothing but work for a long time."

"My partner is the best of men. I believe I will continue to work for him, yes."

"So you want to stay in the city?"

He appeared to ponder her question. "Not necessarily. I admit that I've enjoyed being out of the city for several months. I do relish the quiet." He took another sip. "I believe it would do Mr. Vines a great deal of good for his health as well."

"It sounds like you care for him a lot. Are you close to him?"

"Yes, he's like a father to me." He stared into the fire.

"Are your parents dead?"

He cleared his throat and looked down with a sigh. "No. They are still living."

The way he said it made her curious. "Are you . . . estranged from them?"

"No, I wouldn't phrase it like that. But it has been a good many years since I've seen them."

His answer shocked her. "Why is that?"

Elijah turned toward her and leaned back in his chair. "It's a long story."

"I have plenty of time." She quirked an eyebrow at him, hoping she wasn't being too forward.

With a half smile, he stared down into his cup. "I appreciate that you don't mince words, Miss Rivers."

She smiled back. "I thought it was Jackie?"

A slight chuckle left his lips, and he looked at the fire before turning his blue eyes back to her. "Touché."

"I don't mean to intrude on your personal thoughts."

"No. It's quite all right." He lifted a hand. "You see, my parents are also very wealthy, but they don't care much for anything outside of their own social circle. They traveled once to Chicago, but that was as far west as they wished to go."

"So you don't visit them, and they don't visit you?"

He shrugged. "No. Sadly."

"Do you write letters? Stay in touch?" She knew she was pushing the boundaries of polite conversation, but those didn't apply out West anyhow. Not that she wanted him to think of her as uncouth, but she longed to know more about him.

"Not much. Like I said, my parents like their social status. But they don't even like each other. They're wealthy. Money keeps them busy, I guess."

"What do you mean they don't even like each other?" She couldn't imagine a husband and wife not liking each other.

"It's quite simple really. They live in separate wings of the house and have their own events and appointments to keep themselves occupied. Mother is on the board of several charities, and Father is always overseeing . . . something."

Out of all the outrageous things she'd heard or read in her magazines, Elijah's revelation was the most shocking news to her. She felt her brow furrow.

"I can see this puzzles you."

"I thought marriage was something entirely different, yet you seem to talk about your parents' marriage as if that's . . . *normal.*" The thought appalled her. No wonder the handsome man before her was still single if that was all the example he had.

"Sadly, I've only known people to be miserable in marriage. My parents used to fight all the time. Over the years they must have come to a truce, because now they just go their separate ways. Only occasionally do they go to a ball together — simply to make an appearance."

"How sad."

"What do you mean?"

"While I don't remember my mother, when Dad spoke of her you could see the adoration in his face. He never married after she died, and I could always tell that he loved her very much. Then there are the Liverpools. They definitely have opposite personalities, but they care for each other a great deal. I know they are happily married. I see it every day. And then there are all the stories I've read. It hurts my heart to think that's the example you've seen. Do you not have any married friends? What about the man who sent you here?"

The look on his face changed. "He is . . . another story." He paused and drank the rest of his coffee. "In regard to your other query, our pastor and his wife looked happy enough, but sadly, I only saw them at church. Work and business have taken over the majority of my life."

"Oh. I see." As much as she was drawn to this man, she couldn't imagine having a husband who was overly absorbed in his work. She didn't like how this conversation was making her feel, and by the look on Elijah's face, he wasn't enjoying it either. "Would you like some more coffee?"

"No, but thank you."

An awkward silence stretched between them.

Michael rolled onto his side with a soft snore, and the puppy slid onto the blanket beside him.

The sock in her hands was finished, but she didn't want to get another one. What she wanted was to know more about the man before her — no, she wanted to ease the pain she saw in his face. But it wasn't her place.

"That was a fascinating discussion we had on Daniel this morning."

"Yes, it was, wasn't it?" Thankful for the change in subject, she still thought her reply sounded ridiculous.

The conversation stalled again, but he made no move to leave, which made her feel better. She liked his presence. "Did you need to look for anything else in the ledgers?"

"No. I believe we found what I needed." As he glanced back at her, his gaze locked onto hers.

"Oh, good." She couldn't look away but couldn't come up with anything else to say. The moment stretched as they stared at each other. The ledgers! Dad's letter to her . . . Suddenly her thoughts shifted to his clue. She'd puzzled over it for several

231

days but hadn't come up with anything. "Do you perhaps know the meaning of the phrase, 'A thousand times the worse to want thy light'?"

A quizzical look crossed his face. "Hmm . . . no. It reminds me of Shakespeare, perhaps?"

She stood to her feet. "That's it! It's from Shakespeare. Dad and I used to read through his works when I was younger." Why hadn't she thought of that before? "Now, where is that book?" she mumbled to herself and went to the small shelf Dad had built for their books. They had been his prized possessions.

"I must admit, I have no idea what you're talking about." He stood as well and followed her over to the corner where the shelf was situated. "Is there anything I can do?"

"No. But thank you so much." Not taking her eyes from the shelf, she scanned all of the titles.

"What are we looking for?"

"Shakespeare, of course."

He moved closer and crouched as he looked at the lower shelf.

"Here it is!" She pulled the large volume from the middle shelf and clutched it to her chest. *The Complete Works of William Shakespeare.* Elijah's nearness combined with the elation that poured through her made her heart race. Without another thought, she stepped closer to him and stood on tiptoe to kiss his cheek. "You've helped me figure out a clue. Thank you."

He raised his eyebrows and smiled. "A clue to what?"

"Oh, just something my father wrote to me."

"Well, I'm glad to be of service. With that kind of reward, I will gladly assist you anytime you need me." He stepped an inch closer. His smile and the spark in his eyes did wonderful things to her heart.

Staring up into his enchanting blue eyes, Jackie lost herself for a moment.

Michael snorted and then rolled again, this time making the puppy yap. His groggy voice broke through the moment. "What's all the commotion about?"

Jackie stepped back toward the fireplace. "Sorry to wake you. I was just looking for a book, and Elijah helped me locate it."

The warmth in Elijah's expression hadn't changed as he continued to stare at her. It thrilled her.

As much as she wanted to dwell on those feelings, reality sank in. He would be leaving soon.

Perhaps she would do better to focus on

something else. Like solving her mystery and helping her government.

Even though the handsome blue-eyed man staring at her made her stomach flop about like a fish out of water.

She shouldn't have kissed him on the cheek. Because now she wanted to do it again. And if she read his expression correctly, he'd like that too.

CHAPTER 14

Virginia City
October 22, 1860

Swinging his leg over the saddle, Elijah dismounted the horse he'd borrowed from Jackie. It was too early to meet with the contacts Crowell had set up, so he hoped to see how many people had lived here twenty-six years ago.

Now that he knew Hanna Morris had come this way in 1834, maybe someone else might remember her and give a description. If the descriptions matched, perhaps that would be enough for him to write Mr. Vines.

The thought that Jackie could be Mr. Vines's daughter made him a bit nervous. Maybe because it would put a barrier between him and the woman he'd come to care about. And maybe because he didn't want to hurt her — which would be inevitable if she found out that the man who raised her wasn't the man who fathered her. But the more he thought about it and worried over it, the more his gut told him it was the truth.

He walked into the general store and looked for the proprietor.

A man behind the counter polished a brass bell of some sort. "Can I help you find something?" His graying hair gave Elijah hope that maybe he'd been here awhile.

"Actually, I'm hoping you can. I need some paper and ink."

The man walked out from behind the counter and led him to an aisle in the back. "Right here. We have several weights of paper. The thin stuff used for the Express is at the end."

"Thank you." Elijah picked out his purchases and went back to the cash register.

"Will that be all?"

He took a deep breath. "I was wondering if you've been the proprietor of this establishment for a long time."

"The past thirty years." The man rang up the ink and paper. "That'll be six cents."

"Here you go." Elijah handed over the money. "Could I perhaps ask if you remember someone who came through here?"

"You could, but I doubt I'd remember. My wife is the one that's good at that." He turned to the back of the store. "Marie!"

His voice echoed off the walls.

A plump woman with hair as gray as her husband's came to the front, wiping her hands on her apron. "Whatcha need, Henry?" Glancing up, she spotted Elijah. "Oh, I beg your pardon. I figured Henry needed something."

"This gentleman needs to ask you about someone that came through here."

"How long ago?" The woman patted her hair and went behind the counter.

Elijah prayed she'd remember. "About this time in 1834."

She whistled. "That's a long time ago. We were just getting started and didn't have a lot of customers at that point, so I'll give it a whirl. Who was it that came through?"

"A woman and her baby. The child would have been under a year."

Marie smiled. "A beautiful woman came through that fall. Her baby was teething something awful, so she came in here looking for something for the child to chew on."

"Did you happen to get her name?"

She shook her head. "No, sorry about that. I doubt I'd remember it anyway. But she was a pretty thing. She took her wagon and headed east from here. Which was mighty strange because there ain't much out there."

It had to be her! "What did she look like?"

"Green eyes. I remember 'cause they were so striking. And she had long, red hair. Not something we saw much of back then. Not until the Irish started coming through. But that was more than a decade and a half later. We'd grown a lot by that time too."

His hope deflated. "Well, thank you for your time."

"I'm sorry I couldn't be of more help."

Elijah walked out of the store with his purchases and checked his pocket watch. He still had an hour before he met the first contact. He might as well try every place he could.

After forty-five minutes, he'd visited every establishment in town that had been in existence back in 1834. No one remembered a woman and child.

Only Marie from the general store.

Something didn't feel right. He'd gotten close several times only to find that the woman who came through with a baby had red or brunette hair. Not blond.

What was he missing?

He got back on his horse and headed back to the general store. He didn't have much time, but he wanted to speak to Marie again. He rushed in and found her at the counter. "Ma'am, I'm sorry to bother you again, but I just had to ask. Are you certain that the woman who came through here had red hair? It couldn't have been a dark blond perhaps? Maybe in the light it had a red tint?"

She shook her head. "No. It was red. A deep shade too. My husband had been so captivated by it that he talked about it for days. I told him maybe he should order me a red wig so I could look like her." The woman laughed. "But wouldn't that have cost a pretty penny! What is it with men and red hair?"

A wig! That was it. "Thank you so much. You've been a great deal of help."

Still laughing, she waved at him as he exited.

Elijah ran to the horse, mounted, and headed to the address of the first contact. It all made sense. The different colors of hair. Hadn't Mr. Vines said something about a special order that he'd discovered his wife's maid had purchased from France? That particular maid had been the one responsible for Mrs. Vines's coiffures. But if he recalled correctly, the maid had disappeared shortly after Anna Vines. He'd have to check his notes when he went back to Carson Sink.

If she was as smart as Charles said, Elijah

wouldn't be surprised in the least to find out that Anna Vines had ordered wigs. It would have been an easy way for her to change her appearance.

Arriving at the first address, Elijah switched to the next task at hand.

He tied his horse at the post and knocked on the door.

"Good day." A neatly dressed gentleman greeted him at the door. While the office behind him was a bit of a ramshackle room, the man looked like he belonged back in Kansas City. Not in the dust of Virginia City. The contrast was a bit . . . odd.

"I'm here to see Mr. Williamson," Elijah offered.

"Please come in." The man opened the door and held out his arm in welcome.

"Thank you."

The man closed the door and sat behind a desk. "What can I do for you?"

"I presume you are Mr. Williamson?"

"Yes, my apologies. Now, how may I assist you?"

"I'm here on behalf of Mr. Crowell."

"Yes, yes. He is the one who made the appointment." Williamson drummed his fingers on the desk in an impatient manner.

Elijah cleared his throat. He had specific questions to ask. "Have you had any forgeries come through your office?"

"Forgeries of what?"

"Treasury notes?"

"Not recently. But I hear there's quite a ruckus brewing about the owners of the Pony Express taking Indian bonds. Illegally."

Elijah didn't know what to do with that information. Crowell hadn't said anything about Indian bonds. It wasn't the question he was supposed to ask. "I see."

"Is that all you needed?"

"Yes." He stood. His second question was only to be asked if the man had seen any forgeries. Was this all he was supposed to do? It didn't seem like he'd been of much help. Maybe the next meeting would go better.

He shook Williamson's outstretched hand and turned toward the door. A large stain on the floor caught his eye.

Williamson followed his gaze and stepped in front of him. "Sorry about that — my dog died over there a few days ago. It was quite a mess. She'd gotten caught in a trap. My wife must've moved the rug when she was cleaning." He tugged the small carpet back over the spot. "Thanks for coming today." He patted Elijah's shoulder. "Do you think they are close to apprehending the criminals?" Williamson appeared genuinely concerned, his impatient and curt manner gone.

Elijah leaned a bit closer. "I believe they are. And the sooner the better."

The man nodded. "We don't want anything like this going on in our town. And to think that someone is stealing from the government, well, that is simply unspeakable."

"Yes, it is." He walked out the door with an uneasy feeling in his gut.

"I'm sure I'll be seeing you soon. If I catch wind of anything, I'll let you know." Williamson waved and closed the door.

Staring at the door for a moment, Elijah wasn't quite sure what had just happened. For one, he'd gotten absolutely no information out of the man. And two, nothing seemed to fit. The man. The office. The stain on the floor. It all came down to the fact that he didn't think Mr. Williamson had been telling the truth.

Carson Sink Station

"Jack . . . Ja-ack." Mark's voice penetrated through her thoughts as she looked down at her hands in the soapy wash pan.

"Hmm? I'm sorry. Did you need something?"

The young rider laughed. "Nah, I've just been trying to get your attention for almost a minute now." He shook his head. "Just needed to tell you I'll be headin' out on Timothy's run tonight. He's not feelin' too well."

"Oh. Thank you for letting me know. I'd better go check on him."

Finishing up with the soapy water, she looked down at the pup asleep at her feet. "Look at how much help you are. I didn't even realize he'd been standing there." She took the tub of water out the back door and poured it at the base of the two apple trees she'd begged her dad to plant a couple of years ago. He'd given in to her even though he told her that apple trees probably wouldn't produce fruit. She'd been faithful to water them in the dusty, sandy soil, and they'd grown, scrawny as they were. But no apple blossoms yet. Maybe next year.

She hung the tub on the side of the house and wiped her hands on her apron. Heading to the bunkhouse, she prayed that Timothy's illness wasn't anything serious. The last thing they needed was a sickness to spread among the riders.

"Timothy?"

The bunkhouse was quiet. All the guys were out either doing chores or on one of the runs.

"I'm here." He moaned as he rolled over on his bunk.

"What's ailing you?" She moved closer and stood at the edge of his bed.

Red crept up into his face. "I guess you might as well know. All the boys already do."

She squinted down at him. "What did they do to you?" Placing her hands on her hips, she figured a stern talking-to was in order for whatever prank they'd pulled this time.

"They didn't do nothin'." He sighed. "Except dare me to eat an entire block of Mrs. Liverpool's cheese."

Jackie tried to cover her mirth. "An entire block?" Everyone knew of Timothy's love of cheese. The boys had just taken their jesting a bit too far. Of course probably none of them expected that Timothy could actually do it.

"Yeah. I ate the whole thing. Now I don't feel very good."

"It's no wonder."

"You're not going to make me drink castor oil, are ya?"

The pathetic look on his face made her feel sorry for his discomfort. "No. I won't do that to you. Unless, of course, you don't get any better."

"I'll be better by tomorrow . . . I hope."

Another moan escaped.

"I hope so too. For now, you'd better stay there and pray it doesn't make you sicker."

He nodded.

With a chuckle, she headed toward the door. As she opened it, she turned back to face him. "Was that the cheese she brought me this morning?"

"Yeah. I'm sorry."

No wonder she couldn't find the cheese she thought she'd put in the cellar. Here she'd been so worried that the puppy had gotten into it.

When she entered the door back into the station house, the little ball of fur greeted her with yips and jumped as high as he could. Crouching down to pet him, she rubbed his ears and he licked her hands. "You really do need a name. We can't keep calling you 'the puppy.' "

He wagged his tail and followed her over to the fireplace, where she picked up the volume of Shakespeare. So far, she hadn't found the quote her father had written in the letter. But she'd keep reading until she did.

Michael came in the front door and dove to the floor to play with his dog.

"Have you thought of a name yet?" Jackie peered over the book at him.

"Nah. You know I'm not any good at that. Why don't you name him?" He tousled the puppy's fur. "No, wait. You'll probably give him some dumb Shakespearean name like your horse. Why don't we just call him Spot?"

"You can't call him Spot — there's not a spot on him . . . wait, what did you just say?" His words hit her. "Romeo! Michael, you're brilliant." She jumped to her feet.

"We're not calling the dog Romeo. We already have one of those."

Shaking her head at him, she gripped his shoulders. "No, we're not going to call the dog Romeo. Let's call him Brownie or something like that." She flipped through the large tome. "Romeo and Juliet, wherefore art thou, oh quote of my father. . . ."

"Huh? Sometimes I think you are really strange, Jack." Michael picked up the puppy and fluffed his ears. "You do look like a Brownie. I guess that's what we'll call you."

Jackie laughed as she watched Michael smile at their little dog. She should have thought of getting a pet a long time ago. Finding the right play, she went back to her search while she heard Michael trying to teach the dog how to bark on command.

As she scrolled down the page with her finger, she found it. Act two, scene two. *"A thousand times the worse to want thy light."*

She laid down the book and headed for the desk in her room where she'd stashed Dad's letter. Once she pulled it out, she scanned the page until she found his clues:

With help for your future and keys to your past. To find it, you'll have to remember: "A thousand times the worse to want thy light." He who speaks shelters the treasure that I hope to share with you one day — prayerfully in my old, old age. But until then, I'll keep it hidden. Just in case. It's my back-up plan in the event I do not garner the courage to tell you in person.

Dad was so ingenious to play to her sense of adventure. She smiled thinking of how much time he must have put into this treasure hunt for her. But it bothered her to know that something in that box would tell her some truth Dad had kept hidden.

It couldn't be all that bad. Could it?

Shoving the letter back into hiding, she took a deep breath. Time to go find what he'd left her.

She marched through the living room, driven by the desire to put an end to the mystery.

"Where are you going?" Michael called out.

She looked over her shoulder and saw the confusion written all over his face.

"Keep an eye on Brownie for a little bit. There's something I need to find."

CHAPTER 15

Virginia City

"Mr. Sanders?" Elijah stood at the threshold of another door, awaiting yet another of Crowell's contacts.

The door opened a crack. "Who's asking?"

What an odd greeting. "My name is Johnson. I'm here on behalf of Mr. Crowell."

The door opened wider, and the man tugged Elijah in and promptly closed the door. "I feel like I've been watched all day. I don't know what it is, but it's driving me crazy. Sorry for the lack of hospitality. Where are you staying?" This man was a stark contrast to the smooth, well-dressed man he'd met earlier. Short, stocky, and a bit of a rumpled mess, Sanders ran a hand through his thinning hair.

"At the Station House in Carson Sink."

"Good. It's best you're not in town after we meet. So you know Rivers? I haven't seen him in months."

"I know of him, sir. Marshall Rivers is dead. His daughter is running the station now."

"Marshall's dead?" His face turned gray. "Do you know how?"

Elijah shook his head. "I'm sorry, no. It's been several weeks."

Sanders nodded and sat down hard in the chair. "He was a good man."

"I need to ask you a question, Mr. Sanders."

The other man took a deep breath and looked him in the eye. "Of course."

"Have you seen any treasury note forgeries come through here?"

"More than you would believe."

"Really? How many?"

"At last count, more than thirty. And they weren't for small amounts either. I tried to get a message out to the Treasury Department and Crowell, but it was too little too late."

"Were they all from the same source?"

"No. That's the interesting thing. I couldn't find any patterns whatsoever. My orders were to cash them through and document everything, and that's what I did." Sanders reached into his desk and pulled out a packet. "This is what you need to give

Crowell."

Elijah wasn't sure what rules governed this little game he'd been asked to play, but he decided to follow his instincts. "The last person I met with said something about Indian bonds."

"*Indian* bonds? What about 'em?"

"That there was some kind of ruckus about government officials illegally obtaining them?"

"I don't know what you've been hearing, but that has nothing to do with our job at hand."

"Of course. But it was Williamson who told me that."

"Odd that Williamson would tell you that. Sounds like a bunch of gossip to me. I don't know anything about it."

The odd feeling he'd had earlier was back. "Do you know if I could talk to Williamson's wife?"

"Wife? What makes you think he has a wife?" Sanders eyed him suspiciously for a moment.

"He told me he did." The sinking feeling grew.

Sanders's eyes widened. "Williamson isn't married. When will you see Crowell?" He rushed around the room stuffing things into a leather bag.

"When he returns from Carson City." Elijah turned and watched him. "What do you mean, Williamson isn't married?"

Sanders shoved him toward the door. "It's time for you to go. I hope Crowell makes it in one piece. Things have been feeling iffy —" A grunt left his lips and he tumbled back over his desk.

Time slowed down as all of Elijah's senses went on high alert. The window had shattered a split second before Mr. Sanders fell, and the report of a rifle hung in the air.

Elijah spun around and looked at the room. Ducking behind the chair that was the largest piece of furniture in the room besides the desk, he felt his heart race.

What had just happened? One moment he was talking to Sanders; the next the man had been shot. Screams echoed outside of the building. People must have heard the report. Were there women and children out there? Had more than one person been shot? It had all happened so fast, he wasn't sure.

After several deep breaths, he crawled over to the desk to check on Sanders. If the man was still alive, maybe he could get him to the doctor. But as he looked at his contact's head, the bullet wound told an undeniable story.

Elijah thought he might be sick. He'd never seen anything more gruesome in his life. Blood appeared to be everywhere. What was going on?

Whatever it was, the danger seemed very real. Elijah crawled back over to the chair and noticed that he'd dropped the packet. Counting to one hundred, he waited to see if any more shots would be fired. Would they aim at him next? Was he safe here, or should he slip outside into the crowd of people? At the thought of possibly putting others at risk, he decided to stay put. But after several minutes, he knew he couldn't do anything from here. He looked down at the packet in his shaking hand. Whatever it held, he'd need to get this to Mr. Crowell as soon as he could. Tucking it deep into his boot, he went in search of the sheriff.

Carson Sink Station

"It has to be here somewhere." Jackie scratched her forehead as she looked around Romeo's stall. Dad's letter said, "He who speaks shelters the treasure." The quote was a line from *Romeo and Juliet,* spoken by Romeo. Her horse's name was Romeo. So it made sense to look for the box here in his stall, right?

But after looking throughout the stall, she

realized there wasn't much of a place to hide anything in here. At least not a place where it wouldn't get ruined. What was she missing?

Walking out of the stall, she looked into Romeo's eyes. "All right, big fella. Any clue where Dad hid it? You're supposedly the one who's sheltering it."

Her horse just stood there where she'd loosely tied him to a post in the barn, a patient look on his face as if he knew he'd get his room and bed back later.

"Well, you're no help."

He shook his mane at her and stomped his front right leg on the wooden plank floor.

It gave her an idea. Kissing Romeo on the nose, she giggled and headed back to his stall. With pitchfork in hand, she moved all the straw off the floor. How many hundreds of times had she mucked out this stall? A memory washed over her of a question she'd asked Dad.

"Daddy, why do you have a wooden floor in the barn?"

"What makes you ask that, little one?"

"Mrs. Liverpool said it was a waste of money to build a floor for the horses. She said some people don't even have wood floors in their houses."

Dad's chuckle reverberated throughout the

whole room. He picked her up and placed her on his lap. "That's true, Jack. But I find that it's nice to have a wood floor for when we need to give the horses' stalls a nice good cleaning. If we need to wash the floor, we simply muck out the stall, throw a bucket of water and some soap in there, and clean it up. That wouldn't work very well if it was dirt, now, would it?" He tickled her under the chin.

"No." She giggled. "It would just make mud."

"So, yes, Mrs. Liverpool is correct that it costs more money to put down a wood floor in the barn, but I find I'm able to keep it cleaner that way. And I think that's good for the animals."

She sat straighter on his lap and nodded. "I agree."

He tapped her nose with his finger. "I had a feeling you would."

As the memory faded in her mind, she realized just how smart Marshall Rivers was. Oh, she'd always known it growing up, but she appreciated it much more now.

Once she had all the straw out, the only thing that was left was the blanket that Romeo slept on. She stomped on the floor with her boots. It echoed beneath her rather than sounding solid. Why had she never noticed that before? Probably because there wasn't a lot of room to be stomping around, and with straw always covering the floor, the noise would have been muffled.

So how did she get under the floor to whatever was hidden beneath it?

Crouching down, she started looking in the corners. There had to be a clue somewhere. Dad never did anything halfway.

Pulling Romeo's blanket out of the back left corner, she squatted down to look. It was the darkest corner in the stall. The perfect place to hide something — what, she didn't know. She stood back up. Light from the two barn windows couldn't reach over here. They were designed to let in enough light so that during the day they could grab the horses fast, without having to grab a light, whenever an Express came through. But maybe that was just what she needed. More light. As she went back to the front of the barn, she grabbed a lantern and lit it. She hurried back into Romeo's stall and looked in the dark corner.

Sure enough, there was a hinge. That meant a door was attached to that hinge.

She felt almost giddy. But where was the opening?

Dad was a master at carpentry. There was hardly a groove between the planks, so how was she supposed to lift it up?

"Jack, what are you doing?"

She jerked at Michael's question. "Michael, you scared me. You should know better than to sneak up on someone like that."

He held up his hands. "Didn't mean to scare you, but you've been gone awhile, and I was getting worried. The Express could come through at any minute."

She stood up and put her hands on her hips. "I know. I'm just frustrated."

"Do you need my help? If you frown any harder, that wrinkle in your forehead might decide to stay permanently."

Swatting at him, she gave him a forced smile. "Oh, hush. Now get over in the corner and help me figure out how to open it."

Doing as he was told, Michael got down on his hands and knees but gave her a look. "Open what exactly?"

"The floor, silly." She huffed.

The ground began to rumble beneath them.

Michael jumped up. "Oh boy. Let me get the horse to exchange and we'll come back to this after the Express."

"Sounds good to me." Jackie raced out of the barn and to the front of the station house. The others were already out there getting things ready for the exchange. Paul had the water bucket and dipper, John had the saddle ready for the next horse, and Mr. Liverpool stood there with his blacksmith apron on, the pockets full of tools in case he needed to do any quick fixes on the horse or saddle.

The pounding of the hooves increased as a dust cloud followed from the west. Mark came out the front door of the station, his hat pulled down low and his leather coat almost covering the two pistols strapped to his thighs.

As a new rider pulled his horse to a stop in front of the station and hopped off, Jackie helped to move the mochila, checked the way pocket, and recorded the times. Mark mounted the fresh horse and gave her a nod. "I should be back tomorrow."

"Be safe." She waved and he took off toward the east.

The new rider stepped up to her side. "Could you tell me who the station manager is? You had the keys, so I'm assuming it's you?"

She held up a finger. "Hold on a moment." Watching Mark race off toward the horizon, she wasn't about to break her habit now. The new kid would just have to wait.

Once Mark's image had vanished from view, she turned to the young man beside her and raised her brows. He didn't look like he could be much more than twelve. "How old are you?"

"Fourteen, ma'am."

While she knew there were young riders on the Express, she didn't have any out here that young. "When did you start?"

"I took my oath this morning."

She smiled thinking of the oath. Each rider was given a small leather Bible after reciting it. Dad had made her memorize it and swear the oath too. The words still rang in her ears.

"I, Jack Rivers, do hereby swear, before the Great and Living God, that during my engagement, and while I am an employee of Russell, Majors, and Waddell, I will under no circumstances use profane language, that I will drink no intoxicating liquors, that I will not quarrel or fight with any other employee of the firm, and that in every respect I will conduct myself honestly, be faithful to my duties, and so direct all my acts as to win the confidence of my employers, so help me God."

The memory evaporated as she looked at the young man. "What's your name?"

"Edward. Most people just call me Eddie."

"It's nice to meet you, Eddie. I'm Jackie. Why don't you follow me." She headed toward the station house.

He did as he was told. When he entered the room, he looked up and removed his hat. "Sorry."

"That's quite all right. This is the station house. You will have all your meals here with the rest of us and you are welcome to sit with us in the parlor in the evenings. Every Sunday we have Bible study, which I hope you will attend whenever you are here. We often get interrupted by the Express, but we just come right back to it when we're done." She nodded at John. "Would you help him get situated in the bunkhouse?"

"Sure, Jack."

The young rider blinked. "Did he just call you Jack?"

A chuckle left her lips. "You'll get used to it. My father always called me that, so all the riders followed suit. It's short for Jacqueline." Taking a long look at the kid, she began to worry about him. But her job wasn't to baby the riders; it was to help them do their jobs to the best of their abilities. "You all right? I'm sorry to rush, but there's something I must attend to. I'll fill you in on the rest later."

"Yes, ma'am. I mean . . . I think so. I can't believe I'm an actual Pony rider." He twisted his hat in his hands.

"Well, from what I can tell, you had a

great first day because you arrived early." She patted his shoulder. "Good job."

"Thanks. I rode over seventy-five miles today. That's the farthest I've ever been from home." He rubbed his backside.

Covering her smile with her hand, she nodded. "You'll get used to it. Most of the time you'll just go back and forth from one day to the next, so I presume that you will be here every other day. Make yourself at home. Dinner will be in about an hour."

"Thanks. They told me that Carson Sink would be my other home station. I'm glad to be here."

"We're glad to have you." She smiled.

John took the new kid out the back.

Once the back door closed, Michael gave her a grin, and they both raced out the door to the barn.

Romeo greeted her with a nicker when she entered.

"Sorry, fella, for leaving you there so long. Hopefully we'll be done soon."

Michael was already back in the corner on the floor. "Hey, Jack, hand me that hoe over there, will ya?"

She passed him the gardening tool that she'd lovingly dubbed the snake-killer since she used it more to chop off the heads of snakes than to do any actual hoeing in the garden.

"The blade just might fit into this crack. . . ." He paused as he placed it where he wanted it. "Nah. It's too big. I wonder if my knife will fit. Somehow I need to gain some leverage."

He pulled out his small pocketknife and wiggled the blade down into the crack. In less than a minute, he had the trap door open. Jackie clapped her hands and moved closer.

Michael grabbed the lantern. "You want me to go down the dark and scary hole first?"

"Yes, please."

He sighed. "The things I do for you."

"Hey, at least I feed you. Which reminds me, if you don't hurry up, we won't be having any dinner tonight."

"Bossy, bossy." His head disappeared beneath the floor.

"What do you see?" She leaned over the hole.

"Not much. It looks like Marshall probably stored different things under here over the years. It's actually quite large."

How had she never known about it? She watched the glow of the lantern move around the dark space.

"Look, it even goes beyond the wall of the barn." His voice sounded more distant. "But this is a much smaller space. I'm going to have to crawl."

"All right. But be careful."

"When am I ever not careful?" A thud followed his words. "Ow. Spoke too soon. The ceiling gets a little lower in here."

Suppressing a giggle, she couldn't help but bounce on her toes as she waited for Michael to explore. As much as she wanted to be the one to find whatever Dad had hidden, she had a staunch dislike for dark and dingy places. Especially if spiders were involved. But her excitement grew with every moment that passed.

"Found it!" Michael's voice rang out. She watched as the light grew closer. His head appeared out of the hole.

Lifting up a wooden box, he handed it to her. "It was wrapped in an old slicker, but I left the slicker down there because it was in pretty bad shape."

"That's fine." Holding the box in her arms, she was surprised by the weight of it. Sitting on the floor of the stall, she didn't even care about her skirts anymore. She laid the box in her lap and ran a hand over the top of the lid. Dad had made this. She could tell by the craftsmanship.

"Come on, Jack. You're going to have an angry mob of hungry young men if you don't hurry up and get dinner on the table." He held out a hand and helped her to her feet.

"Thanks for your help. Would you mind closing the door and putting Romeo's blanket back over it? Then he'll need some fresh straw and a bucket of oats before you put him back in."

He shook his head. "You owe me an extra piece of pie."

"Deal." She kissed his cheek and ran to the house with the box in her arms. After placing it under the bed in her room, she washed up as best as she could, scurried to the kitchen, and put on a clean apron. The evening couldn't pass fast enough for her so she could open the box from Dad.

Elijah's face flashed through her mind. She'd miss seeing him tonight, but she hoped his errands in Virginia City were going well.

Besides, she had a mystery awaiting her.

Chapter 16

Virginia City

After spending hours with the sheriff, Elijah was weary. The lawman didn't have any idea who would have wanted to kill Sanders. "Why don't you head on home and get some rest, son. If I have any other questions, I know where to find you."

"Thank you, sir." Turning toward the door, he realized he didn't have his horse. He spun back around. "I left my horse at Sanders's place."

The lawman swiped a hand over his mustache. "I don't remember seeing one when I rode up, but then again, there was quite a panic. Hopefully it's still there. Ya need me to go back with you and look?"

"No. Don't worry about it — you've got enough on your hands. Besides, it's only a short walk from here." While it would have been nice to have the protection of the sheriff, Elijah hated to bring further work to the man.

As he left the building, he hoped that whoever had shot Sanders didn't know he was a witness. The short walk in the cool night air helped to refresh him and clear his mind, but the horrible fact remained that he'd seen a man murdered today. Elijah doubted that Crowell knew anything about the danger that now awaited him. Was there any way he could send word? It was imperative to get this information to the man as soon as possible, but how?

With a sigh, he realized it would be a very long ride back to Jackie's station. And it wasn't a trip he wanted to take at night. It was bad enough when the thought of encountering Indians was very real. And he'd figured out quickly a horse could get sucked into the sand if the rider wasn't careful to keep him on the path. But now, a much more threatening — and evil — presence was among them. The thought made Elijah's skin crawl.

He'd talked to the sheriff about everything that happened at Sanders's. But he hadn't mentioned his visit to Williamson, or the fact that he was for all intents and purposes doing the job of a spy for the secretary of the Treasury Department. His first day and there'd been a murder. That didn't bode well at all.

Shaking his head as he walked, he tried to put the pieces of the puzzle together. Something didn't add up. And it all pointed back to Williamson. But Crowell had said that the man was a trusted contact. Had been for years.

So why had his gut told him that the man was lying?

He was new at this. Maybe he was just letting his imagination run away with him. Spying wasn't his normal business.

But then there was that awful stain on the floor — that definitely looked like it could have been blood — and Williamson's flippant excuse for it and blaming of his wife. Then Sanders said that Williamson didn't have a wife. Why would the man lie about it?

Maybe it *would* be best to wait until morning to ride back. That way he could have another chance to speak with the sheriff. He might be a novice at this, but it was better to be safe than sorry.

The thought of not making it back to Carson Sink wasn't pleasant. Especially since he'd looked forward to seeing Jackie again all day. But he realized that he'd better be smart and she wasn't expecting him anyway. He'd hoped to surprise her.

He should have asked the sheriff about a good place to stay for the night. Oh well, he could ride back over in a minute.

As he reached Sanders's address, his gaze darted around.

His horse was nowhere to be found.

Kansas City
October 23, 1860

"Sir?" Colson stopped digging in the trunk and pulled out a bundle. Handing it to his employer, he wore an expression of remorse. "My apologies. I forgot that these even existed."

Charles examined the stack of three letters. The handstamps traced a trail all the way to the Utah Territory. He couldn't believe his eyes. They'd never been unsealed. "Why weren't these opened? Did I not read them? Why would you keep them from me?" The questions flew out, and he instantly regretted them.

Colson cleared his throat. "At the time, sir, you told me to burn them. You told me to burn all the mail. Every day. You were quite adamant about it. I tried to save anything of import and paid all the outstanding bills while you were . . . incapacitated."

The depth of his depravity overwhelmed

Charles at moments like this. Had he really been that drunk? That angry and hateful? Not caring for anyone or anything? "I'm sorry I put you through all of this while you were in my employ, Colson. It's a miracle you've stayed." He shook his head. "Might I ask why you chose to put these away?" He set the letters down on the table in front of him and simply stared. It wasn't Anna's handwriting. But had she tried to contact him? The thought made his stomach turn. How could he have been so blind?

"Forgive me if it was overstepping, sir, but I thought it might have something to do with your wife. And I thought that one day you might get better and want to see them. But it was a difficult time here and over the course of the weeks and months, I must have forgotten about the missives."

"It's not your fault, Colson. In fact, I need to thank you for saving them. Whatever they hold, I'm glad to have them." As he picked up the stack, Charles's hands shook. All this time, could there have been answers waiting for him? Right here? In his very home? Once he'd found the Lord, he'd searched for Anna and sent investigators out. Then the letter had come saying she was dead. If he'd come to his senses earlier, could he have seen his wife? Apologized to her? Tears sprang to his eyes as sobs shook his shoulders.

No matter how much time passed, the guilt he carried from his former life could still overwhelm him. He knew he was forgiven by God — even though that still amazed him as well — but some days it was hard to even think of forgiving himself. How many lives had he ruined? How many people had he hurt? None worse than his wife and child, no doubt.

After his emotion was spent, he lifted the top envelope and examined it. Five hand-stamps from the postal service covered the back of the envelope. It was yellowed and worn from time and its journey. Charles tore it open. Pulling out the single sheet of paper, he swiped at his eyes so he could focus on the words:

January 19, 1835

Mr. Vines,
  This is a most difficult letter for me to write. I will be completely honest with you: as despicable of a human being as I think you are right now, I know that I am just as much of a sinner. For scripture is clear that all have sinned and fallen short.

I don't want to write this letter, but I feel that God is prompting me. Perhaps He has done a mighty work in you and you have changed your ways. If that is so, then you need to know that your wife and daughter are safe. You deserve to know at least that much.

I will not tell you where they are.

I will protect them at all costs.

But they are well and happy.

For you, sir, I will pray.

Charles took a deep breath and read the letter again. He turned the paper over. No signature. No clue whatsoever to the person who sent the note. But he knew that the words were honest. He'd needed them even as much as they stabbed him in the heart. It was a good thing he didn't read this back then. It wouldn't have done any good, and it would have been burned. Colson had been wise to put these letters away, even though they'd been forgotten, because now they just might help him. Whether simply to bring healing or to help find his daughter, he wasn't sure.

Replacing the paper in its handmade envelope, he took a deep breath before opening the next letter. As much as it would hurt to read the words and be reminded of all that he'd thrown away, he needed to do it.

New determination filled him as he read, then wept. No matter how much it cost, he wanted to send all of this correspondence to Elijah. Perhaps something in the letters or on the envelopes could help him locate his daughter.

Now, more than ever, Charles longed to make things right. To find his daughter, confess to her where he failed, and ask for her forgiveness. Then perhaps one day he'd be able to forgive himself.

Carson Sink Station
October 23, 1860

"Jack. Jack! Are you all right?" Michael's voice penetrated the painful fog that had overtaken her mind. He sounded so far away. Where was he?

The events from last night came rushing back. In her rush to finish washing the dishes so she could look in Dad's box, she'd slipped on soapy water on the floor and hit her head on the table. A massive headache quickly followed and she couldn't see straight, so she'd gone to bed. At least that was what she remembered.

Putting a hand to her forehead, she sat up in bed. The ache had dulled at least. As long as she didn't move too fast. How long had she slept?

Thud, thud, thud!

Michael was outside the door. Knocking — or rather banging. It sounded as if he was trying to break the thing down. "Jack! I'm coming in."

The door flew open and Michael's eyes were wide as he put a hand to his chest. "I was getting worried. You've been asleep forever."

"What time is it?" If she were to lie back down, she could probably go right back to sleep.

"It's after three. In the afternoon."

Throwing back the covers, she jumped out of bed, which made her head swim for a minute. "Why did you let me sleep that long?"

"Because you hit your head pretty good last night." He shrugged. "I thought you needed the rest. But I started to worry when the first Express came through. I grabbed your keys and did it just like you showed me, but when I brought them back, you just turned over and groaned." He leaned up against the doorframe. "Then the fellas and me had to fix our own lunch, which was quite the mess. That's when I went and asked Mrs. Liverpool to come check on you.

She came and said that you didn't seem to have a fever and were sleeping peacefully."

Taking slow steps and hoping that the room would stop spinning, Jackie moved toward the washbasin. Maybe if she splashed some water on her face, she could get rid of the cobwebs and fuzziness. She took a few moments to wash her face and straightened back up. "That's better. My head still wants to throb, but everything is becoming clear again." She smoothed her hair back from her face. Her braid felt like a rat's nest. With deft fingers, she redid the plait and tied the ribbon back around the base.

Hooves pounded the ground outside.

Michael frowned. "That's a good deal early for the Express."

She grabbed her keys and they both headed to the front of the station.

"Jack! Jack!" Timothy's voice yelled for her before he was even within thirty yards.

Michael ran another horse over to her while everyone scrambled for the exchange.

But the look on Timothy's face scared her.

She ran closer to meet him.

Jerking the horse to a stop, he jumped off and ran to her.

"What's happened?" She gripped his shoulders.

"The stage has been attacked. It's not

good." His breath came in gasps. "I rode as fast as I dared."

"Attacked? By whom? Thieves? Indians?" *Oh Lord, please help those people.*

"I don't know. I saw two arrows sticking out of the side of the coach, but there weren't any Indians around. The driver had been shot with a gun. Not an arrow. He's dead. The stage was on its side, pinning the passenger. I tried . . . but I couldn't do anything to help."

She swallowed. It was no wonder Timothy wasn't able to help. All the Pony Express riders weighed under 125 pounds. It would take several men to lift a stagecoach. "We've got to get a wagon out there and help." Turning toward the stable, she was about to give orders to everyone when Timothy's hand on her arm stopped her.

"Jack. There's something you need to know." He looked down at the ground.

"What is it?"

"The passenger is Elijah."

She shook her head. "It couldn't be Elijah. He used one of our horses to ride into Virginia City." But dread built inside her and tears sprang to her eyes.

The young rider gripped both of her arms in his. "I don't know why he was on that stage, but it's definitely him. He knew my name when I tried to lift the coach off him. He's pretty badly hurt."

The ride out to the scene of the attack felt like it took hours. But when they made it, Jackie jumped from the wagon and ran to Elijah's prone form. *Oh God, please let him still be alive!*

Mr. Liverpool and two of the boys had come with her, and she hoped they would be able to lift the stage off of him.

She crouched by his head and touched the side of his face. He looked so peaceful with his eyes closed. "Elijah?"

He groaned but didn't open his eyes.

"We've got to get him out from under here," Mr. Liverpool shouted to the boys. "I need John here" — he pointed — "and Luke here. When I count to three, I need you all to lift with everything you've got." He turned to Jackie. "Jack, it's going to take all of us to lift the stage, so I need you to get your arms up under his shoulders and pull him out as soon as he's free."

She nodded. "I can do it." Hiking her skirts up, she squatted down and lifted up Elijah's shoulders so she had leverage to pull.

He groaned louder.

"I'm so sorry," she whispered into his ear. Who cared if it was proper or not. She couldn't let him suffer alone. "We're going to get you back to the station and all patched up in no time."

Mr. Liverpool and the boys took their positions. He looked at her.

She nodded back and gripped Elijah for all she was worth.

"One . . . two . . . three!"

CHAPTER 17

Eight days later
Carson Sink Station
October 31, 1860
It had been a little more than a week since
Jackie helped to pull Elijah out from under
the stage. But he still hadn't woken up.

As each day passed, the thought that he
might not became harder to bear.

Lord, what do we do?

The doctor was due back today, and she'd
hoped that Elijah would awaken before
then. If he didn't, what did that mean? It
was amazing the man was still alive, but
he'd suffered a nasty break to his right leg,
and several of his ribs had been broken. Dr.
Thompson had said that broken ribs could
be extremely painful and that was probably
why he remained unconscious.

Sitting in a chair by Elijah's bed, Jackie
held her dad's Bible in her hands. She'd
read the entire book of Daniel out loud to

him three times over the past days. No response.

Everyone in Carson Sink had put together a schedule of sorts so that someone sat with Elijah at all times. It hadn't been easy since they all had a lot to do on a daily basis, but they'd made it work. Meals became simpler as people ate in shifts, everyone taking a turn at helping with each other's chores so that there was always someone to sit with their guest-turned-patient. But she refused to leave him at night. The thought of him waking in the middle of the night alone and injured was too much for her heart to bear. So one of the men always stayed with her, keeping watch over her and their patient. Two cots had been squeezed into the room for that purpose, but hers hadn't seen a lot of use.

His soft breathing was the only thing that gave her hope. They attempted to get a few spoonfuls of water and broth down his throat each day, but trying to get him to swallow without choking was a challenge. How long could he survive without much food and water?

"We need you to wake up, Elijah," she whispered and touched his arm. The first few days, she'd talked to him a lot. About anything and everything. But as exhaustion had crept in, her words had left her. What could she say to him anyway?

He'd become her friend. And she'd enjoyed talking with him each night by the fire. But how well did she really know him? The fact remained that she'd wanted to know him better — and had hoped he felt the same. At times, she'd thought for sure that she'd seen it on his face. The difficulty of the situation made her miss Dad and his input even more. And her mother. What she wouldn't give to be able to sit and talk with her.

This wasn't productive. She needed to do something. Maybe she could write some more correspondence. But she'd caught up on everything she could think of while she'd sat by his side the past week. Even the box from her dad had gone untouched all this time, because she just couldn't take the emotional weight of it all. Shaking her head, she forced herself to focus on Elijah. It was selfish to think of herself at this time.

Fiddling with her handkerchief, she looked back at Elijah's serene face. The bruising had faded, and it simply appeared that he slept peacefully. She reached out and touched his cheek. "Please wake up."

Several moments passed and she looked out the window. Perhaps it was time to send a note to his employer. Certainly the man whom Elijah had praised and respected so much deserved to know what had happened.

Encouraged by the job she could do and hoping that it would do some sort of good, she rose from the chair and went to the small desk in the room. He'd received two Express packets from the same address — a Mr. Vines in Kansas City — in the past few days. One was quite thick for an Express letter. It would have cost Mr. Vines a good deal to send it and must be of great import. It impressed upon her even more that she was doing the right thing by sending Vines a return Express herself.

Picking up the smaller envelope that showed a lot of wear from its journey, she studied the address. It was a little smudged, but she was still able to read it. She laid it on the edge of the bed as she brought her writing supplies over to the chair.

After dipping her pen into the ink, she began her letter:

October 31, 1860

Dear Mr. Vines,
    My name is Jacqueline Rivers, and I am the station manager at Carson Sink

Pony Express Station and Stage Stop. We've had the lovely privilege of having your employee, a Mr. Elijah Johnson, stay with us this month.

I'm writing to inform you that a terrible tragedy has befallen Mr. Johnson. Returning from Virginia City, his stage was attacked, and he was injured. He has a broken leg and several broken ribs.

As her pen went dry of ink, she tapped her chin with it. In all the craziness of the rescue aftermath, she hadn't thought again about the fact that he shouldn't have been on that stage. What had made him choose to return that way? And where was her horse? It didn't make sense. She'd have to discuss it with Mr. Liverpool tonight and send a couple of riders to retrieve their mount. If they could find him. Taking a deep breath, she dipped her pen again and went back to the letter, hoping she could get it out today.

While we are doing our best to care for him, he has not woken up yet. The doctor is hopeful that his body is healing and needs rest.

I wasn't certain if there was anyone else I should contact on his behalf, but please know that we will continue to see to Mr. Johnson's health and needs while he recovers here.

Please pray for him, and we will continue to as well.

He is welcome to stay in our care until his wounds heal.

Sincerely,
Jacqueline Rivers

Michael came in to relieve her as she was fanning the paper to help it dry. "The Express should be here soon."

With a nod, she blew on the letter. "Would you mind handing me that envelope I laid on the bed? I need the address for Elijah's employer."

"Sure." He went to pick up the packet, but in his hurry around the bed, he knocked it onto the floor.

"Be careful. It looked pretty worn already."

"Sorry, Jack. Didn't mean to drop it, but it's open."

With a wince, she prayed that nothing had fallen out of it during its travels. Hopefully nothing of import. That wouldn't look good for the Pony Express.

As Michael moved to retrieve it, she noticed the seams of the envelope were open and it looked like a little basket as it lay on the floor.

He leaned down to pick it up and let out his breath in a whoosh. "Well, will ya look at that."

"What is it?"

Michael squatted down next to the open envelope and stared at it.

"Michael, I just need the address. I don't have all day —"

"Jack. Look" — he pointed — "it's *you.*"

Virginia City

Carl paced in front of the fireplace. "I'll take whatever you can have done in a week."

The fat man puffed on his cigar. "What's the rush?"

"My urgency doesn't concern you." He pulled his pocket watch out of his waistcoat and checked the time. "You just focus on getting as many done as you can."

"I'll work around the clock if I have to." Smoke filled the air. "So did you hear about Sanders?"

"What about him?"

"He got hisself shot the other day."

Carl stopped his pacing and looked at the man. He couldn't wait until he was done working with this imbecile. The man had no

284

fear and no manners. "I'm sorry to hear that."

"Dangerous times, you know. Just thought I'd let you know so you could watch yourself."

"Thank you." Sarcasm dripped from the words. Like he needed advice from a two-bit forger. No. He had much more important things on his mind. "Shouldn't you be getting back to work?"

"Sure. I'll get right to it." Another ring of smoke polluted his air as the plump man turned with a smile and left.

Slapping his hat against his thigh, Carl narrowed his eyes. Their forging friend knew too much. But ridding themselves of him would have to wait until after the job was done. Then it would be a difficult cover-up. Maybe he should just take his chances and let it all play out. So what if the plan had changed. Their timeline had moved. They were still on target to get away with one of the biggest thefts — from the government, no less — in history.

He could handle a few thorns in his side along the way. Just like he had before.

As long as he got what he wanted.

Carson Sink Station
Staring at the face that gazed back at her

from the floor, Jackie couldn't believe her eyes.

Michael reached to pick up the small packet.

"No. Don't touch it."

"Why? It's not like we've broken anything, and we didn't break the law by opening mail that wasn't ours. The seal popped open. Right? We can't exactly leave it on the floor. You needed the address, remember?" He picked it up and held it out in his hands. "What do you want me to do with it?"

All she could do was stare. "It does look like me, doesn't it?"

"Yep. If I didn't know any better, I'd think it *was* you. Not that you ever fixed your hair fancy like that or sat for your portrait to be painted." He elbowed her. Just like a little brother, he always knew how to bring her back down to reality.

Blinking the weird coincidence aside, she picked up her pen and the envelope she'd made for her letter. "Quick, turn it over so I can copy the address. I don't want to miss the Express."

He did as she asked and she transferred the address.

"I'll just put this back on the desk." Michael carried the packet over and set it down. "Maybe we should seal it back up so he doesn't think we were snooping while he was laid up."

"That's a good idea. I will simply explain things to Elijah once he's well enough to read his correspondence."

"Then maybe you can ask him who the lady is."

He had a point. But it sparked a different idea in Jackie's mind. A brave and daring one. She prayed she had enough time before the rider came. Dipping her pen back in the ink, she added a postscript to her letter to Mr. Vines before she changed her mind.

P.S. In an effort to obtain your address to send this missive, I had to look at one of your packets to Mr. Johnson. It had been quite worn on the long journey here and the seal popped open. Rest assured, I read nothing of your correspondence and resealed the packet so that Mr. Johnson will have it when he awakens, but I did see the painting. I must inquire about it. The portrait looks like me. Why did you send it, if I may ask? It was quite shocking to see. Are we acquainted, sir?

Once she'd ensured the ink was dry, she folded the letter, inserted it into the envelope, sealed it, and stamped it with the Pony Express stamp.

Michael sat down beside Elijah. "So did you ask him, then?"

"Ask who what?"

"Don't act all innocent with me, Jack. I know you. Did you ask the man who sent that packet about the portrait?"

"I did." Heat flooded her face. "I don't know if it was the right thing to do — it definitely doesn't follow the rules of etiquette — but I did." She put a hand to her stomach to quell the nervousness she felt. How extraordinarily odd it felt to see a painting of herself. Who could have done it?

Who was the woman? Was she related to her mother? Or Dad? That would explain the uncanny resemblance. But it still unnerved her.

"Good. I'm glad you did. It was strange." He patted Elijah's bed. "Maybe if we could get this gentleman to wake up, we could get some answers."

CHAPTER 18

November 1, 1860

A stabbing pain in his foot jarred Elijah's senses. What was that? Why wouldn't it stop? He tried moving his foot away, but the sharp weapon followed it.

The stabbing and burning continued until finally he could stand it no longer. He forced his eyes open and let out a yell. *"Ahhh-owww!"*

Figures came into focus above him. Jackie, Michael, and Timothy were holding him down, while another man he didn't recognize must be the one behind the torture and pain.

"Good, you're finally awake." The man lifted a small, shiny knife with the telltale red of blood into the air.

No wonder he felt like he'd been stabbed. Because he had been.

"Sorry to have to use such force. I'll get your foot bandaged up, and we'll get some nourishment in you. You gave us quite a scare, Mr. Johnson."

"Who are you?" And how did the man know who he was?

"I'm Dr. Thompson. These good people here rescued you after your stage was attacked about nine days ago I believe. They've been taking care of you ever since." He wrapped something white around his foot.

Now that the piercing pain in his foot was gone, Elijah began to feel pain in other areas of his body. His chest hurt. Especially if he took too deep a breath. And what was wrong with his leg? It felt like every muscle cramped at the same time. Pushing up with his arms, he tried to move.

Jackie leaned closer into his field of vision. "Don't try to sit up just yet. You have broken ribs. How are you feeling?"

"Weak. And hungry."

"The hunger is a good sign." The doctor wiped his hands on a rag. "But sadly, you won't be able to eat much for a while. Your stomach won't know what to do with solid food after the famine you've put it through. I've given instruction to Miss Rivers here to give you lots of broths, soups, and then custards for the next couple of days. Then perhaps you can have some bread and after that some meat. Your body has been through quite a trauma. I'm afraid this is going to take a lot of recuperation and exercises for you to be able to walk normally again."

"What do you mean, to walk normally again?"

"It was quite a bad break, and, well . . . it took awhile to get you out from under the stagecoach and then back here. Thankfully, they'd already sent for me, but your leg had swollen a good deal before I was able to set it. And, of course, there's still the risk of developing a fever."

"But I *will* be able to walk again?"

"You should." The doctor tilted his head. "It might need to be with a cane for a while, but you're relatively young and healthy." He grabbed his black bag and patted Elijah's shoulder. "Let's just take it one step at a time, shall we?"

With a nod, he let his head fall back on the pillow. It was all a bit too exhausting. Had he really been asleep for more than a week? How was that possible?

But even as zaps of pain made their way up to his brain, he found himself thankful for them. Thankful that he was alive, awake, and able to feel. It could have been so much worse. "Could I get something to drink?"

"Of course." Jackie brought a cup to him

and lifted his head with her hand. It embarrassed him to need help taking a drink, but he was thankful for her assistance. The pain in his chest was intense, and he doubted he had the strength to take a drink himself.

"I'll come back in about a week." The doctor walked out of the room.

"Thank you, Doctor." Jackie smiled at the man.

"We've been taking turns sitting with ya." Timothy shoved his hands into his pockets. "We didn't want ya to be alone."

"Thanks, Timothy." Elijah lifted his hand to shake the young man's, but it felt like an anvil weighed his arm down.

"I'll get things ready for the next Express, Jack."

"Thank you." She sat down in the chair beside the bed and turned to look at him. "It's my turn to sit with you for a while. Do you need anything?"

"No. I can't think of anything." He looked over at Michael, "I'm sure this has been hard on all of you — having to rearrange your schedules."

"We've been glad to do it. Besides, I still need you to finish teaching me how to swim." Michael's lopsided smile radiated throughout the room.

"A promise is a promise." Elijah attempted

a smile in return. "It just might take me awhile to get to it."

"That's all right. It's too cold now anyway." Michael sent an odd look to Jackie. "Don't you want to tell him?"

"Tell me what?"

Jackie's expression was indecipherable. "Michael, I don't think —"

"You received some Express mail while you were sleeping. I thought it might be important, so I wanted you to know."

An Express for him . . . here? Oh, that's right. He'd sent a letter to Mr. Vines. As much as he wanted to hear from his mentor and boss, the energy was draining out of him faster than a bucket riddled with bullet holes. "Thanks for letting me know, but don't worry about it right now. I doubt I could even read it if I tried." He turned his head to Jackie. "I think I need to sleep — as odd as that may sound since I've been asleep for so long. I just can't seem to keep my eyes open."

In the back of his brain, niggling thoughts about important things that needed to be said or done pressed forward, but the fog pushed them back and he relaxed. Gazing at Jackie, he saw her face diminish as his eyelids weighed down. Everything went black again.

■ ■ ■ ■

Pacing in her bedroom, Jackie wrung her hands. She'd been praising God for hours that Elijah had woken up, but now she'd have to tell him what she did. And she'd have to ask him about the picture. What would he think of her? And what would that do to his fragile health?

Dr. Thompson had said to make sure nothing brought the patient anxiety while he was healing. It would take time for the bones and muscles to knit themselves back together, and he didn't want any undue stress to slow Elijah's progress. Especially since he'd lost so much time already and was in a weakened condition.

It didn't matter what he thought. She had to be honest with him — when the time was right. They'd become friends, hadn't they? Granted, they didn't know each other very well, but she did feel she could trust him. He'd seemed to have respect for her as well.

Oh Lord, what do I do? She crumpled to her knees at the edge of her bed and poured her heart out to the Lord. It was all so confusing.

Before Dad died, things had always been so simple. Not anymore.

The weight of all she had to do pressed on her. The responsibilities, the people she had to care for, the Express, the station, the questioning she was supposed to be doing for Mr. Crowell.

If only she could simply go to sleep and wake up to find everything better, taken care of, and . . . simpler.

Burying her face in the quilt, she knew that was unrealistic, but some days were just so overwhelming.

Weariness flooded her limbs, but her mind spun with all the questions and what-ifs. Would she even be able to sleep tonight? Knowing she'd spent every night watching over Elijah, the doctor had ordered her to sleep in her own bed before she collapsed.

"Get ready for bed, Jack. Get some sleep. You can deal with it all tomorrow." Sometimes talking to herself was the only way she kept going. Pushing up from her kneeling position, she prayed for sleep, but when she got her feet beneath her, her right pinky toe stubbed something hard. *Ow!*

When the shooting pain eased, she took a deep breath and realized it was the box from Dad. She hadn't meant to neglect it, but she'd pushed it to the back of her mind every time she thought of it.

No matter how tired she felt at the moment, it didn't matter anymore. She needed something to get her mind off Elijah. So she pulled the box out from under the bed. Lifting the delicate brass latch, she opened the lid of the handmade gift from her dad.

On top was a folded piece of paper with her name in large letters.

Lifting the box from the floor, Jackie stood up, placed it on the bed and sat down. Staring at the letter, she took another deep breath. Excitement and grief swirled together. Was she ready to read the truth he'd kept hidden? It didn't really matter — reading anything from Dad would be wonderful. She missed him so much.

She closed her eyes for a moment and reached for the letter. Opening her eyes again, she unfolded the note:

April 3, 1860

Dear Jack,

As your twenty-sixth birthday has come and gone, I've realized I have been putting off writing this letter for far too long.

Your mother — God rest her soul — died when she was just twenty-six. She's been gone twenty-three years, yet I can still hear her voice and her laughter.

Some days it feels like just yesterday.

I know that you noticed my reaction to your birthday this year when it hit me like a stab to the heart that you were now the age she was when she died. I couldn't say anything at the time because it caused too much heartache, but I hope this will help to explain. At least a little bit.

You look just like your mother. I know I haven't told you that very much — but it's true. She was small in stature and seemed frail — unlike you — but her spirit was stronger than anyone I've ever known — just like you.

If you're reading this, then I must have never gotten up the courage to tell you in person. Please humor me a bit longer and allow me to say again that I have loved you since the moment I first saw you. And I will always love you. It has been my greatest joy to be your dad.

But this is also the source of great agony for me. You see, I'm not your real father.

She sucked in a breath. She reread the words. No! It couldn't be.

Your mother came here with you as

just a babe in 1834. She'd been traveling for months — running away actually
— and needed a place that was remote
where she could raise you. Why she
chose our little wilderness out here is
beyond me, but I've come to know that
it was God-ordained. You'll notice in the
ledger that it simply says that H.M. and
infant were in room 3. That was you, my
little one. You and your mother. She
asked me not to list her name after the
first night she stayed, and over time the
fear and haunted look left her eyes.
When she finally told me the whole
story, I wanted to protect the two of you
at all costs because I had come to love
you both. She became my best friend.
And I became hers.

Your mother and I loved each other
very much, Jack. But as much as it pains
me to say it, we were never married.
Before you think something awful, you
need to understand that we never broke
God's commandments. It's important
that you know that. It would have been
so easy to pretend she was someone else
— like she had been doing for so long
— to forget her former life and to start
our own life together. But we couldn't.
Because she was still married to your

father. Yes, I guess I should have told you that. Your real father is alive.

When your mother came down with the fever in '37, my heart broke. She faced the end with such grace and humility. The circumstances caused me such anguish. Not only could I not marry the woman I loved, but all too soon she was gone. Before she died, she made me promise to take care of you as if you were my own. I gave my word because I already loved you as if you were my own flesh and blood. We signed documents, and I officially gave you my last name. I have tried my best to honor that promise and to raise you in a godly manner. I know I have failed you in so many ways by not telling you the truth, but I beg for your forgiveness. You will always be my little girl . . . my daughter.

In the case I have made for you are letters from your mother and a journal she kept for a little while. She wanted you to know the truth — probably much sooner than now — and she prayed for your father each and every day.

There are also some treasury bonds that I purchased for you over the years. You come from great wealth, and while I couldn't give you that while I was here,

I wanted to leave you with something from me — something to help provide for you. Now that I'm dead, it's up to you, Jack.

Many of our memories are also in this wooden box. Yes, I'm a sentimental fool. Over the years if you need some encouragement, laughter, or simply to remember, they are here for you.

As you know, the station is yours. Not that a young, vibrant woman would want to stay in the desert in the middle of nowhere, but in case you do, you can do with it as you please. I never did much to the place until your mother arrived. But then she fixed it up and it became our oasis. Feel free to stay, sell it and move elsewhere, or really just do whatever you wish. You don't need my permission to go on with your life. That is my desire for you — live. Be happy.

Above all else, remember that your Father in heaven loves you more than anyone on this earth ever will. He will never fail you like I have and as I'm sure others will in the future. Always be willing to forgive. Over and over again. Your mother taught me that. I want to pass it on to you.

In God's grace, He allowed me to raise

you and love you like my own. It is the most precious gift I've ever received other than salvation. I hope you know that.

Please forgive me.

I love you, my darling daughter. My Jack. Please, don't ever forget that.

Dad

Jackie put a hand to her mouth as the paper trembled in her other hand. Oh, how she missed him. She could hear his voice as she read the words. But Marshall Rivers wasn't her father? The man who had raised her — the only parent she remembered — wasn't her blood after all? It felt like someone had reached in, torn out her heart, and crushed it underfoot.

She let the letter fall to the bed. Why hadn't he told her? Was that why he never spoke much of her mother? But it had been clear how much he loved her — she had to admit that.

Dad had never been false with her. She knew that he loved her dearly. He proved that each and every day. She couldn't have asked for a better father. He was her real father no matter what the letter said.

But then the words tumbled in around her. Had everything been false? Marshall

Rivers wasn't her father. He was never married to her mother. And her mother had run away from . . . what? Was her whole life a lie?

His words washed over her: *"Always be willing to forgive."*

"Oh Dad. I miss you so much." She choked on the words as she spoke to the ceiling. "And I forgive you. I do. I might have to work on it every day, but I choose to forgive you. You *are* my dad."

With a long sigh, she lay back on the bed for a moment and closed her eyes against the tears. In a matter of minutes, everything had changed. But had it really? She still loved her dad. He'd been wonderful. And from everything she knew, her mother had been a wonderful person too. So why did this new knowledge hurt so much? Why did it feel like the world had crashed and tilted on its side?

Then it hit her: Dad had said that she looked just like her mother. The portrait she'd seen! Was that her mother?

Her mind spinning and her heart racing, she sat back up and looked at the beautiful box. There were letters from her mother in there.

Wiping tears from her cheeks she hadn't realized she had shed, she leaned toward the open box. On top, tied with a pink ribbon, sat a few letters.

The one on top had shaky handwriting.

Jackie untied the ribbon and looked at the others. The handwriting on them was elegant and graceful, but it appeared to be the same. She looked back to the one that had been placed on top and decided to read it first.

Running her hand over the letters that spelled Jacqueline, she was overwhelmed by grief but also by joy that she finally had a connection to her mother. Why hadn't Dad let her see these before now? How many times had she asked questions about her mother?

It didn't seem fair. Especially now that she was without them both.

With a tear sliding down her cheek and a new sense of determination, she opened the note.

July 2, 1837

Dearest Jacqueline,

My beautiful daughter. I'm leaving you my journal and a few letters I wrote you while you were a baby. I'd hoped to give you the letters on your sixteenth birthday, but it seems I won't be here for that wonderful day. And that brings me great sadness.

My time is short — I know that. But I wanted to leave you something in my own words. I've asked Marshall to give these to you when the time is right — when you are old enough to understand. There's so much I wish I could explain to you, but you'll have to read about the whole story of your father and me in my journal. I'm sorry that I will never be able to tell you in person, because words on paper just can't convey the depth of everything we've been through. But it seems that God is calling me home.

I've asked Marshall Rivers to raise you as his own. He has been like a father to you these past three years and dotes on you as if you were his own. He took us in — you and me — when, having learned the truth, he easily could have sent us back the way we came.

He's a good man. I've learned so much from him as we've studied the scriptures together. I pray that you will listen to his wisdom as he raises you.

Oh my darling girl. My heart aches that I will not be there to see you grow up, get married, have your own beautiful babies. I wish there was something I could do, but the fever has taken its toll. It has taken me several hours to simply write this letter.

I'm going to ask you to please do me a favor. It may be difficult for you, but I pray it is not.

I wrote your father back in St. Louis a letter and told him I forgive him. Which I do. It took a long time, but God worked in me mightily. I'm asking for you to do the same. I've prayed for him every day since I left, that God would work in his life as well. Because I know that God can do miraculous things.

I want you to know that I loved him very much even though he did some awful deeds.

I'm sorry that I took you from your inheritance, but you deserved a better life than the one we were living. Please forgive me.

I know this will also be difficult for you to understand, but I loved Marshall too. He has been my dearest friend the past three years. In my heart, I longed to marry him — because he showed me each and every day that there were good, honorable, and trustworthy men in this world who love God. But I was legally bound to your father. It is terrible of me to admit my failings to you, my daughter, but I pray that as you get older, you will understand. And I want you to know the truth. All of it.

I have grown weary even though there is much more I wish to say. I pray that Marshall can explain everything that I cannot.

I know you probably will not remember me, my sweet girl, but know that your mother loved you very much. Always and forever . . .

Your mother,
Anna Marie Morrison Vines

Jackie's breath left in a great *whoosh* as she read and reread her mother's name.

The man she'd written to on behalf of Elijah — just today — was Charles Vines. Elijah was here looking for someone. Was it her? Was Charles Vines her . . . father?

Another thought made her gasp for air. The picture she'd seen truly had to be her mother. All these years, she'd wondered exactly what her mother looked like. She'd wondered what she was like. Wondered what her handwriting looked like, what her voice sounded like, what it felt like to be hugged by her. And here, all this time, these letters had been sitting. Hidden.

Anger welled up within her that Marshall Rivers had kept them from her. But then she crumpled with the weight. She'd loved her dad. More than anything. He'd begged for her forgiveness. And she had given it.

A new wave of grief hit. Not just because she'd never had the chance to know her mother, but because she couldn't talk to Dad — Marshall — about all of this now. He understood her like no one else. He'd been her best friend.

Tears that she'd held at bay plunged down her cheeks. Great sobs racked her shoulders and body as she released her emotions. Who was she?

Why, Lord? I don't understand. I feel like I don't know who I am anymore.

Looking back to the letter, she couldn't find why her mother had left her father, but he was still alive!

The man who had raised her she'd loved so dearly. But he was dead.

The loss of her mother — which she'd never truly understood as a child — hit her as if it had just happened.

One by one, every emotion within her welled up and screamed for attention. It was too much.

As she allowed her tears to wash the anguish from her heart, she prayed for wisdom. Every time she thought the pain was too much to bear, she was reminded to cast all her burdens on the Lord. That still, small voice kept telling her that she wasn't alone. She latched onto that truth because everything within her told her she was so very alone.

Jackie curled into a ball and sobbed until no more tears remained. Her head ached, her nose was stuffed, and every part of her body felt completely void of strength.

Wiping the last tears from her cheeks, she took several breaths to calm herself. As much as she wanted to read her mother's journal tonight, it wasn't wise. She needed rest to face tomorrow's duties. They wouldn't stop just because she wanted to stay in bed and cry.

Emotionally she was spent. She had nothing left to give. Yet she had a station full of people relying on her. They had a patient to attend to as well. And thoughts of Elijah brought in a fresh new wagonload of emotions.

Did he know who she was? Was *that* why he was here? She'd thought of him as a friend. And at times had hoped for more. Her heart had begun to open up to the possibility of love.

Could she trust Elijah? Or was he simply playing a part this whole time?

CHAPTER 19

Kansas City
November 2, 1860

"Mr. Vines, there's an Express for you." Colson's voice from across the garden grabbed Charles's attention. "The delivery boy apologized. It had been misdirected to Omaha and sat there for a few days before they discovered the problem."

Charles walked toward his man and met him in the middle near the pruned rosebushes. Colson handed him the missive. He raised his eyebrows. From Elijah. That was good — perhaps there was more information.

"Would you like to come inside and sit by the fire, sir?"

"No. I'm actually feeling quite invigorated by the crisp air today. I'm feeling like myself again." He opened the envelope and pulled out the paper.

"Wonderful news, sir. But please remember the doctor's orders that you continue to rest."

Charles let out a huff. "Good grief, Colson, I've been resting for months, and I've had quite enough of it. There shouldn't be any problem with me walking about, getting exercise and fresh air." Waving the letter in the air, he accentuated his exasperation.

"My apologies, sir. It's only because I don't wish to see you ill again."

"I understand that, Colson. I do. And I appreciate it." He sat on one of the stone benches in the garden. "You've been good to me all these years. I'm just tired of being an invalid."

"Understood, sir. Is there anything I can do for you?"

Charles took a deep breath. "No. I think I'll just read the letter and then come back inside."

"Good, sir." Colson walked back over to the door of the house that led out to the garden, but instead of going in, he turned, put his hands behind his back, and waited.

Charles chuckled. Stubborn man. Of course, he had a stubborn boss to deal with, so that was probably to be expected.

Pulling his spectacles out of his pocket, he put them on and opened the letter.

October 15, 1860

Dear Sir,

After all these months, you've probably become a bit discouraged by all the correspondence I've sent saying that I haven't made any progress. Well, this may be premature, but I believe that I may have news.

As we went through ledgers at the stagecoach stop where I'm staying, I found out that a woman — Hanna Morris — and her infant stayed here for three years. Then nothing else is said of her.

I don't wish to jump to conclusions, but the woman who now runs the stop and Express station was raised by the man who owned it all those years ago. Sadly, he passed away recently, but the woman has blond hair and green eyes. She also told me that her mother died when she was quite young.

She's also twenty-six years old.

Now, all of these might be coincidences, but with the witness I found in a nearby town, I believe this might be your daughter. I'm hesitant to even write that so soon, but I'm hoping to find some other proof. She doesn't have the slightest idea of any of this because she believes the man who raised her was her father, and I've been reluctant to bring her any more grief. He sounds like he was a very good man.

I pray that your health has improved and that this note will give you a bit of encouragement as well. I'm praying for you every day.

If you have anything that could help me discern the truth, please send it to me here.

Before I sign off, might I inquire if you know a James Crowell? He works for the secretary of the treasury and he's asked me to assist him in a matter or two.

All my best to everyone there. I look forward to hearing from you again.

Sincerely,

Elijah

Charles blinked rapidly after reading the note and then read it again. Could it be true? After all this time? The thought thrilled him more than he imagined possible. Looking across at Colson, he smiled. "I need you to send for Dr. Newberry. Tell him I need to see him as soon as possible." Getting to his feet, he had a spring in his step as he headed to the door. "Then I need you to bring a trunk down for me, and you'll need to pack for yourself as well."

"Are we going somewhere, sir?" One of Colson's eyebrows quirked up.

"Yes, indeed. We're going out West."

"Whatever for, sir?"

"To see my daughter."

Four hours later, Charles was itching to leave.

Dr. Nathaniel Newberry was listening to his heart with his long wooden stethoscope tube. That made Charles all the more impatient.

Newberry pulled back and gave him a glare. "You're not being a very cooperative patient today, Charles. What has gotten into you?"

"Nathaniel, we've known each other for ages. Quit stalling. I'm better, aren't I?"

The doctor's head tilted back and forth as he put the instrument away. "You are better. I will admit that, but I'm still concerned that if you go back to your work-crazy lifestyle, this brief respite of good health won't last long."

Charles buttoned his waistcoat and lifted his chin. "Well, it's a good thing I'm not planning to return to my work anytime soon . . . if ever."

Nathaniel narrowed his eyes and put his hands on his hips. "Exactly what *are* you planning to do, Charles?"

"Nothing much, just going on a little trip."

"A business trip or a trip for leisure?"

"Leisure, of course, my friend."

The doctor gave him a smile. "Good. But as much as I would like to think you don't have anything else up your sleeve, I know better. I've known you too long."

"I won't be doing any business, if that's what you are thinking."

"I'm not sure what to think, Charles. But I'll be praying for you. Don't overdo it. Send for me when you return." He grabbed his black bag and walked out.

Colson stepped forward, a smirk on his face. "I'm guessing you're not planning to tell him the truth about where we're going."

"Not at all." He went over and checked the trunk. "I can always send him a letter."

Colson chuckled. "Of course, sir."

"Have you made the arrangements?"

His man looked down at a list he held and used a pencil to point to each item. "Yes, sir. I've hired two men to accompany us and spoke with the Butterfield stage manager when I purchased the tickets. I paid double the price for each of us, just like instructed, so that the stage is all ours. It normally takes twenty-one days and nights to travel from St. Louis to San Francisco. That's in good weather. So it could take up to five or six weeks. The main driver has been all the way to California and back many times, so he knows the way quite well. He's been driving since the line was started in 1858. I told them we would help purchase more horses along the way if need be, but they change the horses every three hours or so. He was grateful for your offer of assistance and said the drivers will be informed."

Charles clapped his hands together. "That sounds rather well prepared to me. Especially on such short notice. Thank you, Colson." He moved to pick up his hat. "This is going to be quite the adventure. We are headed to the great American West." Placing his hat on his head, Charles realized he hadn't thought about one important aspect of travel. Sustenance. "But what about food?"

"I've purchased plenty of supplies in case of emergencies, but there will be food available for purchase at the way stations we visit. Cook has prepared a couple of baskets of your favorite treats for our trip."

"I'm sure this will be an extraordinary adventure. I've gotten so used to the train that I haven't been on a stage for a long-distance trip in quite a while. Are there accommodations for sleeping along the way?"

"No, sir. The stage travels all day and all night. We'll have to sleep in the coach while it travels. Unless, of course, you want to stop."

"And the men you hired. They are trustworthy? Prepared to protect us in case of any outlaw attacks?"

"Yes, sir." Colson closed up the two trunks they would be taking. "The manager told me that the driver has said so far the trail is dry, but snow could fly at any time. So we will keep to a tight schedule until the weather won't allow us that anymore. Up to sixty to seventy miles a day when we can, but that will diminish to twenty or thirty miles a day if the snow comes."

"What of the weather in the mountains?"

"That is the only thing the men are worried about, sir. But the stage continues to run throughout the year. Any snow or ice will just slow us down. Especially if it gets too treacherous around the mountains."

"Then let us pray that the good Lord keeps the snow from flying anytime soon."

"It is already November, sir."

"I know that, Colson. But I'm not going to wait all winter before I try to see my daughter. Besides, Elijah probably needs my help."

November 6, 1860

The pounding sound of a horse's hooves woke Elijah. Blinking in the bright sunlight that streamed through the window, he forced himself to stay awake rather than fade back into the cocoon of sleep.

Ever since the doctor had given him such a rude awakening by stabbing him in the foot, Elijah had been sleeping most of the time. He'd awoken a few more times in the middle of the night and one of the boys had helped him get broth down his throat, but other than that, he didn't remember much of anything else.

For the first time in a long while, he felt alert. And quite parched. Turning his head, he noticed Michael asleep in the chair next to him. "Michael, Michael! Wake up."

"Huh?" The young man sat up straight and wiped at his eyes. "I'm sorry. Did you need something?"

"Could you help prop me up so I could drink? I'm so tired of lying on my back."

"Sure. Jackie brought a few extra pillows in here the other day. Let me grab them." The young man kept talking as he walked to the other side of the room. "You know, she was hoping that once you woke up, you'd be awake a lot more. But Doc said it might take awhile. Here they are." Michael fluffed up each one. "How do you want to do this? Should I lift you up by the shoulders?"

"Yes, that might be the best. I'll push up from the bed with my arms, and you lift from there. Maybe you can shove a few pillows behind me then."

"All right, I'll lift on three. One, two, three."

It took both of their efforts to move him a mere foot, and his ribs screamed in pain, but he was at least a bit more upright. "Thanks, Michael."

The lad then brought over a glass of water. "I just filled the bucket from the stream, so it should still be cool."

"Thank you." With a shaky hand, he took the glass, and once he'd drained it, he was amazed at how much better he felt. The events that had happened in Virginia City came back in fuzzy pictures. Mr. Sanders had been murdered. Elijah's horse stolen. And then the stage attacked. His heart beat faster as his breathing became short. "What happened to the driver? Was he killed?"

Michael put a hand on his shoulder. "Doc said you're not supposed to be getting yourself all worked up. Now why don't you just take a couple deep breaths and calm down."

"He's dead, isn't he?" All the pictures began to sharpen as memories rushed into his mind. What had happened with the stage? He wasn't sure. But he remembered watching a man with a bandanna over his face shoot the driver. The horses had taken off with no one to guide them. The stage crashed.

"I'm sorry, Mr. Johnson. It had to have been an awful thing."

He swiped a hand down his face and tried to calm his breathing. The room swirled and spots danced in front of his eyes.

"Mr. Johnson?"

He closed his eyes. "I'm all right. Just give me a minute."

"Jack is gonna kill me. You're supposed to be calm and resting."

"I'm fine, Michael. Don't fret." He tried to convince himself his words were true and took deep, long breaths, keeping his eyes closed. As much as he wanted to help Mr. Crowell, the stress of the situation was obviously sending his body into a panic. He couldn't allow that to happen. The only way he'd be able to help was by healing, getting better, and telling the authorities everything he knew.

Once his heart slowed down, he opened his eyes and saw Michael hovering over him. "See? I'm all right." But every time he thought about the accident, the pictures of men being shot flashed in his mind and made him nauseous. They had to find the criminals. And soon. Before more people were killed.

"You don't look all right. You've got that look in your eyes again."

"What kind of a look?"

"Like you've just seen a ghost."

Elijah forced himself to take a few more calming breaths. How could he let Crowell know? Or the sheriff? The sooner this was taken care of, the better. Especially since he was a witness now. Twice. "Has the sheriff been out here?"

"Yeah. While you were unconscious. I'm sure he'll come back out here when he finds out you're awake."

"Good." He nodded and looked around the room. He needed something to get his mind off of the horrible memories. He spied the letters on the desk. Hadn't they said something about him receiving some Express letters while he was injured? "Michael? Would you mind handing me those letters?"

"Not at all. Let me get them for you. But

there's something I need to tell you."

"Oh?"

"The top packet fell and the seal was broken, but rest assured, we did not read your mail. But we resealed it. That's why there's a fresh one on there."

"Of course. I understand. Thank you for being honest with me."

"Sure. Hey, do you mind if I go to the privy? I don't want to leave you alone, but since you're awake, is that all right?" He deposited the letters in Elijah's lap.

"Go right ahead. It's not like I'm going anywhere."

"Thanks. I'll be right back." Michael dashed out of the room.

Elijah lifted the first envelope up so he could see it better. It was definitely worn from the long journey from Kansas City to here. He wasn't surprised that the seal had been broken. Especially since there seemed to be something more than just a note inside. The packet had a good deal of weight to it for an Express.

Splitting the new seal, he opened it up and pulled out a letter. A miniature canvas fell out of the envelope, bounced off of his lap, and landed on the floor. He looked down at it. Oh well, he'd have to ask Michael to retrieve it when he returned. He turned his attention back to the letter.

October 18, 1860

Dear Elijah,

It was indeed wonderful to get your letter from the twelfth of this month. It is beyond my wildest imagination to think of the distance between us. You in the Utah Territory. Me back here in Kansas City. But now thanks to the Pony Express, I received your letter in a week! Amazing!

My boy, I hope you are doing well. As anxious as I am for you to find my daughter and for you to return, I know this has not been an easy task. I'm glad you have had some time to rest and gather your thoughts while awaiting my response. To be honest, I'm very thankful you chose to stay there so that I could send this on to you.

Right after you left, I had Colson come and gather some things out of the attic for me. Just in case my time was growing short. (Don't worry, I've been following the doctor's orders and am glad to say that I'm doing remarkably better.) But over the last months, Colson and I have gone through many old trunks filled with memories of years gone by. We found this miniature painting yesterday amongst the items.

All these years, I've been under the impression that I had nothing to remember her by. You see, Anna had thrown all the portrait paintings into the fireplace the night before she left. I can't say that I blame her, but this sweet picture appeared as we were digging through an old trunk.

It was from our courtship. I paid handsomely to have it done so that I could have her with me at all times. I'd kept it on my desk in my office in those early years. Somehow, after she left, it was stashed away with old clothing and documents. I'm passing on this treasure to you because for some reason, I have a feeling and hope that our daughter might look like her mother. As much as it pains me to part with it so soon, I'm holding out hope that it will aid you in your search.

I'm looking forward to hearing more from you.

As always, I'm praying for you.

Sincerely,
Charles Vines

Michael came back into the room at that moment, and Elijah couldn't have been more grateful.

"Would you mind picking something up for me? I dropped it out of this letter."

"Sure." When the young man made it around the bed, an odd look spread over his face as he looked down at the canvas. He picked it up slowly and handed it to Elijah.

Elijah studied the portrait, which made his heart pick up its pace. He raised his eyebrows. "You saw?"

"Uh, yeah." Michael's brow furrowed. "Who is that?"

Elijah ignored the question for a moment and looked back down at the painting. Charles Vines had no idea how helpful the portrait would be. In fact, Elijah now knew exactly where he could find his partner's daughter.

"Mr. Johnson?" Michael prodded.

As he opened his mouth to respond, a knock at the door rescued him. He turned to see the very object of his thoughts standing in the doorway to his room.

CHAPTER 20

Jackie looked from Elijah's face to Michael's and back. "What are you two up to in here?" She smiled and put her hands on her hips. "Have you had anything to drink? You know the doctor wanted you to have broth and fluids."

Elijah nodded, his face a bit ashen.

Michael stood. "Maybe I should go check on the horses." As he walked around the bed and toward her, Jackie understood what was going on. The envelopes were sitting in Elijah's lap.

With a squeeze to her shoulder, Michael left.

"Jackie, would you come sit with me for a while? There's something I need to tell you."

"All right." She wiped her sweaty palms on her apron as she made her way to the chair. How much did he know? Had Michael told him they'd seen the painting? Taking a deep breath, she sat down.

"Could you come closer? I can't sit up all the way, so it's hard for me to see you."

"Of course." The chair scraped across the wood floor as she moved closer. She hoped he couldn't hear her heart pounding from there.

"Michael told me what happened with the seal, so don't worry. I'm not upset." Elijah swallowed and held up the portrait to her. "But I needed you to see this."

Even though she'd already seen it, the painting still took her breath away. "Who is that?"

"This" — he brought the picture back in front of him and stared at it — "is my partner's, Mr. Vines's, wife."

"Is she the reason you're out here?"

"Yes." He sighed. "I should probably start at the beginning. I've been working for a man named Charles Vines for over ten years. I know I've mentioned him to you since I've been here."

"Yes." It was all she could seem to get out. It had all happened so fast. It didn't seem real.

"He is the very best man I know. But a few months ago, his health declined."

"I'm very sorry." Her heart tightened at the thought. Could this man actually be her father? How sick was he? The thought of

327

losing him before she even met him made her heart clench.

"Are you all right?" Concern was etched all over Elijah's face.

With a slow nod, she swallowed down her fear and convinced herself to be patient and listen to what Elijah had to say. "Is he, Mr. Vines, all right?"

"He's been resting and trying to regain his strength. He sat me down one day and asked me to find someone for him."

"Her? His wife?" She pointed to the small painting. Even though she already knew the answer to her question.

Elijah nodded and stared at her. His blue eyes penetrated her heart. "Yes, and . . . his daughter. You see, she left him. And she took their baby with her."

"The woman we were looking for in the ledgers. Why did she leave?"

His lips came together in a thin line as he took a long breath and then let it out in a huff. "Mr. Vines told me that he had turned to liquor to fill the hole in his heart. He had done some horrible things. Said some horrible things. To his wife. I don't want to talk about such delicate matters with you, Jackie, because it's not my place. But those events were what God used to turn Charles's life around. He was completely broken by what he'd done. Now he's a different man. But he asked me to find his daughter."

"Wait. Why not his wife too? Did he not want to find her?" Resentment and anger ignited within her. Defense for the woman who bore her, yet a woman she didn't know.

"He searched for her for more than a decade. Even though he received a letter a few years after she disappeared saying that she died, he still kept looking. He's an extremely wealthy man and he paid many, many investigators over the years to try to find Anna and their . . . daughter."

"Why are you looking at me like that?"

Elijah looked away for a moment. "You must see the resemblance, Jackie. You look just like her." His voice softened with the words. "You're the same age. You look just like her. You were here with your mother. . . ."

Tears began to stream down her face.

"Jackie. I'm so sorry. The last thing I want to do is hurt you. I know you loved your dad very much. He sounds like an amazing man, and I'm so thankful that he was here to raise you. But don't you want to know if it's true? If Charles Vines is your real father?"

Standing abruptly, she covered her mouth for a moment and just looked at him. This man she'd come to care about and yet the same man who was in the middle of the most difficult situation of her life. Running from the room, she swiped at her tears as she hurried to her room and closed the door. She leaned against it and tried to get her breathing under control. It was kind of Elijah to try to tread carefully, but he knew. And so did she.

Going to her bed, she prayed for wisdom. Then, pulling out the box, she ran a hand over it one more time before she opened it and looked at the letters.

Did she really want to share this with Elijah?

It was all so personal and intimate. Words from the man who'd raised her. And then words from her mother as well.

There was so much she didn't know or understand. She didn't have to share the letters with Elijah, but she could at least tell him the truth of what she knew. He deserved that much.

Jackie reached into the box and pulled out the small book that must be her mother's journal. Perhaps tonight she could start reading it. She needed answers. How could everything in her life turn upside down so quickly?

Placing the book back inside the chest,

she decided to go and talk to Elijah now. She shouldn't have left the way she did, but his revelation had been so overwhelming.

When she reached his room, he was asleep. She watched him for a few moments, the way his dark hair slid over his forehead. Never in her life had she felt so drawn to a man. But a giant chasm stood between them. She wasn't who she thought she was anymore. His boss was . . . her father?

As much as she longed to know Elijah better, her heart just couldn't take it right now.

Exhausted after the long day, Jackie went back to her room.

Everything seemed so blurry. Her life had been perfectly in order up to this point. Yes, it had been hard that she'd lost her mother as a child. But Dad had done a wonderful job raising her. She'd loved and respected him more than anyone.

The fact that he wasn't her real father had been a blow, but in reality, it didn't matter to her. Marshall Rivers would always be her dad. But what she couldn't comprehend was the fact that he had never been married to her mother. In her mind, her parents had always had a perfect, dreamlike romance. Now she had to accept the fact that everything she'd thought about her parents wasn't true.

As she unhooked her boots, she eyed the box from her dad. She had so many questions.

Needing answers, she grabbed her mother's journal and sat in the chair by the lamp.

24 December 1834

My little Jacqueline,

Did you know that your name comes from the name Jacob? The pastor at our church in Kansas City told me about the name Jacob when I was expecting you. So if you had been a boy, you would have been named Jacob. Jacqueline is a derivation of that and of the Hebrew meaning "May God protect."

That has been my prayer for you. That God would protect you.

I'm not planning to give this to you until you are much older because it will be very hard for you to understand, but I know it's important for me to be completely honest with you. This past year has been difficult. My name is Anna Marie Morrison Vines, but you will grow up knowing your mother as Hannah. I'll explain that later.

You are Jacqueline Rose Vines. A beautiful name for a beautiful baby.

Your father is a brilliant man. I fell in love with him when I was eighteen when our parents thought we would be a good match. We married that same year. The first thing I want to share with you, Jacqueline, is that you should never be unequally yoked. The Bible warns about it, and I did not take that warning to heart like I should have. You father didn't have much use for God, but I thought I could change him. About a year after we were married, something happened to him. I don't know what. But he changed. He began to drink liquor to excess. Over time, he became a very violent man.

But I still loved him. We still had many moments of laughter and good times when he wasn't drinking. But those became fewer as time passed. I became with child three times before you, my precious daughter. Each time, the baby was lost. Usually after a fit of your father's anger. Which made me very angry with him. I blamed him for our children's deaths. This enraged him, and he said it was all my fault. The cycle of anger and bitterness grew into a nightmare.

I collapsed one day in church, and

after they'd taken me to the doctor, his nurse sat by my side and listened as I told her the whole horrid story. She prayed with me and encouraged me to let go of my anger because it would be worse for the baby. When I finally understood that she was trying to explain to me that I was expecting you, I made plans. Desperate plans, really. In hopes that I could hide from him long enough for you to come into this world. It wasn't easy. But we had a large estate. I would make an appearance every morning when he was coming out of his stupor and pretend to be sick. Since he wanted nothing to do with that, I would hide in one of the other wings. It was a horrible time. At night after his drinking binges, he'd roam the house yelling for me, always trying to find me. I believe that God kept him from finding me. But as soon as you were born and I was strong enough to go, he exploded worse than anything I'd ever seen. Earlier than planned, I ran away. I couldn't risk anything happening to you, my beautiful little angel.

Your father is a very wealthy man. But he is lost, my dear. I pray that he finds the only One who can fill the gaping hole within him — Jesus Christ. His agony was so great, I could do nothing to help him, so he turned to the bottle. The night I — we — left, your father was enraged. But by what I believe was the grace of God, we escaped.

For months we traveled west. Wandering it seemed. Until one day, we came here. To what I thought of as the wilderness. I took a room at Mr. Rivers's boardinghouse and have decided to stay. After months of sleeping in a wagon, it was nice to have a bed again. You've grown so much that you need room to roam and discover.

I feel like this is a good place to call home.

Marshall Rivers is a good man. He loves the Lord and is kind to his workers. Right now he runs a horse ranch, and you love the horses. I can tell it won't be long until you are trying to ride one. I've been helping by washing and cooking. You'll never know the wealth that I came from, so you can't find the humor in that statement. But two things I didn't know how to do a few months ago, I do to help earn our keep now. I've learned a lot. God has humbled me and protected us. I'll do anything for you, my precious girl.

In this journal, I'll try to tell you the whole story. Because you deserve to know the truth. You need to know that your mother is a sinful and flawed human being, just like your father. If not for Christ's sacrifice on the cross, none of us would have the opportunity to have eternity with God in heaven. So please remember that I am not perfect. I have made many mistakes. And the last mistake I want to make is keeping you from knowing the truth.

I'm tired tonight, but I will write more tomorrow.

I love you.

Jackie laid the book in her lap. Another piece of the puzzle had fallen into place. The question of why her mother left had now been answered. And the discrepancy in the ledgers. Hannah was Anna. Just like Elijah had guessed.

He'd alluded to the reason for her mother's departure as well, but having her mother's testimony made it more tangible. Her real father had been a monster.

CHAPTER 21

November 7, 1860

The bed grew more uncomfortable by the hour, and the new splints Dr. Thompson had put on Elijah's leg severely restricted his movements, making it even more difficult to find a position that didn't hurt. On top of that, the doctor had wrapped the new splints in awful-smelling bandages that stiffened over time. It wasn't adding up to be a very good day.

Not that he had energy to do much yet, but his mind was ready to get back into life, and he'd definitely gotten his appetite back. The day couldn't come soon enough when he could eat something with more substance than broth or soup or egg custard.

Mr. Liverpool knocked on the doorframe. "Come on in."

"It seems it is my turn to sit with you again for a while. Although I'm not sure how much longer you'll need one of us to watch over you. You're looking pretty good."

"I have to admit, that's just the encouragement I needed to hear. Thank you, Mr. Liverpool."

"Please, call me Tom."

"Tom. Thank you for being here, but I know this must be pretty tedious for you when you have a number of other things to attend to." Did anyone understand how difficult it was to be a patient laid up — dependent on everyone else? Especially knowing how much everyone had to do around here. "It was different when you all were worried about whether or not I would awaken, but now this is simply for my convenience since I can't exactly get up and fetch things for myself. Feel free to go on about your business. I'm sure I've caused enough upheaval in everyone's schedules."

Liverpool smiled at him. "You're very gracious to be thinking of others, Elijah, but I think we all recognize that this is a very difficult situation for you. We'd like to help." The man pulled a piece of paper out of his pocket. "I was studying in the book of Romans — since I'm still pondering Daniel's chapters — and read a few verses that I thought might encourage you, so I took the liberty to write them down."

"Romans is one of my favorites, Tom. I

really appreciate you taking the time."

He opened the folded paper and added, "This is Romans chapter 5, by the way. 'Therefore being justified by faith, we have peace with God through our Lord Jesus Christ: by whom also we have access by faith into this grace wherein we stand, and rejoice in hope of the glory of God. And not only so, but we glory in tribulations also: knowing that tribulation worketh patience; and patience, experience; and experience, hope: and hope maketh not ashamed; because the love of God is shed abroad in our hearts by the Holy Ghost which is given unto us.' "

Elijah leaned his head back after Tom read. *"But we glory in tribulations."* The words struck him. He hadn't been very appreciative of the tribulations he'd been enduring. Yet the Bible said that tribulation worketh patience, and then experience through patience blossomed into hope. He lifted his head and looked at his friend. "May I be quite frank with you?"

"Of course."

"I needed to hear those exact verses today. For most of my adult life, I've plunged into whatever is in front of me with gusto and drive. This is the first time I haven't been able to simply attack whatever it is that needs to be done. It seems God has put me in this place for a reason, and I need to be willing to wait on Him. No matter how hard that may be."

Liverpool chuckled and laid the paper on the table beside Elijah. "You know, I've told my beautiful bride many times over the years that she has tried my patience. Do you know how she always responds?"

"How?"

"She says, 'Dear, it's my job to help you become more Christlike.' "

Elijah laughed out loud — even as much as it hurt his ribs. "Your wife has got quite a quick wit."

"Oh, my June. She is a jewel, isn't she?" The expression on the man's face showed how much he loved his wife. It did strange things to Elijah. "Well, if you're certain you're all right here by yourself, I'll go ahead and tend to things back at the stables. Two of the horses have thrown shoes."

"Thank you for coming, Tom."

He stood and nodded at Elijah. "You're most welcome. Do you need anything before I go?"

Elijah looked over at the table beside him. "Would you mind handing me my Bible and the paper you brought me today?"

As Tom lifted his Bible, Elijah noticed the

packets from Kansas City.

"And would you mind handing me those letters as well?"

"Not at all. I'll leave the door open and let the others know that if you need something you'll holler for one of them."

"That would be great. Thanks."

As Elijah watched the man leave, he thought about the way Tom Liverpool had talked about his wife. And the expression that filled his face. Here was a man who truly seemed to love his wife and appreciate her. Every time Elijah had seen the couple, they'd seemed happy to be together. Whether out at the picnic or in their little church service, the admiration and affection they had for each other was evident.

A fondness like that couldn't be faked. He'd seen enough of the fake variety growing up. Enough that he could spot it a mile away and sadly had witnessed it in far too many couples. But Tom and June Liverpool were different.

His thoughts went back to Jackie. She'd said the same thing about Marshall and her mother. It seemed she'd had a greater opportunity to witness true love in this little collection of people than he had in all the thousands of people he'd known in the city and in all his travels.

Once again, he felt the longing in him spark to a flame. The thought of being betrayed again was horrific, but what if he actually had a real chance for love? Wouldn't he want to take that?

He opened his Bible to Romans and read through the chapter that Tom had quoted from. If God was giving him this chance to learn, he'd better make the most of it.

Leaning his head back again, he closed his eyes and prayed. *Lord, I don't know what it is that You want me to learn, but I'm willing. I want to know You more. I want to understand Your will for my life. Please help me to discern the correct path. I need patience as I wait to talk to the sheriff and Mr. Crowell. It's a good thing I'm laid up, or I would probably try something stupid. Please help the criminals to be found.*

And Father, You are the Great Physician. I ask You to heal Mr. Vines so that he at least has the chance to meet his daughter. It will be a long time before I can travel and bring her back to Kansas City, but I ask for You to keep sustaining him and encouraging him. Also, God, I need wisdom with Jackie. You know I've come to care for her. But I don't have any idea what I'm to do. Is this Your will? Please guide me. In Jesus' name, amen.

As he opened his eyes, a new sense of calm

washed over him. Maybe the real key was what he'd thought about on his trip out here. Focus on God. Not on his own will.

He placed his Bible beside him on the bed and picked up the second packet from Mr. Vines. It was hefty as if the man had written him quite the missive. But as he opened it up and leafed through the pages, he realized they were letters. Obviously from different people at different times because of the variances in paper and handwriting.

Curious, Elijah began with the top letter.

Elijah,

Colson and I found these letters this week. I don't know if you've come any closer to finding my daughter, but perhaps these will help. I must admit it's almost embarrassing to share such intimate details with you, but I am desperate. Desperate to find my daughter and to apologize to her for all that I've done. I hope you don't think any less of me after reading these letters, but I'm sure there must be a clue in here somewhere. And you're just the man to figure it out.

I miss you, my boy. Please send word as soon as you can.

Charles Vines

Elijah looked at the yellowed sheets behind Mr. Vines's note. The first letter was quite interesting. A mystery person whom Anna had obviously confided in because the sender knew that Vines had not been a good man. But the writer said that while Vines's wife and daughter were safe, he would not reveal their location. Hmm . . . Elijah had never seen anything quite like it. It had to be from a man because he stated he would protect them at all costs. Could Marshall have written this letter?

He quickly flipped to the next page. A different script filled the paper. His heart wrenched when he read the name at the bottom. Going back to the top, Elijah took a breath and read:

July 2, 1837

Charles,

I forgive you. It has taken me a long time to be able to say these words out loud, but time is running short for me.

As I think of God's unconditional love for us — sinners and wretches that we are — I'm amazed at His example of forgiveness. So I ask that you forgive me as well.

I'm dying, Charles. I'm sorry it has

come to this, and my heart aches with the thought of leaving my precious daughter behind at such a tender age, but the fever has taken hold.

I pray that you have found God and His forgiveness. I pray for your soul every day.

I loved you, Charles. With all my heart. I'm sorry for all the ways I failed you. But I couldn't fix you. Only God can do that.

I'm leaving Jacqueline in good hands.

Anna

The shaky handwriting on the page attested to the difficulty the woman had in writing it. But his instincts had proven true. Anna and Charles's daughter's name was Jacqueline. That combined with the fact that Jackie was the spitting image of the woman in the painting was enough proof for him. He flipped to the next page.

July 11, 1837

Mr. Vines,

Your wife became quite ill with the fever, and I'm afraid she will not be with us much longer.

She's asked me to promise to care for

her daughter. I have given my solemn word to her. I will raise Jacqueline as my own and provide the best life for her that I can. Anna's greatest wish is that you have found peace with God. How she still loves you, I do not understand, but it has been a privilege to know her and learn from her example. I will continue to pray that you find God's grace and mercy.

Sincerely,
M.R.

Elijah turned to the last page.

July 13, 1837

Mr. Vines,

I regret to inform you that the fever took your wife this morning. She had been happy these last years.

M.R.

Splotches smeared the ink in one place and crinkled the paper in several others. Whoever it was must have cared deeply for Anna, for their tears marked the page. Elijah remembered Charles telling him about this letter. How it had been delayed for months in the long mail-service route. Especially since he moved from St. Louis to Kansas City. Even though Charles had tried to start over and be a better man, the letter had crushed him.

Elijah sucked in a breath. All the proof he needed was right there in front of him. The last two letters were signed *M.R.* — Marshall Rivers. It was all true. Jacqueline Rivers was actually Jacqueline Vines. Now he just needed to tell Jackie.

CHAPTER 22

After feeding everyone lunch, Jackie wiped her hands on her apron and headed to Elijah's room. She'd tucked the letter from her dad and one from her mother in her pocket.

"Elijah?"

His eyes were closed, but he obviously heard her. "Hmm?" Blinking several times, he focused on her. "I'm sorry. I was asleep again."

She pulled the chair up close so she could talk softly. "I don't want to lose my gumption, so I'm just going to be blunt, all right?"

He scrubbed at his eyes with his right hand. "I'm listening."

"You asked me yesterday if I wanted to know if Charles Vines was my father. Well, what I didn't tell you — and the reason I ran out of the room — is that I already knew." Taking a deep breath, she felt a tear escape her eye. "Dad wrote me a letter —

remember how I was looking for the Shake-speare book?"

His brow scrunched like he was confused. "Yes, but what does Shakespeare have to do with the letter?"

"I'm sorry. It was just a clue. My father hid a box for me. I always liked treasure hunts when I was a kid." Another tear. Another shaky breath. She could do this. "Anyway, I found the box, and then the stagecoach was attacked and you were injured, and I didn't have a chance to open it. But then I did . . . and Dad told me that he wasn't my real father. I have to admit, it crushed me to find that out. My dad was the greatest man I'd ever known. He was amazing. . . ."

Elijah reached across the bed and put his hand over hers. "I'm sure he was, Jackie. I wasn't trying to take that away from you."

"I know that." She squeezed his hand and held on. "But then I read a letter from my mother." Her shoulders began to shake. "So when you asked me about it, I was just too overwhelmed. I'm sorry I didn't tell you that I already knew."

"That's all right. There's no need to apologize." His eyes were filled with com-passion and understanding. "I think you need to read these." He handed her a small stack of letters.

She took them with shaky hands and glanced at each one. Dad's handwriting! And then her mother's on another. "Where did you get these?"

"Charles sent them. He thought they might help me find you."

Ducking her head at the intensity in his gaze, Jackie read through them. She hadn't needed any more confirmation, but these definitely added to the story she'd been trying to digest for the past couple of days. She handed them back to Elijah and brushed a tear from her cheek.

"My mother also left a journal of sorts — it appears to be letters she wrote to me to help me understand. I started to read it, but there's still more." How did she ask what pressed on her heart? "Elijah, I need you to be honest with me. My mother was careful not to bash my father — Mr. Vines — but she was truthful. He sounds like he was a . . . a monster." The tears flowed freely. "He hurt her. Was violent. Did you know that she lost . . ." She couldn't say it; the words choked her. Closing her eyes, she swallowed and started again. "My mother lost three babies before me. Because of . . . him. It's why she decided to leave."

Elijah let out a long sigh and closed his

eyes. "Oh Jackie. I'm so sorry."

She leaned forward and placed her other hand atop his. "You told me that your boss was a good man. The best of men. Didn't you? So how can this be the same person? I need to know. I can't . . . I just can't go on with this facade all around me. But how am I supposed to deal with all this?" She sniffed and begged him with her eyes for the truth.

"I didn't know Charles when he was the other man. The only man I've known is the good one. But he told me himself that he was a despicable person before God got ahold of him. His greatest desire was to find you and set things right. He wants you to know the truth and he wants to apologize."

She ducked her head and held on tight to his hand that she'd sandwiched between her own. When she looked up at him, she thought for sure that what she saw there was love. She'd seen it between Tom and June and had longed for it deep down. "I don't know what to do — my whole life has been good. It really has. Dad led me to the Lord when I was just a young thing. I always believed that he was married to my mother and that he loved her very much. I thought things had been perfect between them and then the fever took her.

"Her loss was tragic and awful, but Dad

and I . . . we made it. Because we had each other and we had our faith. But what do I do with this now? The two people I thought were my parents weren't actually married. Did people think they were married? Or how many people thought they were living in sin, or had a child out of wedlock? Not that I should care about what people think, I know — but the picture I've had painted in my mind all this time . . ." She shook her head and sighed. "Yet they both wrote to me that even though they loved each other deeply, they never broke God's commandments. My mother was actually still married to a man she'd run away from. I feel like it was all a lie! My whole, beautiful life was a lie. It's like a jar that's broken into a hundred pieces. Shattered. So will I not know what real is when it comes? Is this real?"

Elijah pushed himself up with his other arm and winced. He took a deep breath. "Out of everyone I've ever met, Jacqueline Rivers, you have had more real in your life than any of them. Just because they weren't perfect and you didn't know the whole truth doesn't mean that your life is a lie. Believe me, I've seen enough people living a fake life to know the difference."

He squeezed the hand that he held before

he continued. "Why do you think I'm so drawn to you and want to know more about you? It's because you've experienced real love, Jackie. You know what it is. You've had the joys of a real family — even as different as it has been — and you still enjoy that here. All these riders — John, Mark, Luke, Paul, Timothy, Eddie — the Liverpools, and Michael. It's a beautiful thing to watch all of you here. I want that. Long for it. If I've learned anything from all of this, it's that I want to have a family of my own. I've never had the opportunity to experience love like this. I thought I was in love once a long time ago, and she betrayed me. So I've kind of put a barrier around my heart all these years."

What was he saying? She swallowed hard. "But you're going to leave here eventually. I'll never see you again."

He grimaced. "I'm making a mess out of this. I'm so sorry. This wasn't the time for me to . . ." Swiping his other hand down his face, he looked at her sheepishly. "Can we start again?"

"Does that mean you're not going to leave?"

"I'm not going anywhere for a good long while. If you haven't noticed, I can't."

The way he said it made her giggle.

"And I'd genuinely like to get to know you better, Jacqueline Rivers. I'm asking you if you will pray with me about this. Perhaps consider a courtship of sorts?" He winced as he leaned closer to place his other hand atop hers.

"I'd like to know you better too. Of course I will pray. A courtship sounds . . . lovely." She looked down at their hands stacked in her lap. "I'm sorry for falling apart like that."

Elijah nodded and leaned back in the bed. "You had a right to."

"This is going to take a lot of getting used to. I'm not quite sure what to do with myself since I can't talk to Dad about it and I don't remember my mother."

"Give it time. Read the letters and the journal. Savor everything you can. I'll be here. And when I'm healed, we can travel to Kansas City together so you can meet Charles Vines for yourself. You still have family left."

He was right. Although it was hard to fathom that the man her mother had run away from was now desperately searching for her and seeking forgiveness. *God, what are You doing? Because I don't understand. And it hurts. But I will trust You.* "It's hard to think about leaving here. I've never been farther away from home than Carson City. What if I don't like it there?"

"Let's not worry about it now. We've got plenty of time to figure it out since Doc says it's going to be weeks before I can even attempt to walk." He leaned a bit closer. "No one is telling you that you have to stay there. I'll be with you the whole time. And if I know anything about Charles Vines, it wouldn't surprise me in the least if he decided to sell off his whole estate and move wherever you wanted to go."

"Really?"

"Really."

"As much as it scares me to travel like that, I like the idea of spending more time with you." She allowed a smile to fill her face.

"I'm looking forward to it."

His hand inside of hers was warm and strong.

"Looking forward to what?" Michael stood at the door grinning like he'd just found his birthday cake and eaten it all.

Jackie released Elijah's hand and gave the young man — who was growing up way too fast — a look that meant she'd talk to him later about eavesdropping. "None of your business." She sat up straighter. "Did you need something?"

"Yeah, you know I was just teasin' ya. You two were looking so serious." He walked over to her and squeezed her shoulder. "This just came in on the Express."

"I missed an Express?" In all her years, she'd never missed the stage or the Pony Express when it came through. Well, other than when she'd conked her head the other day. But even when she was little, before she had any real responsibilities, she'd always raced outside to see what the stage brought. No one could miss the rumble of the horses as they came through.

"We all knew you two were talking, and we didn't want to disturb you."

"I'm still shocked. I didn't even realize it had come."

"You must have been really engrossed in whatever you were talking about." Michael shrugged. "I'll be out in the parlor if you need me."

"Thank you." She looked down at the missive in her hands. "It's from Mr. Crowell."

Elijah put a hand to his forehead.

Jackie stood up and leaned over him. "What's wrong? Are you all right?"

He let out a huff. "I'm fine. I just remembered that I need to get some very important information to him."

Shaking her head, she sat back down and put a hand to her chest. "You had me worried for a moment. I'm sure he'll understand — you were waylaid and unconscious for a good while."

"Would you mind bringing me some writing supplies? I need to send something as soon as I can. Is there an address on there I can send it to?"

She checked the envelope. "Yes, right here." Gathering the supplies he needed, she handed them to him and sat back in the chair and opened the letter.

Miss Rivers,
    I've been detained in Carson City longer than I expected.

The next section of the letter appeared to be in the code.

"I'll be right back, Elijah." She stood up and ran to her room to retrieve the paper she needed to decipher it.

The forgeries are not originating from here, but they have come through here. Have you heard from Mr. Johnson? Could you ask if he had the meeting we discussed? I haven't heard from him, which concerns me.

I apologize for asking for your services once again, but I am at an impasse. I have an urgent matter that needs to be discussed with Mr. Williamson in Virginia City. Could you get a message to him from me? I can't send an Express; it's too dangerous and might fall into the wrong hands. It needs to be brought to him in person. That ensures both of you protection. Right now, we're unsure of who is to be trusted.

If you can, please tell him, "Sacramento is ready." That's it.

I shall return by the end of November if not sooner. Thank you for the information you supplied; it was of great use to us.

The note continued in regular writing.

Please keep all of this to yourself. It is of utmost importance.

Your friend,
James Crowell

Jackie folded the letter back into the envelope. "He asked if I'd heard from you, so it's a good thing you're writing him. He asked if you had the meeting as discussed." What were Crowell and Elijah working on together? She shook her head. It didn't matter. She had enough going on.

In that moment, she realized she'd never gotten off a letter to the owners. Well, that couldn't wait any longer. She needed to write the owners and tell them the truth today. She felt her life had contained too many lies already.

"That's one of the things I need to write him about. I'll take care of it, so don't worry."

"What?" She gave him a puzzled look and realized he was still thinking about Mr. Crowell. "Oh, all right."

His attention on the letter he was writing, Elijah didn't look up at her.

She stood. "Well, I'd better see to the rest of dinner preparations."

He looked up at her. "Will you come back later?" The pleading in his blue eyes made her stomach flip.

"I'd love to."

The fat man stood in front of him, a greedy smile making his double chin grow. "Just your luck, I finished them all. And they're perfect, if I do say so myself."

Carl flipped through the stack and looked at them. They were good; he'd give the guy that. "It's been a pleasure doing business with you."

"And you as well. Now where's my money?" The man puffed on his cigar like a baby sucking his thumb.

Shoving a potato sack filled with coins toward the obese and uncouth man, Carl allowed a smile to slide onto his face. "Have a lovely day." He put the notes into his satchel and left the building. In just a few days, he'd be done with this whole mess and would have everything he'd ever wanted. Let the rest of the world scrounge around and work their fingers to the bone. He preferred the lifestyle of the rich. In a country where no one could touch him for all the heinous deeds he'd done here. All he needed was money. And he now had that in generous supply.

Now all he had to do was visit the tailor and pick up his custom-made clothing.

The rest was too easy.

CHAPTER 23

Carson Sink Station

November 7, 1860

Mr. William Russell
Mr. William Waddell
Mr. Alexander Majors

Gentlemen,
I'm writing this letter to inform you that by withholding information from you, I wasn't honest. I signed my name "Jack Rivers" on my last correspondence to you because that is what Dad always called me and I was uncertain you would allow me to continue on as station manager. But, sirs, my name is Jacqueline. I'm a woman. I run the stage way station and the Pony Express station here in Carson Sink.

I apologize for my actions.

Sincerely,
Jacqueline "Jack" Rivers

Putting her pen down, Jackie reread the note and wondered if she should have begged them to keep her job. The fact of the matter was she'd deceived them and had to be honest. Whatever action they took at this point, she would have to live with their decision. If they decided she wasn't fit to run the station, perhaps she could suggest Tom Liverpool or even Michael. She could allow for the Express to continue to use her facilities, and maybe over time she could show the owners of the COC&PP that she was honorable and trustworthy.

She felt guilty every time she thought about how she'd misled them. Once trust was lost, it was often impossible to earn it back. She hated to think that might be the case, but she'd have to face the consequences of her actions.

With a deep breath, she tried to clear her mind. She picked up her mother's journal and decided to read a little more to get her mind off her problems.

March 3, 1835

Dearest Jacqueline,

I'm afraid today's entry might be short because you are, quite frankly, into everything you can get to and your naps have been so brief lately that I have a feeling my moments of quiet will soon be over.

But it's all worth it to see your sweet, smiling face. I hate to think of you growing up so fast, but I have vowed to cherish every moment.

What I really wanted to tell you today is that you still have other family around. I have a distant cousin — Caroline Weber — who lives in California. She married a man named Horatio Livingston quite a few years ago, and some time before we left St. Louis, I'd heard that she had a little girl and named her Olivia. So that means you have other family — a cousin! Olivia would be a few years older than you, but not much.

I have to admit, I've been afraid to contact Caroline and let her know where I am just in case your father decides to look for us there. But I do long to see her again and connect with family. She's all I have left other than you.

We used to write letters to each other when we were young. My mother, your grandmother, always loved to look into her ancestry and would often try to find other relatives since her great-great-great-great-great-great-great-great-grandmother, Mary Elizabeth Lytton, came over on the Mayflower. I'll never forget the day she heard back from Caroline's mother, Elizabeth, and then told me about my cousin. We wrote letters for years.

Well, I hear your little voice calling for me, so I'd better finish for now. I'll write more tomorrow.

Love,
Mama

Jackie shut the book and found herself smiling at the thought of a cousin to connect with. But how could she go about finding Olivia Livingston? Surely she'd be married by now. And Mama didn't write anything about where in California.

Maybe once she finished this job for the Treasury, Mr. Crowell might have connections who could help find her cousin. As she pulled out another sheet of paper, she shifted her thoughts back to her letter to Russell, Waddell, and Majors. She'd done the right thing. Now she needed to move forward. If she sent out a response to Mr. Crowell on the Express this afternoon, she could head to Virginia City in the morning and deliver his message to this Mr. Williamson.

Jackie finished a quick response to Mr. Crowell and prepared the two missives for the Express. With a glance to the clock she sighed. The day was almost gone already and she had so much to do to finish up dinner.

November 8, 1860

As the sun was just beginning to crest the horizon, Jackie mounted her horse, Romeo, and looked down at Michael. "I'll be back in a few hours. I just need to deliver this message for Mr. Crowell and I'll come straight back."

"Don't worry. I'll make sure Elijah has everything he needs, and I'll handle the morning Express. The fellas won't like my cooking, but I can even handle lunch if I have to."

With a laugh, Jackie leaned over and tousled his hair. "Thanks. Just make sure you clean up my kitchen."

"I make no promises."

"Let's go, Romeo." With her gentle words,

the massive horse took off like a lightning bolt.

Over the years, she'd trained him with that phrase whenever she'd let him have his head. And her horse loved to run. It had been entirely too long since she'd taken him out for a good long run. Well, today he'd get some exercise. Perhaps she could stop at the general store and see if they had any apples. Romeo loved that treat. Part of the reason she'd begged Dad to plant apple trees was so she could feed them to her horse. He'd told her it was a bit ridiculous and far-fetched to think that they could grow apples out here, but he'd ordered them for her anyway.

Thoughts of Dad made her heart cinch. Biting her lip, she ordered her tears to stop, but one escaped despite her command.

The cold wind whipped at her face and her braid, but she'd always loved the cold weather. Thankfully, they hadn't had any snow yet, but the temperatures had definitely dropped.

Dad always teased her about running outside without a coat. What would he say to her now? Riding at breakneck speed with only her red wool shawl around her. He'd probably tell her that she'd catch her death, shake his head, and race her to the next boulder.

Slowing Romeo down to a canter, she lifted her eyes to the sky. *Lord, thank You for the sweet memories. Thank You for giving me Marshall Rivers as my dad and for all the years I had with him. I know I haven't been handling all this news too well, and I'm sorry for that. I don't mean to sound ungrateful for everything I had. But Father, I need Your wisdom for the coming days. Help me to forgive this man I've just found out is my real father. And guide me in my friendship with Elijah.*

Praying for Elijah brought his face to mind. Never could she have imagined that her world would completely change in the month since he stepped off the stage. He'd become her friend, and she couldn't deny that she hoped for much more. All the romantic dreams she'd had over the years about getting married and having a family — they melded into one image, and it was Elijah's face she saw.

But questions niggled at the back of her brain. He was close to Mr. Vines. Would his seeming interest in her right now be real if she wasn't Mr. Vines's daughter?

She fancied herself in love. But was it real? Everything she'd thought was real before was false. What if Elijah decided that she wasn't good enough for him? He was from the city and obviously used to fine things and amenities. Would he continue to work himself to the bone like he had before?

All this time to herself made her thoughts spin. Gracious, she could make herself mad with all the questions.

"Romeo, there are times that I wish I was like you."

Her horse lifted his head and huffed.

"Life would be so much simpler if I could just run and not have to think about all the problems."

He jerked his head and the reins as if to say, *Let's run.*

"All right, boy. You're right. Maybe we do just need to run."

Pushing her feet deeper into the stirrups, she lifted herself off the saddle and let Romeo fly.

When they made it to Virginia City, her hair was windswept, but the smile on her face couldn't be wiped away. She felt such simple joy riding a magnificent animal like Romeo.

After finding the home of Mr. Williamson, she knocked on the door.

An impeccably dressed man answered and raised his eyebrows at her. "How may I help you?"

"Mr. Williamson, I believe we have a mutual friend."

"Oh?" The gentleman eyed her warily. "And you are?"

"Miss Rivers."

He tilted his head as his lips turned up into a small smile. "And our mutual friend?"

"Mr. Crowell." She lifted her chin a notch. "He works for the secretary of the treasury of the United States."

"Ah, yes. Mr. Crowell." The man gave her a full smile, but it didn't reach his eyes. He allowed her entrance. "What can I do for you?"

"I have a message for you from him."

"Please. Have a seat." He gestured toward a chair.

"Thank you." She smoothed her hair back and realized she should have replaited it before meeting this man.

His fine attire and perfectly polished shoes made her feel quite out of place.

"You said you had a message?" He took a seat behind his desk.

"Yes, of course. The message is, 'Sacramento is ready.' "

"Ah . . ." The man blinked several times and looked down at a stack of papers on his desk. Straightening them, he pursed his lips. "That's good to know."

Since she was here, she might as well do a little more of her work for Mr. Crowell. And Mr. Williamson was supposed to be a trusted contact. "I'd also like to ask you a question."

"Go ahead." The man's expression was hard to read. The message from Crowell must have had quite an impact.

"Several of my acquaintances have informed me that they've been paid in government treasury notes and they've cashed those notes here in Virginia City."

"And?"

"Well, I'm wondering if they've come through this office?"

His face went blank for a moment. Then he blinked. "This office? Let me check." He opened a drawer and shuffled through it.

"Yes, sir." Jackie put on her best smile. Finally some progress. "Thank you for your help. It seems I've hit one snag after another. Especially after the horrible stage accident."

"Such a shame those two men were killed."

"Oh, only the driver was killed. The other man is recovering."

The man's head popped up, and he closed the drawer with a slam. "I'm sorry to say I can't help you."

"Why not? You just said —"

370

"I didn't say anything. I just guessed about your question." The man stood and walked around his desk. Taking her hand, he pulled her up to stand and began escorting her toward the door.

"But . . . Mr. Williamson."

His grabbed her arm.

"Unhand me, sir!"

The grip on her arm tightened. "I will do no such thing, Miss Rivers, and if I were you, I'd go back to my home and stop being so suspicious and nosy."

"How dare you?" She turned and put her hands on her hips.

"Mind your own business, woman." The man sneered, the gentle facade gone. "And don't come back."

Shoved out through the door, Jackie felt the door slam behind her. What was that all about? The man had seemed so nice at first, but then she'd delivered the message and asked him about the notes and his whole demeanor changed. What could it mean?

Her skin crawled from how the man had spoken to her. And he was supposed to be a trusted friend of Mr. Crowell? Perhaps that wasn't true.

November 8, 1860
Elijah woke with a start. His leg felt like it

was burning. What time was it? Light poured in through the window, so he knew it was daytime, but no one was around. Should he call for someone?

Deciding it was high time he tried to do something for himself, he shifted his leg off the bed and grabbed for the chair. Maybe he could use it to pull himself up.

The room spun as pain shot through his bad leg. What was going on? It hadn't felt like this yesterday. He'd just been so tired.

Determined to get up, he used all of his arm strength to pull himself up to stand on his good leg. But as soon as he was out of the bed, spots danced in front of his eyes. "Jackie . . . ," he called, but then everything went black.

A wet cloth was on his face. Elijah yanked at it and opened his eyes. Mrs. Liverpool, Mark, and Michael all hovered over him. "What happened?"

"Apparently you were trying to get up by yourself and took quite a tumble." Mrs. Liverpool gave him a sharp look. "Now, you won't be trying that again, will you?"

"Where's Jackie?" It was odd that she wouldn't be here. Especially after their talk yesterday.

"She went to Virginia City. She should be

back soon," Michael answered.

For some reason, that response made him very anxious. But everything seemed fuzzy. "Why . . . why did she go?"

"Said she had some message from Mr. Crowell for a Mr. Williamson." He shrugged.

Clarity rushed over him as his ears started to ring. "Why didn't she tell me?" Everything he'd witnessed in Virginia City made his heart race. He couldn't let Jackie see Williamson.

"Jack can take care of herself. She'll probably get back and give you quite a scolding for trying to get out of bed by yourself."

"I'm sure she can, but you don't understand. I don't think Williamson is who he says he is." The spots were back in front of his eyes, and his ears roared. "She could . . . be in . . . danger."

CHAPTER 24

Michael was out to meet her when Jackie arrived back at the station. The expression on his face told her something wasn't right.

She dismounted and looked at him. "What's going on? You look like you have bad news."

"Elijah tried to get up while you were gone. He passed out, and his leg is burning up to the touch. He keeps asking for you, but he's not making much sense."

"Take care of Romeo?"

"Sure."

She ran inside and went straight to Elijah's room, where June sat in the chair next to him, bathing his forehead and neck.

"He's got quite a fever, Jackie. I'm afraid there's a problem with his leg. He needs a doctor."

Jackie nodded and sat on the edge of the bed. She touched his forehead and wanted to cry at how hot it was to the touch. "Have you sent for the doctor?"

"Not yet. It's been a little crazy around here this morning. The boys are racing around to prepare the station so they can head out in the wagon. Mr. Liverpool says a storm is coming, and we're running low on supplies."

Closing her eyes, she scolded herself for not staying on top of everything. But with everyone taking turns to sit with Elijah along with performing their normal tasks, she'd neglected one of the most important things — making sure they were prepared for the winter. They all knew it was coming, but she'd been so worried about Elijah. Now it was upon them. "I've got a list I've been meaning to take to town. It's on the desk by the ledger."

"Good." June stood and patted her shoulder. "Don't beat yourself up over it. They'll have plenty of time to grab supplies after they get word to the doctor. I'll give you a few minutes with Mr. Johnson, and I'll go get your list just in case you need to add anything to it."

She placed her hand on Elijah's cheek.

His eyes fluttered open, but they looked glazed. "Why didn't you tell me?"

"Tell you what?"

"Virginia City . . . it's too dangerous."

"Shh, don't worry about it now. You need to rest. We're sending for the doctor."

His eyes closed but then his hand came up and gripped her wrist. "The sheriff . . . he knows. Sanders . . . shot."

The words puzzled her. Who was Sanders? "I'm not sure I understand, Elijah."

His grip remained on her wrist, and his eyes opened again. "I couldn't bear . . . if anything . . . to you . . ." His hand dropped back to his side. "Because I love . . . you."

The last words were such a shock that all she could do was stare at him.

After sending Michael and John out with the wagon to fetch the doctor and get supplies, Jackie went straight back to Elijah's side. Ever since he'd told her that he loved her, he hadn't spoken another word or come around again. Worry built in her gut. She desperately wanted to hear his voice again.

Lord, I don't know what to do, but I'm begging You to please heal Elijah. Please.

She laid her forehead on the bed and let the tears come. Too many things had happened lately. There'd been too much loss. So much upheaval. Yet God was here in the midst. Just like they'd studied in Daniel, even if she were in the fiery furnace, He was there.

The pounding of hooves sounded outside. Timothy had already left on the afternoon Express. Who could that be?

She squeezed Elijah's hand and ran out the front.

As the horse and rider approached, she recognized Mark immediately. But something was wrong.

He reined in the horse and came to a halt, then almost fell off the horse.

"Mark! What's happened?" His coat was covered in blood.

Getting her shoulder up under him, she wrapped his arm around her neck and helped him inside.

A cough shook his whole frame. "The Express . . . it's got to get to San Francisco."

"Don't worry about the Express. I'll make sure it's taken care of." She pulled back his jacket and gasped. "Have you been shot?"

He nodded and passed out.

"Tom!" Their quiet stable manager had been outside to change out the horses. Hopefully he could hear her. *"Tom!"*

The man came running in the front door. "Is he all right? I saw the blood."

"I don't know. Can you go get your wife for me? I need her help." Pressing her hand to the wound in Mark's shoulder, she hoped that he hadn't lost too much blood already.

In less than two minutes, the Liverpools were back — June carrying her basket of supplies they used when anyone got injured.

She moved in and looked. "Keep the pressure on it until I can get some water boiling."

Jackie glanced up at Tom, who wrung his hat in his hands.

"I hate to bring this up, but I need you to decide what to do." His quiet voice was steady.

"What is it?"

"The Express. Timothy just left. Michael and John are out with the wagon, and Mark is injured. Eddie won't be back until tonight. Paul and Luke won't be back until tomorrow because of the specials. We don't have a rider to take this to the next station."

She looked around her. Elijah lay unconscious in the other room. Mark sat bleeding in front of her. All the other riders were gone. She looked back to Tom.

"I would, Jack, but you know I can't. I'm way too heavy. It'd kill the horse to carry me that far and that fast."

June returned with the hot water and put a hand on her shoulder. "It's okay. I'll take care of them both. Tom will be here with me, and hopefully the doctor will get here soon and the boys will return with the wagon."

With a nod, she lifted her hand from Mark's shoulder. "I'll be back as soon as I can."

"The horse is ready to go with the mochila," Tom said.

"I'd better go change." Jackie looked down at her hands. She'd have to wash off the blood and try to dress warmly but without all the weight of her petticoats.

As she ran to her room, her heart ached. First Elijah, and now Mark. What was going on?

Stripping out of her skirts and petticoats, she decided to be practical — if a bit uncivilized — and put on her dad's pants over her knickers. Cinching the waist as tight as she could, she threw on his heavy coat over her bodice and plopped his hat on her head.

When she came out to the parlor, June's eyebrows rose as she took in her attire. "Not a word, my friend. Please."

"I wouldn't dare." June turned her attention back to Mark's wound.

"Take care of them."

"God is watching over us. You be careful."

Tom walked Jackie out. "Tell them what happened to Mark when you get to Virginia City and make sure another rider goes the rest of the way. Do you hear me?"

The tone of his voice made her grin. "Since when do you tell your boss what to do?"

He didn't smile back. "I'm serious, Jack. All of this isn't coincidence. You need to be careful. And there's a storm coming. I can feel it in my knees."

She laid a hand on his arm. "I'll be careful. I promise." Looking up, she realized he'd changed out the horse for Romeo.

"I figured you'd be more comfortable on your own horse."

"And he can run like the wind. Thank you." With his help, she climbed up on Romeo's back for the second time that day. "I'll be back as soon as I can. Please ask the doctor to stay until I return."

"Will do."

Leaning over her horse's neck, she whispered toward his ear, "Let's go, Romeo."

Romeo took off without hesitation. Jackie positioned herself above the saddle and hunched down as much as she could. It was a good thing she'd tied Dad's hat down with the chin strap or it'd be long gone.

The ride to Virginia City passed in a blur, but the whole way she'd kept an eye on the clouds overhead. Tom was right. A storm was coming. Sooner rather than later.

She passed Doc Thompson on his horse about halfway to Virginia City and sighed with relief. At least Elijah and Mark would have help. Now she just had to get the mochila to the next station so the Express could get to San Francisco. Whatever was in the way pocket must be pretty important for another special Express to have been sent.

By the time she reached the edge of town, the wind had picked up and barreled toward her from the west. Riding hard to the station, she prayed for the storm to hold off until she could get home.

She pulled Romeo to a quick stop. The next station manager was out with a fresh horse and ready for the transfer.

Jumping off her horse, she removed the mochila as fast as she could and gave it to him. He placed it on the next horse.

"Jack?" He finally got a good look at her. "What are you doing riding?"

"Mark came in with a bullet wound with this packet. Whatever it is, it's important and needs to get to San Francisco. Timothy had already left on the regular westbound route, and my other riders weren't back from their routes this morning. We had an emergency that had me send Michael and John into town, so I was the only one available." She climbed back up on Romeo. "Look, I've got to get back. You've got another rider who can go?"

"Sure." The man shouted commands over his shoulder and then turned back to her. "It looks like a pretty good storm is coming, Jack. Ya better be careful."

"Will do. Tell your riders to be careful too. I don't like that one of my boys has been shot." She wrapped her scarf around her face to combat the icy air that was getting colder by the minute.

With a flick of the reins, she headed back out of town as the snow began to fall. Rather than ride all the way through town, she decided to take Romeo on the outskirts so he could run full out again. The faster they could get back, the better. Maneuvering her way to the edge of town, she sighed when she could let her horse run.

But as she rounded the corner of an empty stable, a gunshot went off.

Time seemed to stand still as she watched a man — who didn't look any older than twenty — fall to the ground.

Romeo reared, and she clenched her knees to his sides to keep her seat.

It was then that she saw the face of the shooter.

Mr. Williamson — if that was his real

name — still held the gun aloft. He grinned at the body on the ground.

It didn't seem real.

She gasped.

Romeo didn't stop because of her shock. He leapt back into a full run.

Keeping her head down, Jackie struggled to know what to do. Flying on the back of her horse away from that horrific moment helped her to breathe. But her heart raced in rhythm with Romeo's hooves.

What should she do? Should she turn around and go find the sheriff?

A shot pinged off a boulder to her right.

Romeo surged ahead and she ducked as low as she could on his back. Did the man have a horse to chase her? Had he recognized her? She closed her eyes as the image of the man who was shot flooded her mind.

But she opened them back up and risked a look behind her. The man was just a speck now, but he still stood where she'd left him. Letting out a deep sigh, she turned forward again.

Could he recognize her in these clothes and with her face covered? The thought made her shiver. If he did, he knew her name from the other day and could certainly find her.

Oh God, help us. Please. Please don't let

him know who I am!

Home. She needed to get home. Hopefully she wouldn't be shot on the way.

Then she would decide what to do.

CHAPTER 25

With her head up against Romeo's neck, Jackie could barely see through the blizzard-like conditions. They were so close to home — she only hoped her faithful horse could find the way.

She couldn't bear pushing him as hard as she had on the way to Virginia City. But he'd sensed the storm as well and had moved at a quick canter. Even so, he'd slowed considerably over the last few miles as the snow had gotten deeper, coming down in a sideways blur of white.

The cold had seeped into every bone of her body. If they didn't make it soon, she feared they would be stuck out in the storm.

Romeo lifted his head and whinnied at her. She patted his neck. "I know, boy. I'm sorry. You can do it. I know you can."

Then the most beautiful sight was before her.

Home.

As they rode up to the front door of the station house, she noticed a stagecoach was sitting outside.

Tom and Michael ran out to meet her.

"Jack! You're all right!" Michael practically pulled her off the horse into a hug. "I was getting so worried."

Tom just gave her a smile and took Romeo to the stable, his hand on the guide rope above his head. While she was gone, they'd strung the ropes to help them get from building to building. Every winter they had to do it. Just in case of a whiteout.

"How's Elijah? And Mark?"

"Doc got Mark all patched up. He's in the bunkhouse asleep."

"Doc is with Elijah now."

As she walked in the door, she saw the stage driver and his second man in the parlor. Then she gasped as Mr. Crowell stood.

"Mr. Crowell. There's so much I need to tell you."

He stepped toward her. "Let's go into the kitchen."

"All right." As much as she wanted to see Elijah, she knew that Mr. Crowell's sudden arrival must be very important.

Once they were in the farthest corner of the room, he whispered, "Did you get my message to Williamson?"

"I did. This morning. But sir, as soon as I started asking questions, he changed his demeanor. He shoved me out the door and told me to keep my nose out of his business. And there's more." It was hard to believe it had happened. "I just saw him shoot another man."

Crowell closed his eyes for a moment, and his lips formed a hard line. "I just learned that Sanders has been killed as well. It appears we had someone infiltrate our contacts." He looked down at her. "There's some news that I don't want to have to share, but I must."

"What is it?"

"We've received several letters that incriminate your father as the forger. One of them stated that your father had a box at the bank filled with the forged notes. When we went to the bank, they were there."

"What? You know Dad didn't have anything to do with this."

"I'm sorry, Miss Rivers. But I'm afraid we're going to have to shut down your station until we can determine the truth."

Her heart sank. They were shutting her down?

Michael ran out of the guest hallway. "Jack. Come quick. You too, Mr. Crowell.

Elijah won't stop going on and on about you."

They all headed to Elijah's room.

When she saw him, his eyes were glassy, his face red.

The doc stood over him. "The pain from opening the wound woke him up, but I don't know for how long. The fever is pretty bad. He keeps saying he has to talk to Crowell."

"That's me." Mr. Crowell moved closer to the bed.

Elijah's face contorted when he laid eyes on the older man. His eyes looked frantic. "Sanders was shot. . . . Williamson lied. . . ."

"I know, son." Crowell looked to her. "Was Elijah there — in Virginia City — the day Sanders was killed?"

She nodded. "Yes, and then the stage was attacked on the way home. We never could figure out why he was on the stage. Unless our horse was stolen?" None of it had made sense.

Crowell shook his head in disbelief. "So he tried to kill the only witness. Elijah."

Jackie gasped. "The stage attack — that was . . . someone trying to kill him?"

Crowell shoved his hat back on his head. "I'm afraid it sounds as if that's so. It's high time we stopped this fiend." Marching toward the door, he threw over his shoulder, "Might I borrow a horse?"

"You'll never get anywhere in this blizzard." Michael met the man at the door. "You're going to have to wait until it passes."

James Crowell nodded and looked back at her. "I'm sincerely sorry for all this. You have my word I'll get to the bottom of it."

Taking a seat next to Elijah, she laid her hand over his arm. "Thank you. I have faith that you will, sir. But I also need you to know that my dad had nothing to do with this. You know that, right?"

Crowell grimaced. "I believe that to be true, but I have to prove it."

"I have confidence that you will. You said that I had your word?"

"Yes."

"There's something I need to show you." She stood and went to her room. Gathering the bonds her dad had left her in the box, she took them out to the parlor where Crowell waited. "My dad left these for me. I wouldn't want you to think I was hiding anything from you or keeping any secrets."

"We'll take these as evidence. I appreciate your honesty."

"I stand by Marshall Rivers's innocence."

He nodded. "And I hope to return these to you if they're real."

She lifted her chin. "Well, until the storm passes, you are welcome to stay in your room here and we will help you with whatever provisions you need."

November 19, 1860
Another week and a half had passed with Elijah in and out of consciousness. The fever had finally broken yesterday, so the doctor was hopeful that he would awaken permanently soon.

Her days had been restless since Mr. Crowell had announced that he was shutting her down. Of course the blizzard had kept everyone housebound for three days and then the Express riders had all gone to Virginia City to help out with the runs from there. It had become all too quiet without her boys around.

The shutting down of one of the stations would be devastating to the Pony Express if it lasted for long. The horses and riders couldn't go on without being switched out.

But even as she worried over the situation, she prayed that God would take care of it all. The sooner they caught the forgers and cleared her dad's name, the sooner life could go on the way it should.

Until then? Well, she was determined to pray.

June had been in and out visiting with her. Encouraging her. Chatting about this or that from *Godey's.* But what Jackie really wanted was to be able to talk to Elijah.

So much had transpired. Her life had been a whirlwind since they met. A month during which her whole world had been turned upside down.

Walking over to the window, she peered through the ice-covered glass to the white world around them. Normally she loved the snow, but now it seemed like a hindrance.

Patience. She needed to work on her patience. Was she trusting God to handle this situation or not?

Turning back to watch Elijah as he slept, she walked back to her chair and picked up her mother's journal. She'd read almost the whole thing over the past few days, and it had done her heart a lot of good. While it had been painful to read about her parents' past, she was thankful for the lessons her mother shared. Lessons she wished she could have learned in person from the woman who bore her. Several images of her mother smiling and laughing had come back to her over this time. Each one had made her cry tears of joy.

One in particular had become a favorite memory that she went back to over and over. They were chasing a tumbleweed, and their giggles had floated up into the air together. It wasn't much, but she clung to it.

Running her hand over the pages, she looked at the journal where she'd left off and flipped a few pages. It almost hurt to realize that she was at the end. This must have been right before Mom contracted the fever.

With a deep breath, she looked down at the entry.

June 1, 1837

Dearest Jacqueline,

You have grown so much, my sweet. It is such a joy to watch you run around and play. Enjoying life, laughing, smiling, jabbering on and on about the horses, the bugs, the rocks, the dirt — whatever you fancy at the moment. Today as I laughed with you over the suds and bubbles floating out of the washtub, I realized that I have done a grave disservice to you. And I plan to fix that starting right now.

I've told you about your father. I've told you what happened and why I took you away. But I haven't told you about the man I fell in love with.

Charles was handsome and charming, with a smile that could light up a room. You inherited that smile, and I love it every time I see it. But he was more than just a dashing young man. He was also intelligent and very business savvy. He took the dowry from my father and practically doubled it overnight. He could make a fortune every day of the week.

What I loved most was that he could make me laugh. I think that is what I missed most when he went down his dark path. The laughter. We'd always had so much fun.

But we had been very young. Immature. Naive. We were not prepared for what was to come.

When those dark times came, I now believe he became very depressed. Because he couldn't figure out what was missing in his life, he filled the void with liquor.

My beautiful girl, I never want you to think of your father as a horrible man. And as you grow up, I will do my best to honor him when I speak to you. But it would be dishonest of me if I didn't tell you that I am still very afraid of him finding me. Especially if he hasn't changed. But if he has found God and turned his life around — I would receive him with open arms. I want you to know that. The reason we are so far away from where you were born is because I wanted a place to hide. I wanted a place where he could never find us. It would crush me if something happened to you because I didn't protect you from him.

Then there is the side of my heart that God is working on. I've chosen to forgive him. Like God forgives us.

So what I have prayed for him the past few years is that he finds the Lord. It is also my prayer for you, little one. God is the only One who can fill the hole in your heart. We are sinners. All of us. Because of that sin, our punishment should be death. But Jesus paid the price for us. Our debt is paid. As you grow, I long to tell you more about our great God and how much He loves us.

I hope to share all of this and more with you in reflective conversation as you grow older. I long to point out my favorite scriptures and all that God has taught me.

But as you've just awoken from your

nap, that is my cue to stop for the day.

I love you, my sweet one.

Mama

As she closed the book, Jackie let the words sink into her heart. She couldn't have known what was coming. But God did. Gratefulness filled her heart to overflowing that God had seen fit to place her here. Her mother had taught her first about God. And then Marshall Rivers had as well. He may not have been her father by blood, but he was her *real* dad. And she would never forget him.

Chapter 26

November 21, 1860

Elijah opened his eyes a crack. The room was dark. As his eyes adjusted, he noticed two figures were with him. One was slumped in the chair across the room, and another — Jackie — had her head resting on the edge of his bed.

He reached out a hand and laid it on her head. The silken strands of her hair were as soft as he expected.

She roused and lifted her head to look at him. "Elijah?"

"Mm-hmm."

A heavy sigh left her lips. "I'm so glad you're awake. We've been praying for days."

"What happened?"

"You had a puss-filled wound in your leg. Doc had to open it up around the break in your leg. He said the damage was close to getting into the bone itself."

"No wonder it feels like my leg's been run

over by a hundred horses." He leaned his head back and watched her. "It's so good to see you, Jackie."

"It's good to see you *awake.*"

"Was Crowell here? I thought I remembered talking to him."

She nodded toward the chair in the corner. "You did. Mr. Crowell?"

The sleeping man roused. "Elijah! You're awake." He jumped up from the chair. "Sorry, son. I came in on the stage and fell asleep almost immediately in the chair when I found you still weren't awake."

Jackie stood and offered Crowell her chair. "Please, sit. I'll get you both some refreshment."

"Thank you." Crowell looked at Elijah after Jackie left the room. "She's still having a difficult time with the fact that I shut the station down. But just so you know, I had to. To protect her."

"I appreciate you doing that. Especially with a killer on the loose."

"The sheriff told me that you were the only witness for the Sanders killing?"

"Yes, sir." He tried to shake the cobwebs from his head.

"But you didn't see anyone?"

"No."

"What about the man who shot the stage

driver — could you identify him?"

"I didn't get a good look at him. His face was almost completely covered."

"All right then. Tell me what happened at Sanders's office."

As Elijah recounted the conversations he'd had with Sanders before the man was shot, Jackie returned with a tray.

Crowell looked up at her. "You told me the night you came back from Virginia City that you saw the man you knew as Williamson shoot another man?"

"Yes, sir." She nodded. "I was riding to the outskirts of town so I could let Romeo have his head. The snowstorm was moving in fast. I came around the corner of a deserted stable and saw it plain as day."

"You're sure it was Williamson?"

"Definitely. I can even describe the man he shot."

"Oh, we're pretty sure we know who he shot. The sheriff found the body. But right now we're trying to figure out the connection."

Elijah took a deep breath. "You're pretty sure that the man Jackie and I saw as Williamson wasn't the actual Williamson, right?"

Crowell's jaw clenched and unclenched. "Yes. Especially after you told me what

Sanders said before he was killed. We just have to catch whoever it was that was impersonating our man." He stood and put on his hat. "I need to get back to Virginia City and meet with the sheriff again. But rest assured, we'll take care of this." He laid a hand on Elijah's shoulder. "You need to heal. And take care of Miss Rivers here."

"I plan to do just that."

Jackie gave the man a stiff smile as she stood. "I'll walk you out. Do you need a horse?"

"That would be wonderful, yes."

As the two left the room, Elijah laid his head back on the pillow. It was exhausting just talking. But maybe once he got some food inside him, he'd be able to regain his strength.

Strange recollections filled his mind. Had he woken at all during the last few days? He couldn't tell if he'd dreamed it or not. But he did know that his focus had been on Jackie. Even if he hadn't woken, he knew he'd heard her voice.

The object of his thoughts returned, and her smile was genuine. "Mr. Crowell told me that he knows Dad was innocent of any wrongdoing. He said it might take a little time, but he's going to prove it."

"That's wonderful news." He furrowed his

brow. "But I didn't realize that anything was amiss."

Sitting back down in the chair, she leaned forward with her elbows on her knees. "I told you while you were battling the fever. I'm sorry. Apparently several letters surfaced at different Pony Express stations, implying that my dad was the forger and kept forged treasury notes at the bank. When they went to the bank and found forged notes, they had to shut down the station."

"Wow. Well, I'm glad that Crowell knows the truth."

"Me too. I was beginning to worry."

He reached out a hand to her. "I'm sorry I wasn't a help to you during that time. I'm guessing that's why it's so quiet around here?"

Jackie let out a huff. "Isn't it awful? I can't wait until my boys are back. I've never wished for anything more in my life."

Laughing with her, he looked deep into her eyes. "Well, I hope they come back soon, because I need to ask Michael a question."

With a frown, she looked at him skeptically. "And what question would that be?"

"Well, as the man of the house — and your adopted brother — I need to ask him for his permission to court you."

"Oh, do you now?" She quirked an eyebrow.

"Yes, I do."

She gripped his hand. "Well, this may be considered completely inappropriate in polite society, but I need to tell you something."

"Go ahead." It was his turn to be caught by surprise.

"I love you."

As the words washed over him, he felt like he'd heard them from her before. "I can't tell you how happy it makes me to hear you say that."

"I don't know if you remember telling me that when you were so sick, but I've been begging God to heal you. And I told you last night that I loved you in hopes that you would wake up." A smile split her face. "I guess it worked."

"It most certainly did." As he stared into her beautiful green eyes, he prayed for the Lord to heal him quickly. Because he wanted to wrap his arms around this woman forever.

November 26, 1860

Charles sat on the edge of the seat in the stage and stared out the window.

"Sir, I don't believe that will help us arrive any faster," Colson teased.

"Oh grief, man. Give me the courtesy of letting me be excited. We're almost there."

"My apologies, sir." His man leaned forward as well. "I must say that it has been good to see you have such a zest for life again."

"We'll have to tell good ol' Newberry that my heart just needed something to look forward to." He clapped his hands together. "I can't wait to meet her."

"What if Elijah hasn't told her anything? What if it's not her?"

"I'll have to take that as it comes. For right now, let me dream."

"Of course." Colson leaned back against the seat. "I'm looking forward to a hot bath and a decent bed. Do you think we'll be able to find that out here?"

"It doesn't matter to me." He wanted to bounce on the seat, but that seemed childish. "I'll sleep in the barn if I have to."

The driver pounded on the roof of the stage. His voice bellowed through the walls. "Carson Sink comin' up."

Charles leaned back and told himself to breathe. After all these years. He swallowed and choked down his fear.

The stage rocked and swayed as it came to a stop.

Colson opened the door and stepped out.

Charles put on his hat and followed.

After the driver handed their bags down, he leaned over the edge. "I think they're closed for business right now."

"Doesn't matter. This is where we need to stop."

"Suit yourself." The driver lifted the reins and put the team back in motion.

Charles turned toward the adobe structure that must be the way station. The door opened and out stepped a young woman who was the spitting image of his Anna.

His breath caught in his throat.

"We're closed, but may I help you?" Her puzzled expression was endearing as she tilted her head and wrapped her red shawl about her shoulders a bit tighter.

"My apologies, miss, but my employer and I were hoping we could find some rooms at your establishment." Colson had stepped forward with his starched manners in place.

Not able to contain himself any longer, Charles stepped forward and stuck out his hand in greeting. "My name is Charles Vines. And you are?"

CHAPTER 27

Jackie gasped and covered her mouth with both of her hands. Blinking rapidly, she felt tears pooling in her eyes. Before her stood . . . her father. She couldn't take it all in.

"Miss?" The taller man who'd asked for rooms looked as if he wasn't quite sure what to do with her reaction.

Clamping her lips together for a moment, she lowered her hands and let out her breath slowly. "I'm so sorry. Please come in."

The men came in with their bags, and she shut the door behind them. "My name is Jacqueline Rivers."

Mr. Vines nodded with his hat in his hand.

"I know who you are," she blurted. Not the best way to start a conversation.

"I know who you are too." He swiped at a tear that slipped down his cheek. "You look just like her." He looked around. "Anna?"

Silence hung for a few seconds before she could respond. "She's dead." Those two words stabbed her in the heart as if she'd just lost her mother yesterday.

"Perhaps I should give you two a moment alone." The other man who had obviously traveled with her father started for the door.

"No, please. That's not necessary." Charles held up a hand. The man's hat was shaking in his hands as he took a deep breath.

Taking pity on them both, she pointed to the parlor. "Perhaps we could sit down?"

"That would be nice. Thank you." Her father walked toward the fireplace but didn't sit.

Jackie sat in her favorite chair and placed her hands in her lap. She'd been praying about this very moment but had no idea it would come so soon. She'd thought it would be months down the road.

"If you know who I am, then you know that I sent Elijah to find you." He paced in front of the fire as his man took a seat across from her.

"Yes."

"I came as soon as I received his letter stating that he hoped he'd found my daughter. Colson here thought I was a bit out of my mind for taking such a chance, but I could no longer sit and wait."

She managed a nod.

He stepped closer. Then to her surprise, the older man got down on his knees in front of her. "I can't take it any longer. Jacqueline, I'm sorry. I'm so, so sorry. I don't deserve your forgiveness, but I'm asking you for it — no, I'm begging you for it. It took your mother's courageous act to finally get through to my stubborn self. I hate the man that I was. But if not for her — and for you — I never would have found that I needed a Savior."

Tears rushed to her eyes. "So you found Him?"

"I did. Or rather, He found me."

She came out of the chair and knelt with him there in the middle of the floor. "Mama prayed for you every day. That's all she ever wanted for you." A new emotion filled her heart for this man she'd just met. It bubbled up inside of her. She grabbed his hands.

He sobbed at her touch and placed his forehead on their clasped hands. "I didn't deserve her. She was such an amazing woman. And I will have to live with my regrets for the rest of my life, but will you — my daughter — forgive me?"

The agony in his eyes as he lifted his face to look at her was almost her undoing. Hot tears streamed down her face, and as her vision blurred, a new picture appeared before her.

It was her.

At the foot of the cross.

Watching her Savior be the willing sacrifice for *her* sins.

Pleading with Christ to forgive her.

She was no more deserving of forgiveness than the man who'd humbled himself before her now. Yet Jesus had forgiven her. The power of the image in her mind made her heart pound. There was no decision to be made. She blinked so she could see. "I forgive you."

He laid his forehead back on top of their hands and sobbed.

Jackie leaned forward and wrapped her arms around the man who'd carried this burden for so long. As they cried together, Jackie released all her anger, fear, and doubt. She felt clean and whole.

As Charles Vines — her father — cried with her, he kept thanking God. Over and over.

The tears came in earnest then. *Yes. Thank You, God. For forgiveness. For grace. For a wonderful mom and dad. And for bringing my other father to me.* She imagined God had looked upon His child — her father — in all his misery and shame and welcomed him with open arms. Like the prodigal who had come home. She wanted to rejoice. Looking to the ceiling, she smiled through her tears and could imagine her mom and dad rejoicing as well. What a beautiful picture. Jackie smiled through her tears at Charles Vines. A man she didn't know . . . yet loved.

Her father lifted his face and stood to his feet, pulling her to stand with him. Wrapping his arms around her, he said, "For this child I have prayed."

Jackie hugged him back and closed her eyes. God had done an incredible thing, and she would be forever grateful.

Elijah sat on his bed and tried to listen to what was happening. All he knew was that a stage had come in and Jackie had gone to see who it was. It worried him a bit. Especially since the station was shut down. Hopefully there wasn't an emergency.

But as he listened, it didn't sound like there was a flutter of activity or chaos. Only voices.

But then they stopped.

After the quiet lasted for several minutes, Elijah worried a bit more. Then the minutes stretched even longer. He couldn't wait any longer and shouted as loud as he could from the bed, "Jackie?"

Footsteps sounded down the hall.

Her tearstained, joy-filled face was the first thing he saw.

"What's happened?"

"My father is here." She clamped her lips together as the tears flowed down her cheeks.

"Elijah, my boy!" Charles entered the room behind his daughter and came to the bed with open arms. "What's happened to you?"

Shock at the health he saw in the man's face — which was also a bit tearstained — Elijah stammered, "Wha–what are you doing here?"

"Colson and I took the stage. It was awful if I do say so myself. But it got us here." Charles hugged him hard. "You found my daughter. Thank you."

His gaze shot back to Jackie, who glowed. "I did. And I'm so glad I found her."

Charles's eyebrows shot up. He looked to Jackie and then back to Elijah. "Oh, this is perfect. My two favorite people have met." He sat on the edge of Elijah's bed. "Now, who's going to tell me what happened to you?" He looked toward the door. "Wait just a moment. Colson! Colson, come in here."

As they spent the afternoon catching up

on all that had happened since Elijah arrived in Carson Sink, laughter and a few more tears filled the room. And even though he couldn't walk, he felt so much better.

"You look like you have something to say." Charles knew him quite well.

Elijah wiggled his eyebrows at Jackie and turned back to his mentor and partner. "Yes, sir. I believe I do."

"Well, let's hear it."

"I'd like to ask your permission to court your daughter."

Charles crossed him arms over his chest. "Oh, well now. I'm not so sure about that. I might have to think on that for a while."

Colson and Jackie laughed.

"That's not funny, sir." Elijah gave his partner a pointed glare.

"I know. I'm sorry." The man looked a bit sheepish. "Of course you may." Then he clapped his hands together. "So it appears we'll be staying in Carson Sink for quite some time."

Elijah nodded. "Not only is it necessary for my leg here, but the place has grown on me." He smiled at Jackie.

Vines grinned. "It doesn't matter where we are. As long as we're together. I say let's stay for as long as you like."

"Then maybe one day we can travel to

Kansas City?" Jackie gave a sweet smile.

"Whatever you want." Elijah took her hand. He wanted to spend every moment with her that he could.

"And it's not like we have any responsibilities. Goodness knows we've made enough money over the years."

Jackie's brow furrowed as she sent Elijah a questioning look.

He lifted her hand and kissed it. "It seems there are a few details I might have left out."

November 28, 1860
The pounding of horses' hooves sounded outside the station. Jackie put down the darning she was working on and looked at the men around the room. "I'd better go check on that."

"I'll come with you." Her father followed after her.

As she opened the door to the station, she saw Mr. Crowell, Mark, Timothy, Michael, John, Eddie, and another man she'd never met dismounting their horses.

Mr. Crowell looked over his horse at her. "Your station is back in business, Miss Rivers."

Clapping her hands together, she ran to greet each of her boys. "I've missed you all so much! Where are Paul and Luke?"

411

"They'll be here after their runs."

She hugged each one of them.

"We've missed you too, Jack. And we've missed your cooking." Timothy made a face. "I never want to eat anyone else's food ever again."

Laughter rounded the group.

"We should get you all inside."

"Let us take care of the horses. We'll be in soon." Michael nodded to the other boys. Seeing him take on such leadership and responsibility made her heart swell with pride.

"I'll get some refreshments ready for you."

She led the others inside. After she closed the door, a large, portly man held out his hand. "The name's Trevor Hudson, miss." The puff from his cigar made her eyes water. "I've heard a lot about you."

"Oh, well, it's nice to meet you, Mr. Hudson."

Mr. Crowell held out an arm. "Could we join Mr. Johnson in his room? He'll want to hear all of this."

"Of course." They went to Elijah's room, and she gave him a big smile.

Mr. Crowell didn't waste any time. "I'm happy to say that it's all over. Trevor here was the key to catching Carl Blackwood — whom you would recognize as the man who pretended to be Williamson. He killed our man and then posed as him."

"That's awful. But I'm so glad you caught him. How did you do it?" She couldn't believe it was finally over. Watching that man get shot had given her nightmares.

"Well, it wasn't easy. We've had Trevor here in place as a forger — he's an expert on treasury notes — ever since Carl killed the last man he'd had working for him. He'd been feeding us information about how Carl was doing it and we were able to track the notes that Trevor made here since he left a special mark on each one. What we hadn't figured out was how Marshall had been implicated in it all. Carl obviously hadn't been doing it alone, but since he seemed to kill off all his accomplices as he went, we couldn't find the trail. But once you delivered the message that Sacramento was ready, Carl killed his nephew — the man you saw him shoot — and headed straight for San Francisco rather than Sacramento to cash in his forgeries. He headed straight into our trap. We caught him red-handed. Then when we returned to Virginia City, we found his nephew's belongings and all the other proof we needed. It didn't take much for Carl's sister to turn on him and tell the whole shady tale."

"How much money did he steal?"

"One hundred thousand dollars in gold was found on him when we caught him. He was planning on doubling that in San Francisco."

Elijah whistled. "That's a fortune."

Mr. Crowell nodded. "Yes, it is. And it would have been a terrible blow to the economy." He walked up to Jackie. "All these so-called letters that were seen as evidence against Marshall Rivers?" Mr. Crowell tossed them on the desk. "They were all mysteriously delivered around the same time. And look at the handwriting. They're all written by the same person. Then we noticed that there isn't one legitimate postmark on any of these." He shot her a smile. "They're *frauds,* Miss Rivers. Written by Carl's nephew and planted to implicate your dad. The man who raised you — Marshall Rivers — is exonerated of any accusations against him." He held out another stack of documents with his other hand. "I believe these are yours. They're real."

She stood to her feet and hugged the man. "Thank you. Thank you." She took the documents and clutched them to her chest. "It was so sweet of him to do this for me. I think I'd like to give them to the boys."

Tears streamed down her face. "I wish you all could have known Dad — Marshall. He was such a good man."

Mr. Vines — her real father — walked toward her slowly. "He sounds like the best of men and someone I would have greatly respected. Just look at how well he raised you."

CHAPTER 28

February 7, 1861

Elijah gripped Jackie's hand tighter as they walked down the street and back. "I can't believe it's already February."

"And look at how well you're walking. There's hardly a limp anymore." The smile that she gave him just about melted him.

How he longed to make this woman his wife. "Thank you for helping me with my exercises all this time. I know it hasn't been easy for you."

"Oh, pshaw. With Father helping so much with everything at the station, I've had plenty of time to help. Besides, it has given us more time together."

"Not much of a courtship, huh?" He lifted her hand in his and drew it to his chest as he stopped and turned toward her.

"I beg to differ." Only a few inches separated them. "It has been" — she licked her lips — "wonderful."

Tipping his head down toward hers, he watched her green eyes sparkle in the sunlight. "It has been, hasn't it?"

"Mm-hmm." She blinked and lifted her face closer to his.

"Oh, just kiss her already. We're all getting tired of your constant googly eyes at each other anyway," Michael teased.

Elijah chuckled but kept her close. "You know, he's sounding more and more like his big sister every day."

"Oh?" She raised an eyebrow. "How's that?"

"Bossy, bossy."

Jackie laughed and put her other hand behind his neck. "Why *don't* you kiss me already?"

"Bossy." He gave her a quick peck on the lips but didn't pull back. "Because I want to ask you a question."

"All right. I'm listening." She inched closer.

"Will you marry me, Jack?"

"I thought you'd never ask." Jackie kissed him. "Yes."

Elijah released her hand so he could wrap her in his arms, and then he kissed her with all the love he held for her.

Applause rang out around them.

Jackie pulled back. "I didn't realize we had

417

an audience." Her cheeks a deep pink, she looked into his eyes. "Oh, what does it matter. I love you." With a passion he wasn't ready for, she kissed him back.

When they pulled apart, Elijah's heart was thrumming in his chest.

Jackie grabbed his hand again as they turned to their friends. "We're getting married!"

Charles walked toward him with his hand outstretched. "That's wonderful news. When?"

"Oh, how about St. Valentine's Day?" Elijah threw out.

"But that's in just a week." Jackie gave him an odd look.

"And that's already too long to wait."

February 14, 1861
Jackie sat in her room in the beautiful gown her father had paid a small fortune to have made in just a few days. In a few minutes, she'd walk out and become Mrs. Elijah Johnson. The thought made her heart soar.

A knock sounded at the door.

"Come in." She stood and picked up the bouquet she'd made out of the ribbons Dad had given her over the years.

"You look beautiful." Her father looked on with pride. "Are you ready?"

She gave a giddy nod. "And more excited than I've ever been."

"That young man out there is the best man I've ever known. I know he'll cherish you and love you."

"I know." And she did. With all her heart.

"Is there anything else you need on this special day?"

"I can't think of anything." Jackie loved the time she'd had to spend with her father. But an idea struck. "Actually, there is something I'd like to ask you to help with."

"Of course, anything." His eyes always lit up whenever she asked him to help her with anything.

"Mama wrote in her journal to me that I have a cousin in California. It's a distant cousin, but still, I'd love to see if we could find her." She hated asking something that might bring him pain from the past.

"I would love to help you, my dear. In fact, California would make a nice trip. You, me, and Elijah could take a little trip there."

"Oh, could we?"

"As soon as you want to go, I say we should head west! I've always wanted to see the Pacific Ocean."

Jackie clapped her hands together and gave her father a huge hug.

He pulled back, a sentimental expression

on his face. "I want to give you something."

"Father, you've given me so much already."

"Oh, hush. I'll have none of that. Allow me to shower my daughter with whatever I want. You know, I might not be around forever."

She tried not to giggle at the dramatic look on his face. Even though she knew he had been quite sick last year, his health had only continued to improve.

He pulled his handkerchief out of his pocket. "I have paid a small fortune for this piece *twice*. I gave it to your mother because I loved her so much and thought with my own will I could love her forever. But I was wrong. I didn't understand real love. So I'm giving it to you now as a reminder that *God's* love is forever. And it's only through His love that you and Elijah will be able to navigate this life and love one another the way He designed for a husband and wife." He opened the cloth to reveal the piece.

She didn't even look at the gift for a moment. His words had reached down into her heart and touched her very soul. When she looked down, she saw the back of a brooch where the word *"Forever"* was etched. "Oh Father. It's lovely."

"Just like you are." Elijah's voice floated

over to her from the door. "I hope I'm not intruding."

She shook her head and smiled.

Father took the brooch and pinned it to her ribbon bouquet. "Something from both of your fathers on this special day." Then he turned and escorted her toward the door.

Jackie put all her effort into keeping the tears at bay. She looked at the man who was about to be her husband, and her breath caught.

"I have a request." Elijah blocked the doorway.

"All right?"

"Could we pray together before the ceremony?"

"I'd like that. Very much."

He leaned in and captured her lips. Right there in front of her father. Which she didn't mind one bit.

Every nerve ending in her body tingled as he deepened the kiss.

"Ahem."

They pulled apart.

"I thought you said you wanted to pray?" The teasing look in her father's eyes made them both laugh.

"Yes, sir. But I needed to kiss her first so I could focus."

Heat crept up her neck at the passion she

saw in her almost-husband's eyes.

"Very wise. I knew you were smart, Elijah Johnson." Father patted him on the shoulder and squeezed past him through the door. "Why don't you two come out here into the parlor so that after you pray together, we can all pray for you as well?"

Elijah wrapped an arm around her waist and looked into her eyes. "I can't think of a better way for us to start our married life."

"I can't either." Oh, how she adored this man. *Thank You, Lord, for bringing Elijah to me.*

Elijah took her hands and put his forehead down on hers. As soon as they closed their eyes, he began, "Gracious heavenly Father —"

The unmistakable sound of an incoming Express interrupted and Jackie couldn't help giggling. Out of habit she turned to the door, but Michael stopped her with a wave of his hand.

"Now don't go getting hitched without us. We'll be right back."

Gathering her close once more, Elijah started again. "Lord, we praise You and thank You for this day. Father, Jackie and I stand together wanting to dedicate our lives to You —"

The door crashed open. "Did I miss the

wedding?" Timothy stood in the doorway out of breath.

Everyone gathered in the parlor laughed.

"No." Jackie looked into Elijah's eyes and remembered his kiss. "We were just about to get started."

"Well, what are you waiting for? I'm hungry."

NOTE FROM THE AUTHOR

So much fascinating history surrounds the Pony Express. And plenty of legends and myths as well. But what most people don't realize is that it was a huge financial flop. Even though it was twice as fast as its competitors, the riders, horses, and stations required to keep it running were extremely costly. During the Paiute wars when it had to shut down, it's estimated the Express lost at least seventy-five thousand dollars. Financial problems were very real. William Russell — one of the owners — was arrested in December 1860 and indicted in January 1861 on possession of stolen Indian bonds, but the case was never brought to trial because of the start of the Civil War. By the time the Express ended, it is believed that the endeavor lost as much as two hundred thousand dollars.

So although the forgery of the treasury notes and my villain were completely of my own imagination, the ideas are based on the historical facts surrounding the Pony Express.

While I used the real man who was secretary of the treasury during the time — Howell Cobb — the man who was his secretary (Mr. Crowell) is fictitious.

It was also fun to add into the story how far west Anna originally went. This is where I took artistic liberty, because the first documented white women to travel over the Rockies were Narcissa Whitman and Eliza Spalding in 1836. There were white women in what we now think of as California at this time, but they'd traveled by sea to get there. (From what I could find, they were missionaries like the Whitmans and Spaldings.) So I stretched it and had Anna come west in 1834 by wagon because of her desperation. Several men had traveled west by wagon at this time, but it wasn't common for women. What better way for her to hide than to do something out of the ordinary? In 1834, what is modern-day Nevada was still Mexico. By 1860 it was the Utah Territory. To see fascinating maps of the US through history, here's a great link:

http://alabamamaps.ua.edu/historical maps/unitedstates/1826-1850 b.html

To see a map of the Pony Express stations,

check out these links:

https://nationalponyexpress.org/historic-pony-express-trail/stations/#nv

http://www.waymarking.com/waymarks/WM7A1J_Pony_Express_Carson_Sink_Station

To learn more about the stations, visit the following sites:

https://www.expeditionutah.com/featured-trails/pony-express-trail/nevada-pony-express-stations/

https://www.expeditionutah.com/featured-trails/pony-express-trail/

https://www.nps.gov/parkhistory/online_books/poex/hrs/hrs8a.htm#149&#13

Some wonderful books I would recommend to read that I purchased at the Pony Express Museums include *The Pony Express Trail: Yesterday and Today* by William E. Hill; *Pony Express* by Fred Reinfeld; *Riders of the Pony Express* by Ralph Moody; *Here Comes the Pony: The Story of the Pony Express* (an educational activity book and great resource) by William E. Hill; and my personal favorite, *The Saga of the Pony Express* by Joseph J. DiCerto.

As always, I pray you have enjoyed this intriguing glimpse into history as we've journeyed with Jackie and Elijah.

Thank you, readers.

Kimberley

ACKNOWLEDGMENTS

The last two years of my life have seemed like a whirlwind of deadlines, sickness, surgeries, cross-country moves, and plain ol' chaos. God has been so gracious to get me through, but there are many people I need to thank. Especially for helping me get this story into your hands.

Darcie, Becca, Kayla, and Tracie — I *never* would have made it through without you. Thank you.

Jeremy, you will always be my hero. Thank you for all you did to help make another story happen. I love you!

Becky Germany and the whole Barbour team — you are amazing.

Becky Durost Fish, for another whirlwind of edits. I have so enjoyed working with you. Thank you, thank you!

And always a huge thanks goes out to my

readers. I couldn't do this without you!

Grab on to joy!

Kimberley Woodhouse

ABOUT THE AUTHOR

Kimberley Woodhouse is an award-winning and bestselling author of more than twenty fiction and nonfiction books. A popular speaker and teacher, she has shared her theme of "Joy through Trials" with more than half a million people across the country at more than two thousand events. Kim and her incredible husband of twenty-five-plus years have two adult children. She's passionate about music and Bible study and loves the gift of story.

You can connect with Kimberley at www .kimberleywoodhouse.com and www.face book.com/KimberleyWoodhouseAuthor.